FEED THY ENEMY

SUE PARRITT

Copyright (C) 2019 Sue Parritt

Layout design and Copyright (C) 2019 by Creativia

Published 2019 by Creativia (www.creativia.org)

Edited by Marilyn Wagner

Cover art by Cover Mint

This book is based on a true story. The names of all characters have been changed to protect those persons still living. Some places and incidents are the product of the author's imagination or are used fictitiously.

All rights reserved. No part of this book may be reproduced or transmitted in any form or by any means, electronic or mechanical, including photocopying, recording, or by any information storage and retrieval system, without the author's permission.

In loving memory of my dear parents, Nick 1913-1978 and Jean 1921-2009

ACKNOWLEDGMENTS

Many thanks to Miika Hannila and staff at Creativia for enabling me to share my father's story.

ONE

They are in the garden when the phone rings, he, bent over a spade digging up potatoes, she, pulling out weeds with great gusto and throwing them onto the adjacent lawn. He watches her sprint across the grass and up the concrete path alongside his new wooden shed, her shapely sun-browned legs moving with the same power and grace she displays when swimming or cycling. Fifty-three last birthday, Ivy retains the trim figure Rob admired all those years ago in the goods office at the central railway station. A petite woman, she was and remains, a complete contrast to his first post-war girlfriend, the tall, voluptuous redhead seated at the adjoining desk, long pale fingers tipped with scarlet nails, striking typewriter keys as if her life depended on it. That relationship was over almost before it began, Edna's avant-garde attire and flamboyant behaviour overwhelming a mild-mannered railway clerk, still recovering from four years of war service. Why had he asked her out in the first place? Almost thirty years on, he still doesn't know the answer.

Leaning on the spade, Rob smiles as he remembers the day one of the older clerks took him aside following one of Edna's more colourful tales related over lunch in the cramped staff room. 'Robert, I think you should know that both girls caused great consternation in the office during the war whenever a troop-carrying train pulled in to the station,' the fifty-something clerk confided in a low voice, colour dusting his pale cheeks as though the very mention of Edna and Ivy's exploits made him somehow complicit.

Too late, Rob wanted to say, thinking of his evening date with Ivy, but being a relatively new employee, remained silent.

'The moment boots were heard marching across the platform,' the clerk continued, 'the girls would rise from their desks, fling up the office windows and resting their breasts on the windowsill, wave and shout warm welcomes. Responses were always greeted with requests for billet addresses in exchange for promises of evening outings and a tantalising glimpse of cleavage.' The clerk leant closer. 'Summer troop arrivals were the worst, the girls attired in thin blouses or dresses with low necklines during warm weather.'

Rob found it difficult to maintain a serious expression, being fully aware that Ivy had dated men from Commonwealth countries and numerous Americans besides during the war. Prior to the clerk's disclosure, they had been dating for weeks.

Still smiling at his wife's wartime escapades, Rob picks up another potato and tosses it in the old enamel basin at his feet. His back is stiff from repeated bending, so he straightens up, wincing as he stretches arthritic fingers. Through the nearby bay window, he can see Ivy perching on the arm of an easy chair, holding the telephone handset to her ear. He's wondering whether to go inside to make a pot of tea when a familiar gesture, fingers raking through her short curly hair, alerts him to sudden irritation. Displeased, he wants to wrench the handset from her fingers, berate the caller who has destroyed the tranquil ambiance of their shared spring afternoon.

When Ivy returns to the garden, Rob senses her altered disposition long before he notices pursed lips and the heightened colour dusting cheeks already tanned from spring sunshine. Disappointment hangs over her like storm clouds mustering in a summer sky.

'Our cruise has been cancelled,' she announces in a clipped voice.

'Whatever for?' he asks before she can enlighten him.

'The shipping line's gone bankrupt.'

Swearwords froth in his mouth, but before they can be expelled, neighbour Harold appears beside the garden shed that backs on to their shared fence. Harold Jenkins is the epitome of courtesy and never swears. Curses metamorphose into banknotes that hover above Rob's head just out of reach. 'Does that mean we've lost our money?'

Ivy shakes her head. 'Only the small deposit. Our travel insurance will cover the rest.'

'Thank God for that. So, what now, how can we organise another holiday in just a couple of weeks? I imagine the insurance money will take an age to come through.'

Ivy smiles. 'Not a problem on both counts, love. We've been offered a two-week coach tour of Italy and the travel agent said her company is happy to cover the cost until our insurance pays up.'

'I see.' He tries to envisage well-ordered olive groves, unspoilt villages clustered on hillsides, ancient ruins shimmering in summer sunlight. He fails, scorched earth and smoking ruins making his eyes water.

'She wants a definite answer today.'

Frowning, Rob thinks of the friends who suggested he and Ivy join them on the cruise. 'We'd better phone Alf at once,' he says, drawing a finger across his left cheek to wipe away moisture. 'He and Dawn may not have been offered the coach tour and it wouldn't seem right to go without them.' Looking down, he studies the potato resting on damp soil at his feet.

'Our travel agent and theirs have already liaised. Alf and Dawn are happy to take the coach tour.'

Lifting the spade, he slices the potato in half. 'Decision made then.'

———

Seated either side of the dining table, a well-ironed cloth disguising its shabby surface, husband and wife concentrate on miniscule lamb chops served with generous portions of home-grown potatoes and broccoli. Silence suits them both, she, dreaming of ancient monuments, art galleries and cathedrals; he trying to blot out disturbing wartime memories.

'Rome, Florence, Venice,' Ivy exclaims suddenly, raising her eyes heavenward. 'It's going to be wonderful!'

Rob neatly arranges his knife and fork before lifting his head and looking across the table. 'I'm not certain I want to go.'

Sea-green eyes flash fury. 'You agreed this afternoon. It's a bit late now to change your mind. The booking will have been made.'

'But I wanted to cruise the Aegean, explore tiny islands, experience the wonders of antiquity.' He sighs. 'Sun, sea and glorious food.'

Ivy jabs a last potato with her fork. 'There'll be plenty of sun and glorious food in Italy, plus countless antiquities. And the travel agent said most of this tour follows the coast. Besides, we can't let Alf and Dawn down.'

In no mood for argument, Rob picks up his knife and fork to continue eating, each mouthful chewed and swallowed without acknowledgment of taste. Unblinkingly, he endeavours to focus on gradually emerging white china as images of the Italian coastline move in slow procession through his mind. Messina, Salerno, Naples, Anzio – targets on maps for Allied eyes only.

FEED THY ENEMY

Wartime maps and holiday destinations are far from Rob's thoughts the following Monday, as he unlocks the small door at the rear of Harrison's Supermarket and steps into a dark storeroom. After reaching for the light switch, he waits a moment for the fluorescent tube to connect, then lifts a grey dustcoat from a nearby hook, replacing it with his sports jacket. The dustcoat is faded from copious washing and fraying on the hemline but at least it protects the well-pressed navy-blue trousers, white shirt and tie he always wears for work. Unnecessary neatness for a storeman, he acknowledges, but essential for his self-esteem. Buttoned up, he skirts a pile of cardboard boxes to retrieve the hand trolley he had parked out of harm's way the previous Friday, discovers to his annoyance that someone has shifted it. 'Damn cleaner most likely,' he mutters, moving to check the other passageways.

Abandoned in the centre aisle, the trolley lies on its side, waiting for an unsuspecting staff member to trip and skin a leg or ankle on its rough metal base plate. Resisting the urge to aim a kick at its balding tyres, Rob bends to right the beast, gasps as pain shoots through his lower back. *Bend your knees and keep your back straight,* he thinks, recalling his doctor's advice. Heavy lifting, bending and stretching have taken their toll during his two years of employment at the supermarket. At the end of each working day, each muscle throbs and he longs to immerse his weary body in a warm bath, an unlikely proposition during summer months when the central heating that also heats water has been turned off and they have to use the immersion heater instead. Baths are a once a week affair in the Harper household, the cost of heating sufficient water daily, prohibitive.

Taking small careful steps, Rob pulls the trolley to the end of the passageway where tomatoes from the Channel Isles wait to be transferred to the vegetable section, then slowly lowers the base plate to the concrete floor. 'Bend, lift, stack,' he repeats throughout the wearisome task, the mantra taking his mind off aging muscles. Sounds of imminent opening time filter through the swing doors leading from storeroom to supermarket: high-pitched laughter from teenage cashiers whose mini-skirts leave nothing to the imagination; heavy footsteps in the meat section adjacent to the doors as Terry the butcher, red-faced and rotund, surveys and reorganises his domain.

Trolley piled high, Rob inches his way forward, his breath coming in short sharp bursts, as he navigates an adjoining passageway stacked to the ceiling with cardboard cartons. At the first turn, he cautiously sets the trolley upright to wipe already damp palms on his dustcoat prior to tackling the next aisle. Wooden crates containing trays of Jaffa oranges from Israel arrived late on Friday and are creating an extra hazard by protruding into the walkway. 'Damn,' he exclaims when a careless sideways shuffle results in contact with the crates' rough edges. Pulling up his right trouser leg, he examines the skin above his sock, notes beads of blood decorating a two-inch scratch, an annoying injury only minutes into an eight-hour day.

As he inhales the fragrance of sun-kissed oranges, his gaze shifts to the purple cardboard trays visible through slatted timber. Manufactured with indentations to keep each orange separate from its neighbour, the trays prove useful for storing produce from his own tiny orchard – three apple trees, one plum, one peach, one pear. Mr Harrison has no objection to his taking home any number of trays as non-perishable rubbish is collected from supermarket bins on a weekly basis. Every autumn Rob uses newspaper to wrap apples and pears individually, ensuring his crop keeps for months stored beneath the household's three beds. Peaches are eaten as they ripen, the old tree rarely producing a decent crop. Ivy bottles some of the Bramley cooking apples for pies, crumbles or sauce; others she leaves under the beds to be cooked at a future date. Baked apples, their cores removed and replaced with sultanas and brown sugar, are one of Rob's favourite puddings. Licking his lips, he wonders what delight Ivy will serve this evening. His first question on returning home is always, 'What's for pudding, love,' first course of little consequence to a man with a sweet tooth.

After checking that blood hasn't trickled into his sock, Rob grips the cracked rubber handles and begins to manoeuvre the trolley into the slightly wider passage leading to double swing doors. A tricky right, the operation requires total concentration, so he slows to a crawl, and is almost home and dry when the trolley clips a pile of cartons containing tins of pineapple. They fall sideways in a perfect demolition, crushing several crates of oranges and sending Rob flying. Sacks of King Edward potatoes save him from serious injury, but he feels dazed and remains sprawled on lumpy hessian when the manager rushes in.

'Not again!' The man's bulk towers over the mound of crushed crates and boxes. 'How many times have I told you to be careful with that trolley?'

'I'm so sorry Mr. Harrison.' Rob struggles to his feet.

'Sorry won't replace damaged stock, Robert. I'll see you in my office when you've cleaned up this mess.' And kicking escaped tins aside, he strides towards the doors.

Defeated, Rob sinks to his knees and hangs his head.

———

Dinner is a subdued affair, Rob seeking the courage to confess he's been sacked; Ivy distracted by a letter from their daughter, Sally, who lives in a small town fifty miles away. 'A new sister on the orthopaedic ward is making life difficult for the younger nurses,' Ivy remarks, looking across the table. 'Sally says her constant criticism and impatience has led several student nurses to resign before their final exams. Such a waste of all that training.' She sighs. 'Poor Sally, if only I could just pop over and give her a hug,'

Rob raises his head, tempted to answer that hugs will be off the menu permanently soon, Sally having decided to join older sister Frances and her husband James in Australia. Reluctant to raise what remains a sensitive subject, she'll be leaving the country within three months, he concentrates instead on spearing strips of cabbage with his fork.

'I'd hoped she could get home soon,' Ivy adds, 'but she hasn't a free weekend before we go on holiday.'

Cutlery slips from Rob's fingers onto the plate, splattering the cream tablecloth with globules of gravy. 'We can't go on the tour now,' he blurts out. 'I've lost my job.'

Ivy flinches, then leans forward, green eyes demanding an explanation.

'That damn trolley again.'

A long silence follows, Ivy's mouth moving in slow motion as she digests bad news and a last forkful of cabbage.

'You could still go,' he says, relieved to have thought of a solution. 'Alf and Dawn would keep you company.'

'And leave you alone for fourteen nights.'

'I could get some sleeping pills from Doctor Hughes.'

'Sleeping pills aren't the answer, Rob. A holiday would do you good.'

'But I need to find another job.'

'You need to get out of the house and I don't mean into the garden or the shed.'

FEED THY ENEMY

Rob pushes his plate into the centre of the table and gets to his feet. Two steps and he has turned on the television set tucked in a corner away from the fireplace; a further three and he's seated in his favourite armchair, adjacent to the tiled hearth. The BBC news has already started; he stares at the familiar presenter, ignores the nearby clatter of plates and cutlery, the muttering about having to wash a tablecloth that was clean on this evening.

The national news bulletin, bleak as usual with its reports of industrial disputes, power cuts and IRA bombs, matches his mood, confirming what he has believed ever since the nineteen-seventies began. Everything in Britain is falling apart, the economy crippled by strikes and excessive wage demands, unemployment at its highest level since the war and the Troubles in Northern Ireland out of control. Slumped in the armchair, a draught from the open door leading to the hall, chilling the bare skin between socks and trousers, he shudders at the prospect of searching for work in such a depressed environment. There's no doubt about it, their daughters are the smart ones, abandoning the sinking ship before it's too late. When explaining her reasons for emigrating, Sally maintained she saw no future for herself in Britain, a sentiment Rob endorsed.

Frances and James have sponsored her, offering a home with them, which speeded up the immigration process. Secure accommodation plus nursing qualifications should ensure a bright future for a twenty-one-year old.

In preparation for her arrival, James, a practical man, has built a room in the space under the house between the garage and laundry, a combination lounge and bedroom with French doors leading out to the rear garden. Meanwhile, Frances has purchased a second-hand wardrobe and bed and is saving up for carpet and a new three-piece suite. Clearly, she expects her sister to stay for some time. For her part, Sally has volunteered to make curtains in between looking for work as Frances detests sewing of any kind.

Rob envisages the whole family gathered together under one roof at some future time, but, before long, reality pulls him up short. Even if he wanted to leave his homeland, there is no point in a sixty-year-old with an unacceptable employment record and a long history of mental illness applying to emigrate to Australia. He sighs loudly and for the first time in years, his thoughts return to a distant decade, a distant land and the crash in the Sahara Desert that should have ended his life.

FEED THY ENEMY

After a protracted but successful dogfight with a German fighter, they were heading back to their base in south-western Egypt, when a second Messerschmitt appeared from nowhere. The RAF pilot, Colin 'Smudger' Smith, veteran of countless desert ops, immediately took evasive action and as the Martin Baltimore levelled out hundreds of feet below, he and his crew believed they had outrun the enemy. But the Messerschmitt 109 had a distinct advantage over its opponent, a fuel injection system that allowed the fighter to dive quickly without losing speed, and Smudger soon realised they were heading straight into the enemy's path. Prompt action by both pilots avoided a collision, but gunfire from the machine gun mounted on top of the Messerschmitt's nose cone, peppered the Baltimore, sending it corkscrewing over massive dunes tinted blood-red by the setting sun. As Smudger tried to regain control, black smoke bled into the cloudless Egyptian sky, a stain on an otherwise perfect desert backcloth. A final flash of flame seared the right wing and the Baltimore plummeted earthward, coming to rest, nose first, in a massive wind-moulded sand dune.

Inside the aircraft's metal and Perspex dorsal

turret, rear gunner Sergeant Robert Harper gingerly lifted his head and surveyed his surroundings before descending into the smoke-filled fuselage. Minutes later, his head, still encased in flying helmet and goggles, emerged from a side hatch. Gripping the edge of the hatch, he levered himself out and jumped on to the sand. He landed on hands and knees close to the blackened wing and quickly manoeuvred into a sitting position, his back to the now silent aircraft. Incessant desert wind wailed a sorrowful refrain that filtered through his Mae West life-jacket and blue-grey battledress, even penetrating the black boots half-buried in sand. Scrambling to his feet, he turned to grab the wing, thick flying gloves protecting his hands from heated metal, and pulled himself back to the fuselage. 'Smudger, Jim, Stuart,' he called, peering through the open hatch, his voice hoarse as though he had been shouting throughout the entire afternoon.

There was no response, so he forced his body back into the aircraft, determined, despite the risk of imminent explosion, to rescue his injured colleagues. After a brief interval, he resurfaced ashen-faced, blood smeared over bare hands, fell to his knees in a futile posture of prayer. Anger oozed from every pore, sizzled on exposed skin.

'They've bloody well abandoned me,' he yelled, finding his voice at last. 'Left me alone in this godforsaken desert. What the hell did they think they were doing?' He straightened his back, shook his fist at the empty sky. 'We were a team, a bloody good team, so why didn't you take me with you, you selfish bastards?'

―――

Barely conscious of the slim fingers stroking his wrist, Rob continues to stare at the television screen. 'Please come to Italy with me,' Ivy pleads, her breath a wisp of breeze on his sun-reddened cheek. 'How can I celebrate our twenty-sixth wedding anniversary on my own?'

At last Rob raises his head but can't bring himself to turn and face her. 'You deserve a medal putting up with me for so long,' he mutters, glancing at the framed photograph on the mantelpiece – small daughters and parents enjoying a long-ago holiday on the Channel island of Guernsey.

'Don't be ridiculous,' she counters.

'No, I mean it. Our marriage hasn't exactly been a bed of roses. All those years when I was in and out of hospital and you were left alone with the girls, struggling to manage on the sickness benefit. And even when I was working, the jobs were poorly paid. Remember?'

Ivy remains silent.

'We couldn't have bought this house if you hadn't earned extra cash by taking in guests from the hotel next door to the flat when they'd overbooked. I'll never forget how you slept on a blow-up mattress on the lounge floor with Frances night after night, so I could have her bed. And what about all those foreign students you cared for once we'd moved here? Washing, ironing, cooking, taking them on outings. It must have been a chore, summer after summer. There's no doubt about it, Ivy, you're the one who's kept the family together.'

Stroking stops and the pads of her fingertips press into his skin. 'Oh Rob, please don't bring up all that again. Just come with me to Italy. The holiday is paid for and afterwards we can manage for a while with my job and your war pension.'

It took them long enough to give me my dues, he reflects, recalling annual train journeys to a shabby London office, where he had to plead his case before three grim-faced military men sitting, stiff-backed, behind a heavy wooden table. Fifteen years of deliberations, fifteen years after demob to achieve a minor victory. The RAF medic's upper-crust voice repeats in his head: *'Mr. Harper, we shall be recommending to the Ministry of Pensions that the further disability Depressive State be accepted as attributable to service and added to Stomatitis Ulcerative, which has already been accepted. You will be informed within six months of the Ministry's decision and your War Pension Order Book annotated as necessary.'*

'A pittance,' he says aloud, twisting around to face his long-suffering wife. 'Twelve shillings a week for nearly four years of war service.'

'Better than nothing,' Ivy answers in her usual optimistic manner. 'How about a cup of tea and a slice of cake while we study the tour itinerary?'

TWO

The remainder of the evening passes without further discord, a favourite comedy programme diverting Rob's attention from the wartime memories evoked by photographs in a holiday brochure Ivy picked up from the travel agent. Night is another matter, quietness and darkness joining forces to create an unbearable atmosphere that only minutes after climbing into bed, infiltrate a mind still reeling from the unexpected events of the past forty-eight hours. Questions come thick and fast, lacking sufficient space between them for considered responses. A limited timeframe – only fifteen days remain before they're due to fly to Italy – providing an inadequate period for Rob to consider employment options. There's no way he can register for unemployment benefits and then announce he'll be unavailable for job interviews due to a two-week holiday abroad. Age is another concern that dominates his restless thoughts. By the time they return home he will be sixty-one, too old to apply for any job requiring sustained physical work. Previous occupations come to mind, a lengthy list proclaiming to anyone perusing his employment history, his inability to retain a position for, at the most, more than a couple of years.

Beside him, Ivy snuffles in her sleep, a reminder of his own insomnia. The prospect of sleep unlikely, he slides out of bed, quietly locates slippers and dressing gown and creeps from the room. At the foot of the stairs, he spends a few moments deciding whether to make a hot drink or try reading the library book commenced a few days earlier. Cocoa wins out, a heaped teaspoon of sugar added to enhance the flavour. He carries the steaming mug into the dining room and positions it on the hearth tiles while he draws back the curtains. Bathed in pale moonlight and deep shadow, his beloved garden slumbers peacefully. The evening breeze has died away, nothing stirs in vegetable beds or fruit trees. For several minutes, he stands leaning against the wide curved windowsill, calmed by the thought of runner beans, carrots and tomatoes growing quietly, proof he can contribute something to the household.

Seated in his armchair, he cradles the mug in both hands and sips slowly, grateful for the soothing full-cream milk warming throat and stomach. A digestive biscuit would add to the comfort, but he has left his dentures in a glass on the bedside cabinet and can't risk waking Ivy by retrieving them. Dunking would solve the problem, but for some reason, tonight he doesn't relish the thought of soggy biscuit floating in cocoa.

After replacing the empty mug on the hearth, he lies back in the chair, hoping to doze until dawn, but his eyes feel gritty as though sand has blown from beach to cliff-top, through municipal gardens and winding streets into the dining room. He blinks rapidly to dispel the irritation, sighs as a second wave of sand distorts his vision. Reading is also out of the question; he wouldn't be able to focus. He tries to relax, push unbidden thoughts into the garden where shadows can swallow black bitterness.

Pinpricks of light begin to flicker behind closed eyelids, portents of migraine that threaten to destroy even a modicum of peace. Annoyed by this additional sign of neurological weakness, he

FEED THY ENEMY

rises quickly and with scant regard for the early hour, stomps through dining room and kitchen to what the family refer to as the back door, even though it's situated in the centre of a side wall. He pauses to pluck the key for the shed, from a hook by the sink, before crossing to the door. The old lock groans as he turns the key always left in situ; then, as he pulls the door towards him, hinges creak despite the care and attention he regularly gives them. Undeterred, he walks out into the cool night air, avoiding contact with the Ford Anglia parked behind high latticed gates and approaches the shed with quickening steps. After fumbling in his dressing gown pocket for the key, he manages to open the well-oiled padlock and slide back the bolt with barely a sound. Automatically, he reaches for the light switch, taking care not to trip over the step as he moves inside. Light from a one hundred-watt lamp floods the small space, shutting out dreaded darkness. He pulls the door shut and exhales deeply.

Before long he's perched on an old stool facing the single window, his hands resting on the workbench he constructed from old floorboards found in the loft, his mouth concentrating on the squares of Cadbury's dairy milk chocolate melting on his tongue. He keeps a bar or two in an old biscuit tin stored on the shelf beneath the bench, chocolate perfect for wet weekend afternoons when gardening proves impossible and Ivy sits chatting in the dining room with her friends. He could join the women for afternoon tea, there's always a good spread of homemade cakes and biscuits. No one would mind, he's known most of the women for years, Ivy having a predilection for long-term friendships, but he can't face the inevitable questions about work or health.

He's peeling silver foil from the last two squares of chocolate, when a sound on the roof stays his hand. More a beat than a flap, the noise continues at regular intervals, becoming louder as though the neighbour's cat has climbed onto the shed and is drumming its paws on the green roofing felt. Furious, he slips off the stool and makes his way outside, careful to close the door behind him. There's no way he'll allow the detested feline sanctuary in his shed; it causes enough havoc in the garden. Looking up, he spots the reason for chocolate interruption – a piece of roofing felt has come loose on a corner and is banging against a rafter in pre-dawn breeze. Quickly retracing his steps, he selects nails and a hammer from the workbench drawer, places them in his dressing-gown pocket before picking up the stool and carrying it out to the concrete pad in front of the door.

Slippered feet carefully balanced on the stool, he has finished securing the roofing felt and is gazing up at a myriad of stars when footsteps behind him induce a total body freeze. Light from the shed illuminates the scene, no chance of slipping unnoticed into shadow.

'Come on Rob, that's enough star-gazing for tonight,' Ivy urges, her soothing voice a welcome panacea for night terrors.

Fingers release their grip, the hammer clatters to the ground. Holding on to the doorframe, he eases himself into a sitting position, then slides off the stool and stands in the pool of light as though uncertain what to do next.

Smaller fingers reach around him, switch off the shed light and close the door. A bolt slides into place, a padlock clicks shut. Perfectly composed, despite being woken in the early hours by the sound of hammering, Ivy slips her left arm around Rob's waist and leads him into the house.

———

The following afternoon, Doctor Hughes accedes to Rob's request for medication to calm anxiety, although he refuses the request for a stronger anti-depressant. 'My advice is to leave your worries behind for two weeks and enjoy the holiday,' he says, reaching for a prescription pad.

'That's what my wife says,' Rob remarks as the doctor scrawls.

'She's right you know.' The doctor smiles as he hands over the prescription. 'Italy in early summer will be marvellous.'

Rob manages a fleeting smile.

Three nights of dreamless sleep improve Rob's mood and restore his energy levels to such an extent that, by Friday afternoon, he has dug over two garden beds, mown the lawn and planted more vegetables. Eager to help Ivy, who works two full and three half-days a week as a secretary in the office of a large department store, he has also taken advantage of fine weather to do several loads of washing. Standing by the dining room window, he looks out at clothes and sheets flapping in the breeze, pleased with his day's work. If the weather remains fine the following day, he'll suggest a drive in the country. They can pack a picnic lunch and folding canvas chairs, sit in dappled sunlight in one of the nearby New Forest's picnic grounds. The purchase of a second-hand Ford Anglia five years earlier has broadened their horizons and Rob will be forever grateful to his late mother-in-law for the legacy that enabled them to pay off the remaining mortgage and buy their first car.

Soon after the primrose-yellow car was installed behind the driveway gates, he sold the moped used for travelling to and from work, relieved he no longer had to face journeys up and down the lengthy bypass, exposed to wet or freezing weather. Two years later, daughter Frances drove them both to work in the opposite direction, Rob having secured a temporary clerk's position with the company she'd joined as a clerical officer at age seventeen. Sharing the car didn't bother him – Frances often asked to borrow it on Friday and Saturday evenings – she was a good driver and he understood why her boyfriend James couldn't afford a car on an apprentice electrician's wages.

Despite fine weather, the picnic fails to eventuate, Edna, Ivy's friend from their railway office days, being home on leave from Zambia where her husband works as an engineer. Rob declines the invitation to afternoon tea, knowing the two women will appreciate having time to catch up on news and waves Ivy goodbye as she pedals off on the short ride to her friend's bungalow near the beach.

Gardening, followed by watching cricket, occupies the entire afternoon. On warm summer days, Rob carries the television set into the garden, threading an extension lead through an open window. In between weeding and planting, he sits in a deckchair, retrieved from the shed, to watch play. Sometimes neighbour, Harold, leans over the fence to ask the score, but that seems to be the extent of his interest in the game; he never accepts Rob's invitation to join him.

Engrossed in the English captain's well-played century, Rob fails to hear the side gates open or a bicycle trundle towards the shed, and almost jumps out of the deckchair when Ivy calls a bright, 'hello, I'm back.' She leans the bicycle against the shed before walking towards him. 'Good match, love?'

'Excellent. We should win this one.'

Behind him, Ivy places her hands on his shoulders. 'Good afternoon then.'

He reaches up to pat her right hand. 'I haven't been sitting here all afternoon, you know. I weeded a patch by the pear tree as well.'

'Where Frances used to grow carrots for her guinea pigs?'

He nods. 'Thank goodness we supplemented

their diet. The poor creatures would have starved to death if they'd had to reply on her meagre crop. Never one for gardening, our Frances.'

'Not like Sally with her beautiful display of flowers around the apple tree.' Ivy sighs. 'I'm going to miss them next spring.'

He notes the pensive tone, envisages the sadness clouding her sunny face. 'I'll plant the same varieties just for you.'

'Thanks, love.' She moves away from the deckchair to flop down on the grass beside him. 'I'd really appreciate that, it's going to be hard having both girls in Australia.'

'Did you have a good afternoon with Edna?' he asks, anxious to change the subject. Neither of them had expected their younger daughter to leave the country.

Her face lightens. 'Marvellous. We talked and talked as though we hadn't seen other for years, not months.'

'Plenty of yapping fluid consumed then.'

A hand shoots out to smack his wrist. 'Cups of tea, you mean.'

He smiles. 'Slip of the tongue, my dear.'

'Oh, I don't think so.' She fiddles with a loose thread on her blouse. 'Edna said it's Ron's birthday on Monday.'

'Do they plan to celebrate?' He turns back to the television.

'Yes, tonight.' Wound around her finger, the tread snaps as she pulls it tight. 'We're invited to join them, a new restaurant not far from here. Ron's offered to pick us up to save you driving.'

Clouds mobilise and swiftly cool late afternoon warmth. 'Right,' he mutters, quickly refocuses on screen activity. 'Out! Never! Get some new glasses, umpire.'

Ivy gets to her feet, pads across the lawn and disappears behind the shed.

———

When he enters the bedroom two hours later, she's sitting on the low stool in front of the dressing table mirror, applying lipstick. Absorbed by the cricket, he has forgotten the imminent outing and for a moment queries why she's wearing the dress bought recently in the sales, an absolute bargain she assured him, even without the added staff discount.

'Hurry up and get changed, Rob.' Ivy replaces the top on the lipstick. 'Edna and Ron will be here soon.'

He moves over to the bed, sits shoulders slumped, staring at his feet. 'I don't think I can come, love. My stomach's a bit upset. It must be those pills Doctor Hughes gave me.'

'A good dinner will settle your stomach. You hardly ate anything last night.' She reaches for a brush to arrange the short curls framing her face.

'I think I'd better just have a sandwich and a cup of cocoa, then go to bed early.'

Quick as a sniper on a hillside alerted by sliding pebbles, she twists around and points the brush at Rob. 'One of these days you'll realise there's more to life than growing vegetables and fixing things around the house.'

'Sorry, love, I just can't face going out tonight.'

Ivy lowers the brush. 'Shall I tell them your ulcers are playing up?'

'Thanks.'

The brush lands on the bed inches from his right thigh. Ivy rises fast, smoothing the stiff fabric of her new dress before grabbing her handbag from a bedside chair as though Rob is about to steal it.

Down in the hall a bell rings, twin tones floating up the stairs into the bedroom.

'Good, they're early.' She hurries across the room to the door.

'Is there anything I can do for you while

you're out?' he asks, hoping to salvage something from an awkward conversation.

'No thank you,' she answers without turning her head and sweeps from the room, slamming the door behind her.

———

Dozing in front of the television, Rob remains unaware that a new programme has started. A bleak landscape fills the screen: leafless trees, bare fields, a half-demolished farmhouse surrounded by tyre-churned mud. Beyond the abandoned farm, a low ridge, devoid of vegetation, merges with a leaden sky. Sombre music compounds the desolation. The camera zooms in on a group of British soldiers dug in behind the ridge, some crouched beside machine guns, others sitting on stony ground, awaiting orders from a baby-faced officer.

A burst of gunfire rouses actors and viewer, an empty cup, kicked by a slippered foot, rolls onto fireplace tiles and smashes against the protruding metal grating. Alert to imminent danger, Rob surveys the room, then backs towards the door, his right arm raised, level with his waist, his fingers curled around an imaginary weapon. The doorknob twists beneath his left palm; holding his breath he draws the door towards him, peers into the dim hall. Satisfied no one is lurking in the shadows, he creeps across carpet runner and linoleum to kitchen safety.

Despite cavity brick walls – they built to last in the nineteen-thirties – he can still hear gunfire and the occasional explosion, most likely grenades thrown at the advancing enemy, so after retrieving the padlock key, he turns the key in the back door and heads into the night. Heavy cloud camouflages the small wooden building, hunched beside a fence, stained dark brown with creosote oil. Keeping close to the wall, he sidles forward until all that remains between house and shed is six feet of concrete path. Breeze rustles foliage on a nearby tree, he listens for further night noises, hears only the rumble of a distant train. Two steps and he has returned to shadow, is fumbling with padlock and bolt, his fingers refusing to cooperate.

At last, he enters the shed, closes the door quietly and heads for the workbench. A strip of moonlight filters through the window illuminating a hammer and an open box of nails lying next to torn pieces of silver foil.

Clouds clear, relief cools clammy skin.

Grateful for solitude – how can he rationalise being spooked by a television programme?

– he pulls the stool from beneath the bench and sits down heavily. Fingers fiddle with silver foil, he licks his lips, can almost taste the chocolate melting in his mouth. Reaching under the workbench, he grabs the biscuit tin and after setting it on the bench, removes the lid.

No chocolate!

How could he have forgotten to replenish the supply? Wait a minute, what about the two squares left on the bench the night he fixed the roofing felt? Eyes oscillate over hammer and nails, fingers push torn foil aside, fingertips examine the bench's scarred surface.

No chocolate!

Easing his backside from the stool, he steps sideways to flick the switch on the left of the door. He searches diligently but uncovers no sign of errant chocolate. 'Ivy must have taken it when she got her bike out,' he says aloud, irritated by the theft. He stomps back to the stool and is about to sit when he remembers eating chocolate during the afternoon. Two squares, sun-softened from days lying on a bench adjacent to a window, two squares enjoyed with a cup of tea while cricketers enjoy their own break at Lords. Remorse floods his face, deep down he knows Ivy would never interfere with anything in his shed. Retrieving or returning her bicycle – there's nowhere else to store it out of the weather – are the only reasons she ever enters his domain. Seizing the tin, he jams on the lid before his eyes can alight on a faded brown envelope lying at the bottom. This isn't the time to reflect on past relationships, he must return to the dining room, clear up the evidence of a shameful incident before Ivy comes home.

THREE

The remaining days until the holiday pass peacefully, solitary pursuits a welcome respite to a former storeman, jaded from two years spent in the company of dolly-bird shop assistants prattling incessantly about boyfriends, hair colour and the latest fashion. Terry the butcher was pleasant enough, but rarely spoke of anything other than cuts of meat, while the supermarket manager only addresses his staff when he has something to complain about.

Apart from gardening, Rob uses the time to hone his kitchen skills, making bread for the first time in years, an accomplishment gained a decade earlier in the commercial kitchen of a psychiatric hospital as part of occupational therapy. He also makes marmalade using the large bag of oranges Ivy's brother, Jack brought around late one afternoon. Jack purchased the fruit cheaply in the market that lines either side of the neighbouring town's high street twice a week. 'The girls are a bit sick of oranges,' he said to explain the gift. Jack and his wife have two teenage daughters. 'I bought a bag last Saturday too.'

'I reckon you should leave the shopping to Pam,' Rob replied, recalling previous gifts of cut-price and often over-ripe fruit.

The two men spent a pleasant couple of hours sitting in the garden, Jack on leave from his job in the drawing office of a local aircraft manufacturer. The family had planned to spend the week sailing along the coast to Devon, but his younger daughter's chest infection put paid to that idea. Over cups of tea and slices of Ivy's fruit cake, they discussed a range of topics, none designed to provoke negative reactions, a deliberate tactic on Jack's part, Rob assumed, for which he was grateful. He felt certain Ivy would have told her brother about the trolley accident, but Jack made no mention of it, or the resulting dismissal. During a lull in the conversation, Rob almost raised the subject, knowing Jack would find the incident amusing, but on second thoughts decided against it. Unlike crushed fruit, some subjects were best left buried.

Likewise, neither Rob nor his old friend Alf Simpson raise the matter of their months together in wartime Italy when they finally meet at the hotel in Rome. The late alteration of holiday plans meant the two couples were unable to travel on the same flight as previously planned. Having arrived hours earlier, Alf and his wife, Dawn, have already met fellow tour members over lunch, mostly middle-aged couples according to Alf, with a sprinkling of older women. 'Widows, I imagine,' he remarks as he shows Rob around the pleasant foyer and adjacent lounge while Ivy unpacks. 'Probably on the lookout for a Latin fellow, bit of holiday romance, if you know what I mean.'

'Probably just having a holiday,' Rob answers, reflecting that his mate's interest in the fairer sex never wavers.

'Tour guide's a bit of all right.'

'Man, or woman?' Rob asks, deliberately provocative.

'Woman of course, about twenty-five I reckon.' Alf smiles wistfully. 'Her name's Patrizia.

Tall, long black hair, beautiful...' His hands sketch a voluptuous figure in the air.

'I don't need to know all the details.'

'Bella donna, bella donna,' Alf murmurs, his hands sculpting full breasts.

'Belladonna is a poisonous plant,' Rob says, determined to silence his friend before someone overhears. 'Not something to tangle with.'

'Spoilsport.'

'No, I just prefer to behave like an English gentleman.'

'Since when have you been a toff?'

'Born with a stainless-steel spoon, I was.'

'All right, you win. I never could compete with your quick wit.' Alf glances at the ornate grandfather clock standing sentinel-style to one side of the reception counter. 'Oh Lord, it's five-thirty!' He turns back to Rob. 'We'd better get on move on. There's a tour of the city before dinner.'

Rob groans inwardly. He would prefer a cup of tea and a rest before dinner. It has been a long day - up early, taxi to the bus station, coach to the airport, flight to Rome, taxi to the hotel.

'No need to look so glum, mate, Patrizia said there won't be much walking involved this evening. The coach will take us to the Piazza Augusto Imperatore. Old Mussolini had it built to commemorate the 2000th anniversary of Emperor Augustus' birth. Ordered all the existing buildings except a couple of churches to be demolished. Typical. Bloody tyrant.'

'A veritable mine of information, aren't you?' Rob replies, unwilling to comment on a long-dead dictator.

Alf grins. 'I hang on Patrizia's every word.'

―――

The city tour proves interesting and far from tiring, frequent stops and a slow pace giving Rob and his fellow travellers ample time to experience sights including the Spanish Steps and the fountains in the Piazza Navona, water tumbling over exquisite sculptures. Dinner is spent 'al fresco,' outside a small restaurant located in a side street. Rob savours every mouthful of the splendid gelato dessert.

Following the meal, the tourists head for the coach waiting around the corner to return them to the hotel. Weary, but pleased he made the effort to attend the tour, Rob settles into his seat and strokes Ivy's bare wrist. Her enthusiasm was infectious, her delight palpable as she gazed with awe at Baroque architecture and Bernini sculptures. It had been the same during their visit to

Australia the previous year, her passion for travel evident from the moment they stepped on the plane. An unexpected legacy from a grateful neighbour had funded their Australian holiday, Ivy and Rob caring for the ailing bachelor during the months following his stroke and prepared to continue until he secured a nursing home place. Clifford's death ten weeks after moving to the home was a surprise, but nothing compared to the shock experienced on receiving a copy of his last will and testament from a local solicitor. Ivy and Robert Harper were the sole beneficiaries!

'We'll spend it on travel,' Ivy, a frustrated traveller for years declared when the cheque arrived. 'Australia first, of course. I'm dying to see this country Frances raves on about in her letters. Imagine, kangaroos hopping about all over the place and beaches stretching for miles.'

Rob smiles to himself as he recalls his less exuberant response. 'I don't think you'll find many kangaroos in the streets of Brisbane, my dear.'

The coach pulls up outside their hotel. 'What a wonderful evening,' Ivy says, squeezing his hand. She flashes a brilliant smile. 'I can hardly wait for tomorrow.'

Beside her, Rob stifles a yawn.

After a wake-up call at six, forty tourists board the coach an hour later to visit Vatican City, Patrizia advising there will be fewer crowds at an early hour. This proves correct, the queue for the Vatican Museum short, but when they emerge, Saint Peter's Square is awash with thousands of tourists and Rob finds it difficult to keep their new guide in view - outside the museum, the willowy Patrizia had handed over her flock to a local guide of short stature.

An early lunch in a side street restaurant outside the Vatican walls is a welcome break, although too short as far as Rob is concerned. Hurried back to the coach, he barely has enough time to catch his breath before they are herded into the Colosseum like early Christians destined for a premature death at the paws of hungry lions. Except, according to Patrizia, Christians were never thrown to the lions in this arena. The steep staircase to the second level, the only one accessible, provides an excellent view of the entire edifice but results in Rob puffing and panting as though he has run a four-minute mile.

On their return to the hotel, Rob collapses in a foyer armchair, reluctant to stand in the inevitable queues for the lifts. Totally exhausted, he questions how he'll survive the rest of the trip but as his heartrate slows, he decides to read the British newspaper lying on a low table nearby, Ivy having returned to the room to write postcards to the girls. Days old, the paper contains the usual depressing news of strikes and rising unemployment, so he replaces it on the table and is about to leave when Patrizia appears.

'Ok now, Mister Rob?' she calls, striding towards him.

'Fine thank you. I was a bit breathless that's all. The heat most likely.'

'Then you must take great care in the south. It will be much warmer there.' She gestures towards the bar located to the right of the foyer. 'Come, join me for a drink and tell me what you thought of my city.'

'Thank you, Patrizia, I would be delighted,' he replies, envisaging Alf's expression when learning of this unexpected invitation.

In no mood for idle conversation with the garrulous Cockney widow walking several paces ahead, Rob chooses the stairs rather than one of the lifts tucked around the corner from the hotel foyer. Although their room is on the fifth floor, his legs, aching half an hour earlier from endless sightseeing, appear to have discovered a new lease of life and carry him with ease up the wide marble staircase leading to the first floor. At the top of the stairs, he hesitates and looks around for a sign indicating the fire stairs. Finding nothing, he hurries past the lifts, where he discovers a door marked *'Uscita d'emergenza.'*

Dim lighting in the stairwell forces a slower pace up the remaining flights, giving his breathing a chance to return to normal and the slight chest pain he has experienced in recent months, following exertion, has receded by the time he pushes open the door to the fifth-floor corridor. Turning to the right, he quickly locates the room and inserts his key in the lock. As expected, Ivy is sitting at the small round table near the window, her pen poised over a postcard. She doesn't look up as the door closes behind him.

'Hello there,' she says brightly, 'I thought you'd be back sooner. Been chatting?'

'Yes, to Patrizia.'

'That's nice, dear.' She lowers the pen and begins to write.

In two strides, Rob has crossed the room and is bending over her as though about to kiss her soft brown curls. 'You lied to me.'

A wavy line of blue ink defaces motherly greetings.

'You said we were going to Sorrento after Rome.'

Bewildered by his harsh tone, Ivy raises her head. 'That's right. Why, did Patrizia tell you the itinerary has been altered?'

He slaps the table with the palm of his hand sending postcards fluttering to the floor. 'Patrizia said Sorrento is only a day trip. We're *staying* in Naples.' He takes a deep breath before ejecting a second accusation. 'You deliberately spilt tea over that page of the brochure, ripped it out before I had a chance to read it.'

Ivy shrinks away from him, huddles against the window.

'Want to stir dark memory, do you?' His normally pale cheeks flush with anger. 'Want to spoil my holiday?'

Ivy straightens her shoulders. 'You've got to face up to your demons, Rob. The war finished almost thirty years ago.'

Ignoring her advice, he walks over to the bedside table and picks up the telephone receiver. 'Aeroporto Fiumicino, per favore.'

'Oh no, please don't go home,' she cries, the chair tipping over as she jumps to her feet. 'Talk to me, Rob. Surely we can sort this out.'

The hand holding the receiver shakes as he attempts to erase the visions floating before his eyes: a war-torn city viewed from the window of a transport aircraft, street after street of bombed buildings, burnt trams and piles of rubble, the dark shadows of ships sunk in the harbour. Technicolour scenes fade to be replaced and by the black and white footage of a Pathé News bulletin viewed in the intact basement of a Neapolitan cinema. Allied tanks and trucks rolling into the city, thousands of inhabitants emerging from damaged but still standing buildings, lining the streets to welcome the victorious troops with applause and cheers. '180 Allied raids, more than 20,000 civilian casualties and still the Neapolitans clapped and cheered,' he informs her, post-war statistics crystal-clear in his mind. Shaking his head in disbelief, he slowly puts down the receiver and falls back on the bed.

When next he opens his eyes, Ivy is sitting beside him, stroking his right arm, her fingers warm and tender. 'Try to think instead of the family you told me about all those years ago,' she murmurs, her red lips barely moving. 'They must have clapped and cheered every time you brought them food.'

'But I don't even know if they survived the

war!' He sniffs. 'The situation in Naples was still pretty grim when I left in late forty-four.'

'Well, now you have a chance to find out.'

A frown creases his brow. 'What are you suggesting?'

'While we're in Naples, why don't we go to the Town Hall or wherever they keep the records, then at least you would know for sure what happened to them.'

A simple assignment. Ask a local government clerk a few questions, wait for answers. No emotional involvement; an English tourist simply making enquiries about a family he once knew. 'Some of them could still live in Naples, I suppose,' he remarks nonchalantly, raising himself to a sitting position.

Ivy smiles. 'Now, I must finish those postcards before dinner, or we'll be home before the girls receive them.' Rising quickly, she retrieves the scattered postcards before resuming her seat at the table.

Suddenly Rob sits bolt upright, stares bright-eyed into a possible tomorrow. 'I could buy a map. The Portici area wouldn't have changed that much. I'm sure I could find the street, not certain about the apartment building though, they all looked the same to me. But if that didn't work, I could ask in the local shops if anyone knew their whereabouts.'

'Surely they'd have moved by now?'

'Probably not. Italian families tend to stay in the same neighbourhoods. I'll ask our driver if he can point us in the right direction. I'm sure Patrizia said he came from Naples.'

'But I thought you didn't want to rake up the past? It's one thing to find out if the family survived the war, quite another to deliberately look for them.'

Rob turns towards her, notes the worried expression, her lower lip moving from side to side as teeth chew soft flesh. 'I don't believe I have any choice.'

Ivy frowns and releases her lip.

'Think about it. Alf and Dawn ask us if we want to join them on a cruise. Normally we'd have to decline, especially after last year's visit to Australia, but thanks to Clifford we have enough money for another holiday. Then the Aegean cruise is cancelled, and we end up on a package tour of Italy. Venice, Milan, Florence, Rome and....'

'Naples,' Ivy interrupts, and for the second time that afternoon trips over the chair in her haste to reach Rob's side.

They emerge from the lengthy embrace as

flustered as young lovers caught by a parent returning home sooner than expected. Getting to her feet, Ivy endeavours to smooth out the creases in her cotton sundress, while Rob tucks shirt back into trousers before swinging his legs over the side of the bed.

'Think I'll have a shower before changing for dinner,' she remarks, heading for the bathroom.

Rob glances at his watch. 'I'm just going to pop down and see Alf for a minute. He's probably in the bar by now.'

'Whatever for?' she calls back. 'You'll see him at dinner in less than an hour.'

'I need to catch him on his own, let him know about our plans for tomorrow.'

Ivy swings around, one hand still holding the door handle. 'Surely you don't expect him to walk suburban streets looking for a family *you* befriended thirty years ago?'

'Why ever not? It was Alf who solved the problem in the first place.'

'What problem?' she asks, but Rob is heading for the door.

A group of middle-aged and older men stand around the bar, most casually dressed in lightweight trousers, open-necked short-sleeved cotton shirts and the footwear referred to in England as 'deck shoes.' Rob recognises some of them from the day's tours. English seems to be the predominant language, so he presumes they are all tourists. The few women present, clad in smart evening wear, sit to one side of the bar in black leather bucket chairs arranged around a low glass-topped table. From a distance, Rob surveys the crowd, expecting to see Alf perched on a stool or propping up the bar as he would be in his native Yorkshire, but there's no sign of him. Unwilling to linger in case fellow travellers spot him and suggest he join them for a drink, Rob quickly retreats, but as he approaches the open door, a sideways glance reveals a couple of armchairs in a corner, one of which appears to be occupied. Turning on his heel, he hurries over.

Dwarfed by the overstuffed armchair, thin Alf sits legs crossed, quaffing a large glass of white wine rather than his usual brown ale. 'Well, this is a surprise, old mate,' he calls on noticing Rob. 'Take a seat and let me buy you a drink.' He hands Rob his half-empty glass before getting to his feet.

'Lemon squash for me,' Rob calls after him, but Alf fails to hear the request, his hearing aid still sitting on the bedside table in his room.

Before long he returns carrying a large glass of wine. 'It's a local drop, not bad.'

'Thanks.' Rob takes several sips before divulging his Neapolitan plans.

Alf understands Rob's desire to look for the family they both knew in forty-four, but has no wish to join in the search, maintaining there's no point in digging up the past. Switching the conversation to present day Naples, he becomes atypically animated, chatting about the guided tour of the Museum of Antiquities Dawn has booked for the following afternoon.

Puzzled by Alf's enthusiasm, only this afternoon he was complaining about having to jostle the crowds in art galleries and museums, Rob keeps his thoughts to himself and makes no further reference to his own arrangements. He would welcome Alf's company, but at least Ivy has agreed to accompany him, despite her initial reservations. 'To the next leg of our tour,' he says, raising his glass.

'I'll drink to that!' Alf grins and drains his glass.

———

As the bedside clock makes its slow progression towards dawn, Rob relives the hours following the phone call from the travel agent, witnessing anew the horrific images that had filled his head when Ivy wanted to discuss their altered holiday arrangements. Eyes wide open, he lies contemplating whether such vivid recollections are a warning not to mess with memory. Reason answers in the affirmative, but he dismisses the response, reluctant to relinquish his, by now, overwhelming need to look for the Zappetti family. Instead, he endeavours to recall advice from the numerous psychiatrists visited during the past quarter-century. Convinced one of them had said that revisiting a scene of trauma could bring closure, he settles back on the pillow, his decision made.

Sleep remains elusive.

When the only available space is a hotel bedroom, insomnia poses a problem not encountered at home, where he can slide out of bed, grab his dressing gown and quietly make his way downstairs to the dining room. Once installed in his armchair, library book in hand, he can bury dark thoughts beneath captivating narrative. And if that fails, there's always his garden refuge. He built the original shed from pre-war bricks, most of which remained in one piece following his demolition of the blast wall that still shielded the kitchen door and window when they purchased the house back in late fifty-six. The previous owner couldn't have been in a hurry to forget *his* war, witness not only the blast wall but also the army uniforms, boots and Brodie steel helmets discovered in the loft. Rob burnt the unwelcome relics in the back garden, black smoke from the bonfire darkening an already grey February sky.

They moved in during the second week of January, a bitter sleet falling as the removalist unloaded furniture from an ancient van. The girls, aged six and three, danced all over the house, excited at the prospect of so many rooms, especially the small back bedroom already designated a playroom by Frances. Meanwhile, Ivy bustled around emptying boxes while Rob directed the placement of lounge, dining and bedroom furniture from their small two-bedroomed flat. Half-empty, the spacious house seemed as cold inside as out, but Ivy, concerned about their lack of funds – only nine pounds remained in the bank after solicitor's and estate agent's accounts had been settled – refused to light a coal fire in the dining room until nightfall. The meagre supply of coal purchased the previous week, remained piled against the blast wall outside the kitchen and God only knew how they were going to afford enough fuel to see them through what was promising to be a severe winter.

Warm but restless in a Rome hotel room, Rob recalls Ivy's relief when her father casually mentioned he'd ordered a lorry load of coal for them as a house-warming present. Rob felt a little embarrassed, his father-in-law, Will, having already spent weeks painting and wall-papering every room, the bank insisting on these renovations as a condition of the mortgage. Nevertheless, he welcomed the kind gesture, the first of many during the late fifties when living in a house neglected by its former owner necessitated extensive maintenance. Six years after they purchased the house, Will suffered a stroke while painting the upper storey of his own house and fell from the ladder. Taken to hospital, suffering a fractured skull and other broken bones, he survived for three days, unconscious and unresponsive. Rob still missed the old man's company. Generous and uncomplaining, despite frequent ill-health, his father-in-law had been a welcome replacement for the drunken parent Rob had disowned five years before the war.

Turning onto his back, Rob focuses on the sliver of pale light visible through a gap in the thick curtains. Soon he'll be able to get up, consign reminiscences of any flavour to memory's deep shaft where they belong. Daylight demands

FEED THY ENEMY

an acceptance of the here and now, especially during a holiday, once way beyond his means.

———

Inside the air-conditioned coach, Rob slouches in his seat, exhausted from an almost sleepless night. Unable to suppress a yawn, he glances at Ivy and is relieved to see she appears totally absorbed by unfamiliar vistas, her head and shoulders turned towards the window, her face almost touching the glass. Patrizia has advised the journey will take about four hours, including a brief lunch break, so after making himself comfortable, Rob closes his eyes, hoping to sleep until the coach stops at a roadside café.

He has almost succumbed to sleep when Ivy grabs his left wrist. 'Just look at that gorgeous village,' she exclaims, her voice high-pitched with excitement. 'Tiny houses clinging to the hillside and wildflowers everywhere! It's so picturesque!'

'Beautiful,' he murmurs without opening his eyes.

'Really, Rob, how can you even contemplate sleeping when there's so much to see?'

Heavy eyelids flutter. 'Sorry love, I can't keep up your pace,' he answers wearily, the eight years between them feeling more like twenty today. 'Rome wore me out.'

'Then you'd better recharge your batteries before we reach Naples. Who knows when we'll get the chance to come this way again?'

'Who knows indeed.' He sighs, relishing a draught of cool air on his face, the support of a well-designed seat. Sleep comes swiftly, a pleasant respite from the night-mind's relentless wandering.

The tourist coach rolls south past fields burgeoning with crops, livestock grazing on verdant pasture, ancient vines climbing slopes, olive trees standing in serried rows. Bucolic tranquillity seemingly untouched for generations.

Deep in dream, Rob remains unaware of the picture-postcard landscape unfolding on either side of the Rome-Naples road. Cramped in the fuselage of an Avro York transport along with seventy others, he is leaving Italy to take up ground crew duties at an air base in Lincolnshire. The aircraft has seating for only fifty-six passengers, so with others of lower rank, he sits cross-legged in the aisle. Almost thirty years have vaporised in the shimmering summer heat, the date January twenty-eight, nineteen forty-five, the ground temperature plummeting as the aircraft heads north. Naples is a recent memory, a shattered city, his shattered dreams. Who knows if he will ever have the chance to come this way again?

The aircraft began to level out, so Rob relaxed his grip on the adjacent seat frame to stretch stiff fingers, taking care not to touch the airman in front, an intolerant individual judging from the comments made when their two bodies had touched during take-off. Eyes half-focused on the man's broad back, a sudden stinging sensation drew Rob's attention back to his outstretched hands. Aghast, he watched wind-whipped sand smother nails, knuckles, skin. Shaking his head to banish the mirage, he craned his neck to catch a glimpse of the receding land, framed in a tiny window. But instead of the west coast of Italy, he saw the North African coastline and beyond it the vast Sahara, mile after mile of sand dunes rippling like a golden ocean in relentless desert wind.

Fragments of past nightmares flickered behind closed eyelids. *So, it's back to the desert as usual,* he thought, oblivious to the frown puckering his forehead. *Burning days and freezing nights, shifting sands and shadows that refuse to fade despite the passage of time.*

Before long, the intensity of cobalt sky and yellow sand dissolved to blessed blackness, but respite was short-lived, a camel and rider emerging from behind an immense dune as a red sun rose above the horizon. Clad in traditional Bedouin garb, ankle-length white cotton robe known as a tob, a sleeveless coat and kufeya headgear held in place with a band of camel hair the man appeared to be scrutinising a dark shape lying on the sand some distance ahead, a shape that to the sixty-year old dreamer seemed strangely familiar. He watched the Bedouin reach for the rifle slung on his back and tuck it under his right arm. Camel and rider drew closer, the shape revealed as a man in RAF battledress lying on the sand, his head, still encased in a flying helmet, resting on folded arms. Dismounting quickly, the Bedouin walked over to the body and poked it with his rifle butt.

The airman stirred and struggled to sit up.

Astounded, the Bedouin stepped back and pointed his rifle menacingly at the man's head, prompting him to say in a shaky voice, 'English, RAF. Plane crash, other men dead.'

The dream dune faded, reformed as a small oasis fringed with date palms. Outside a large

FEED THY ENEMY

tent a group of men sat cross-legged eating from a communal dish, the rescued airman among them chewing thoughtfully. A short distance away, women dressed in the long flowing black dresses called galabeyas, their hair covered with embroidered headscarves, cooked on open fires, pausing now and then to check on children playing nearby.

Suddenly, a Messerschmitt Bf 109 appeared in the east and swooped low over the oasis, shattering early evening harmony with protracted gunfire. Palms splintered, peppering the precious water with unripe dates. Women and children flung themselves on the sand; their men scooped up rifles, fired wildly at the German fighter. Lying on his stomach near the tent, the airman heard the roar of a powerful Daimler Benz engine as the plane gained height, waited for diminishing sound to signal its departure. Around him the other men lay down their weapons and carried on with the meal as though the violent intrusion had been only a minor irritation. Women rose slowly and helped smaller children to their feet. Animated conversation accompanied the hiss and splatter of frying food, hands gesticulated, black eyes flashed.

Appetite diminished, the airman rolled over and sat up, hugging his knees as he watched the fascinating interplay of a nomadic community. When a young woman stepped away from her fire and walked over to a group of children sitting nearby, he noted with interest the upturned faces, the babble of high-pitched voices, several pointing fingers. A nod of her head and she turned on her heel, raced towards the water and vanished among the shattered palms.

Still sitting near the tent, the airman was contemplating the likelihood of rescue in the foreseeable future, when high-pitched screams pierced the darkening sky. Jolted back to reality, he watched the young woman emerge from the trees carrying a tiny blood-soaked child in her arms.

FOUR

THE POSSIBILITY OF RESCUE CAME SOONER than expected, the Bedouin leader escorting the airman to his tent the following morning, where a radio sat in state on a square of colourful carpet. Most likely the radio had been taken from an abandoned lorry or tank, although from where the airman stood in the tent entrance, he couldn't tell whether it had previously belonged to Allied or Axis troops. But whatever its origins, the leader appeared to know how to operate it, and when loud crackling subsided, he signalled for the airman to step forward.

'Thank you.' The airman smiled and walked over to the radio.

'RAF,' the leader said, pointing at the airman's chest. 'Good.'

The airman smiled again and reached for the combination transmitter and receiver held in the leader's outstretched hand. The field radio had British Army markings.

Within hours of the transmission, Sergeant Rob Harper, rear gunner, was sitting beside Pilot Officer Greenwood in a RAF fighter, winging his way back to the squadron. The flight passed without incident, there was no sign of enemy aircraft in the cloudless blue sky or troops on the move across the vast desert below. Viewed from high altitude, the makeshift base appeared as a series of white lines running parallel to one another, adjacent to a single black line edged with grey dots. On approach to the site, lines metamorphosed into white tents erected in neat rows and a black rubber runway sprayed with oil for use and rolled up when moving to a new location, while grey dots morphed into aircraft parked on hard-packed sand. From the passenger seat, Rob looked down at the runway and noticed a gap between two aircraft as though the maintenance crew were still waiting for the downed Baltimore to return. Gulping back a sob, he turned away from the window and peered at the instrument panel.

Greenwood, never a talkative type, remained silent until the aircraft was taxiing along the runway, when he remarked, 'Good to be back, eh old chap?'

'I wasn't sure if I'd see the base again,' Rob replied without shifting his gaze. 'Can't say I fancied living with Bedouin for the duration.'

'Food would be hard to take, I reckon. Don't they eat sheep's eyes?'

'I believe so. Didn't see any myself.'

'Strange way of life, wandering through the desert with a herd of goats or sheep.'

'Each to his own,' Rob murmured, anxious to terminate the conversation.

Greenway cut the engine and turned off the runway. Wheels dug into sand and the left-hand wing tipped slightly, missing the last aircraft in line by inches. 'Out you get, Harper. I'll see to this old crate.'

'Thanks for the lift, sir.'

The pilot nodded and turned *his* attention to the instrument panel.

Ever conscious of protocol, Rob headed for Wing Commander Middleton's tent, positioned at the end of a row, but the tent flap was closed and there was no response to his 'Sergeant Harper reporting, sir,' so he headed for the large tent that served as the Officers' Mess. After repeating his salutation and receiving permission to enter, he found the Wingco seated at a table, a beer bottle cradled in one hand.

'Welcome back, Harper,' Middleton called before Rob could salute. 'Take a seat.'

'Thank you, sir. It's good to be back.' Rob perched on a canvas stool nearby.

'A full report can wait until this evening, Harper. I expect you'll want to celebrate your safe return first.'

Rob nodded, unwilling to admit he would prefer to snatch some much-needed sleep. Jammed between two snoring Bedouin men, he'd slept fitfully the previous night.

'Bad luck the others bought it.'

'Yes, sir.' Rob swallowed hard. 'Will we try to retrieve the bodies, sir?'

'No, Jerry's in the vicinity. We can't risk more casualties.'

'Right, sir.' Rob stared at sand pock-marked with boot-prints, tried to erase crash-site images.

'Bedouin leader proved a good sort.'

Rob looked up. 'Yes, sir. Good thing he had a radio.'

The Wingco nodded. 'Well, must get back to work.'

'Yes, sir.' Rob rose quickly, saluted and hurried away in the direction of the tent he shared with Alf Simpson and Gordy McIntyre, both maintenance crew.

But sleep had to wait, Alf waiting in a strip of shadow near their tent and insisting on escorting Rob to the Other Ranks' Mess, a single collapsible table positioned beneath a tarpaulin strung between tents where numerous colleagues had gathered to toast his safe return with the daily beer ration. Embarrassed by their raucous laughter, the endless slaps on the back and unearned congratulations, Rob yearned to retreat, find solace in sleep from the clouds of survivor guilt that swirled around his weary body. No one mentioned Smudger or Jim or Stuart, no one toasted their memory.

Long after midnight Rob was still tossing and turning on his narrow stretcher, his face bathed in perspiration despite the freezing temperature. His mouth felt dry, his gums sore as though he'd been chewing bones not the tiny cubes of unidentifiable meat and vegetables served up in the mess for dinner.

Shaving next morning, he peered into the tiny mirror propped against his kitbag and tentatively touched swollen lips. Greenwood's remark about sheep's eyes came to mind, so he assumed the swelling had been caused by spices in the Bedouin food. Accustomed to bland RAF rations, he had experienced a burning sensation with each mouthful of what he imagined was goat curry scooped up with a piece of flat bread. The tip of his tongue encountered a rough patch on his palette; he explored further, came upon tiny raised circles of flesh that felt tender to the touch. Intending to view the evidence, he tried and failed to open his mouth wide.

The Medical Officer succeeded, his metal instrument forcing Rob's lips apart. 'Nasty mess in here, Harper,' he remarked, shining his torch into the infected cavity. 'It looks like what we called Trench Mouth in the last show.' Removing the instrument, he tossed it in a dish on his desk and switched off the torch.

'But I haven't been anyway near a trench, sir,' Rob managed to croak.

'There are various causes: poor hygiene, emotional stress, poor diet.'

'Yes, to all of those, sir.'

'No surprise there.' The MO walked back behind his table, a piece of ply resting on a canvas stool, a picked up a pen and began to write on a small notepad. 'Stomatitis ulcerative,' he said half to himself.

'So, what's the treatment for these ulcers, sir?'

The MO tore off the sheet of paper before answering. 'I'm going to evacuate you to the nearest field hospital. I want to be certain the ulcers heal properly. There's not much hope of that if you stick around here. He handed over the paper. 'You can fly out with Greenwood this evening. He's going east to pick up some medical supplies for me.'

'How long do you think I'll be in hospital, sir?'

'A week maybe, depends on how you respond to the treatment. Report to the Wingco before you leave. Oh, and take your kit. You never know, we might have moved camp by the time you're ready to return.'

'Yes sir, thank you.' Rob got to his feet and hurriedly left the tent, the pain in his mouth and on his lips ten times worse than before the examination. He longed for an ice-cold drink to numb the stinging ulcers, but he had already consumed the half-cup of lukewarm water handed out to each man first thing in the morning and it was too early for the beer ration.

Harsh morning light streamed through open canvas flaps, illuminating the mainly young patients lying on narrow stretchers either side of a large tent, part of a field hospital situated some distance west of Cairo. Propped on a pillow, the new arrival discreetly observed the men around him, the extent of their injuries shocking even to a seasoned airman. Bedding tossed aside during the night had exposed a plethora of amputations, dried blood staining bandaged stumps, while directly opposite his stretcher, the patient's eyes and head were swathed with spotless bandages, the face beneath unlined by age. *The bloody consequences of war*, Rob thought, looking away quickly and turning his left cheek to the pillow.

'It's not healthy in this climate to lie with your face against the pillow,' a female voice snapped, destroying his fragment of peace. 'On your back at once, Sergeant Harper.'

Rob turned over and focused his attention on the canvas roof.

'That's better. I like an obedient patient. It makes my job a lot easier.'

'It must be tough nursing some of these blokes,' he remarked without shifting his gaze.

'It must be tough being a rear gunner.'

Rob shivered. 'It is, especially after almost three years.'

'Three years! My God, you really are a survivor!'

Rob looked down, noted her immaculate uniform, the white cap perched on neat blond curls. 'I might have defied the odds, sister, but right now I feel a bit of a fraud taking up space in a hospital bed without even a minor war wound. Heaps of ops behind me and here I am grounded by a mouth infection.'

Her grim expression softened. 'Think of it as a well-earned rest, Sergeant. There's no point in feeling guilty. I'd make the most of it if I were you.'

'I'll do my best.'

She smiled and hurried away.

———

But as day crawled into a second Egyptian night, the survivor began to dream of desert conflict and casualties that he alone inflicted. Hour after hour, he flew around Saharan oases, a grinning rear gunner cradling his Browning machine gun. Below him, Bedouin children sprawled on yellow sand, their limbs at odd angles, blood seeping through small garments. Appalled by the consequences of his actions, his throat pulsed with silent screams. Waking before dawn, he lay shivering, perspiration drying on his fevered body, his mind struggling to banish nightmare. He had anticipated images of his dead mates or the downed Baltimore to haunt his dreams – when handing in his report, the Wingco warned this could happen – not relentless unprovoked aggression. The Bedouin had saved his life, enabled a return to his squadron, his people; a subconscious desire to harm them made no sense.

Morning brought a modicum of comfort. Nurses bustled around the ward dressing wounds, bathing, feeding, their cheerful voices expelling night terrors.

After a few days of rest, medication and skilful nursing, Rob's ulcers began to heal. Nightmares continued but were less frequent now his fever had abated. When morning light woke him – at dawn nurses opened the tent flaps to allow cool air free passage through the ward – he learnt to dispel gruesome night images by concentrating on pleasant pre-war memories: girls with scarlet lips, summer picnics by forest streams, victorious football matches. Post-breakfast, he

FEED THY ENEMY

passed the time by assisting the overworked nurses, running errands from tent to tent, feeding the severely wounded, reading to the sightless. Only one tent, standing apart from the others adjacent to military vehicles, remained off-limits. Rob assumed it contained valuable medical supplies.

On the sixth day, he was reading a letter to the young soldier whose eyes were swathed with bandages, when Sister James, she of the permanently pristine uniform, approached the bed. 'When you've finished here, Sergeant Harper, please report to MO Adams.'

Rob looked up. 'Will do, sister. Do you think he'll discharge me today?'

'I'd say so. The infection has cleared up and transport's available.'

'Good, I want to get back. I'm getting bored sitting around here.'

'Wish I could say the same.'

All of a sudden, a hail of piercing screams and plaintive wails swept through the tent like a desert sandstorm.

'What the hell's going on out there?' Rob demanded, fearing the field hospital was under attack.

'Nothing for you to worry about,' Sister

James rushed out of the tent, closing the rear flap behind her.

The young soldier propped himself up on his elbows and leant towards Rob. 'I've heard 'em scream before. Most likely it's a couple of nutters on the move.'

'Nutters?'

'Blokes who've lost their minds somewhere in this god-forsaken desert. They ship 'em home soon as possible, me mate said.' The soldier gestured towards the stretcher to the right, where an even younger man lay still as a cadaver, the empty space beneath his blanket indicating both legs had been amputated above the knee. 'Makes sense when you think about it. Bad for morale, us lying here listening to lunatics. Might start us thinking about the madness of war, eh mate?'

Rob shivered, recalled flaming aircraft spiralling earthwards, the occasional glimpse of a German pilot ejecting from his damaged plane, or a head slumped over the controls, scenes that vanished before they could register in his mind. Prior to the desert crash, he hadn't dreamt of burning flesh or severed limbs or dying moans. Total exhaustion had ensured sleep enfolded him, smothering moral discernment, recharging his body for another day or night of combat. The North African sky had become his entire world, shimmering sapphire without a cloud to hide behind, or coal black night peppered with stars and gunfire. Month after month, he carried on fighting, obeying orders without question, dismissing the rumours of imminent defeat. When new faces arrived in camp, they looked up to him as an older, experienced rear gunner. He had defied the odds, survived three years of desert warfare.

In recent months, the tide of war had begun to turn, Rommel on the run, so why had his unscathed body retaliated as though defeated by the prospect of an Allied victory? What could he say now to the sightless soldier who would never witness his baby son's faltering first steps? 'Sorry, mate, got to get back to base,' he said, folding the letter and placing it in the soldier's right hand.

Flying away from the sordid evidence of war wounds to a different camp in a different country, Rob contemplated future engagements with uncharacteristic stoicism. Whatever his eventual destiny, he vowed to meld with his new team as seamlessly as windblown sand, confident he could return to the role of rear gunner without a backward glance. The squadron depended on his experience, he owed it to his dead mates to continue the fight, help push the enemy into the Mediterranean.

On the ground, faces new and old greeted him warmly before bombarding him with tales of the relentless push to the coast. The mood in camp was buoyant; there was talk of a posting to Italy when the North Africa Campaign concluded.

Months later, camped around a sand-strewn airfield close to the coast, the squadron's fifth Tunisian location in four months, talk still centred on Italy. The invasion of Sicily by Allied forces had started in early July, so a full-scale invasion of mainland Italy couldn't be far away. The squadron was to be posted to southern Italy, so the rumour went, although the Wingco refused to confirm or deny it. Ever optimistic, youthful airmen dreamed of full-bodied women and full-bodied wine. For Rob, older than most by some years, the prospect of a return to Europe filled him with hope that before long he could return to his land of misty skies and verdant fields, live the peace, content he had done his duty to king and country.

Contrary to expectations, the squadron was sent to Malta the following month, tasked with bombing tactical targets in Sicily. Once the Italian island had been secured, the airmen spent their time flying back and forth to mainland Italy on bombing raids to support the British and Americans forces that had invaded Salerno and Taranto in early September.

Despite his initial conviction, Sergeant Robert Harper did not accompany the squadron. Deemed unfit to continue as a rear gunner, his nerves shot to pieces following the desert crash, he was transferred to a Personnel Training Centre where he performed general duties as an Aircraft Hand, assisting tradesmen in aircraft maintenance plus dismantling and cleaning equipment. A second transfer saw his final months in North Africa spent at a Base Personnel Depot in Tunis, where his methodical mind and prodigious memory proved invaluable to RAF administration, the movement of innumerable personnel to Italy involving a veritable mountain of paperwork.

Another year had turned before fresh orders came through for Sergeant Harper. Like his former squadron, he too was headed for Italy, but his destination was a Base Personnel Depot on the outskirts of Naples rather than the Foggia Airfield Complex near the Adriatic coast. Allied forces had entered Naples three months earlier following a four-day armed uprising by civilians against the remaining German forces. Days after the receipt of orders, Rob and several others from the Tunis base relocated to the southern suburb of Portici where a large villa with extensive grounds, abandoned by its Fascist owners following the city's liberation, had been appropriated by the RAF. But while the other men unpacked in the barracks, a converted shed at the rear of the property, Rob's kitbag remained untouched, its owner lying on a hastily improvised examination table, a desk covered with a sheet, in what had been a dressing room.

A Medical Officer, called in from city headquarters, had just finished stitching a deep gash in Rob's lower right leg sustained during the rough crossing from Malta, where the transport aircraft had stopped briefly en route from Tunis. 'Not a bad job if I do say so myself,' the MO remarked, standing back to survey his handiwork. 'There shouldn't be too much of a scar. Just keep your weight off it for a few days and for God's sake keep it clean. You don't want the wound getting infected. I'm not the best at amputations.'

Rob heard a throaty laugh. 'I'll take good care of it, sir.'

'Keep the leg elevated for a few hours. Bit of a lie down will do you good.'

Rob struggled to a sitting position and stared at the rough stitching holding his skin together. It bore no resemblance to the neat work observed at the Egyptian field hospital, and as for the MO, he looked ancient enough to have retired at least a decade earlier.

'I had a peek in the cellar while I was waiting for this room to be set up,' the MO remarked as he secured a dressing to Rob's leg with a light bandage. 'Thought I might find a few bottles of wine, a chap at HQ said some of these villas still have supplies.'

'Any luck, sir?'

The MO shook his head. 'Cellar's a bloody disgrace, mountains of empty bottles piled against the walls, floor littered with rubbish.' He looked up. 'They should get some of you men to clear it out.'

Rob remained silent, envisaging the vermin that inhabited the cellar, the spiders that lurked in dusty corners. Spiders, particularly large specimens, terrified him and rats induced a similar dread. He twisted around and was about to put both feet on the floor when the MO barked, 'Wait, I'll fetch the crutches. Left them on the veranda.'

A crash followed by a string of expletives, suggested the MO had collided with some of the equipment stacked in the narrow corridor, leading Rob to question the man's sobriety.

Twenty-four hours later, Rob felt sufficiently proficient at using crutches to accompany two of his barrack mates to a makeshift bar the pair had discovered nearby at the end of a narrow street littered with rubble from bombed apartment blocks. The local effervescent wine they insisted on buying went straight to Rob's head, so by the time the threesome re-emerged into the night, crutch confidence had waned, and he struggled to remain upright. On either side of him, his fellow drinkers sang loudly, their own gait erratic, the uneven terrain a danger they appeared content to ignore.

Suddenly, stars danced before Rob's eyes, his stomach churned, and a stream of vomit flew from his mouth.

The man on his left stepped sideways with the grace of a ballet dancer. 'Good shot, mate! Missed us all!'

Rob felt a moment of panic as his good leg buckled beneath him.

FIVE

Waking next morning in a long room reminiscent of a medieval banqueting hall, Rob thought momentarily he had died and gone to heaven. Plump painted cherubs trailed garlands of flowers across a high ceiling, strips of gossamer fabric entwined between their thighs. Blinking, he looked down, saw sunlight streaming through casement windows, gilding seasoned wooden floor with more gold than decorated the edges of the pale blue ceiling. 'Where the hell am I?' he asked a woman clad in angelic white, who stood at the foot of his bed, writing on a clipboard.

'Some minor duke's palace, I believe,' Nurse McGill answered, her accent indicating a Scottish upbringing. 'The Yanks requisitioned it a few months ago. They needed a solid structure away from the waterfront. Jerry still strafes the port occasionally.'

'We've got them on the run though, haven't we? Soon we'll be chasing them out of Rome.'

'Well I don't advise you to do any chasing for a wee while. Jerries I mean.'

'What happened last night, nurse? I remember vomiting and feeling a bit faint on the way back to base but after that it's a bit of a blur.'

'It's lucky your mates were sober enough to flag down a passing jeep and ask the driver to take you to hospital,' she said, fastening the clipboard to the foot of his bed before moving towards him. She turned back the sheet, bent to check his dressings. 'Why on earth didn't you mention the wound infection to your MO?'

'Didn't want to bother him. I thought it would clear up in a couple of days.'

'So now you're bothering me instead.'

'Sorry about that. I promise to behave in future.'

'I should think so, and make sure you tell me if there are any further problems.' She rearranged the sheet and straightened up.

'Cross my heart, nurse.'

She smiled, then glanced down at the watch pinned to her uniform above the swell of ample breasts. 'Well Sergeant, I can't stand here chatting.'

Watching her walk away, he noted her shapely figure and immediately recalled Alf Simpson's incessant chatter as they dismantled the squadron's final Tunisian camp. His mate had dreamed of dark-haired Italian beauties with soulful brown eyes, all eager to express their gratitude for liberation from German control, but from the news that had filtered across the Mediterranean, Rob doubted his former squadron would have time for fraternising with the locals. So far, Allied troops were making slow progress in their march north, German defences proving difficult to breach. Alf, a boilermaker in civvy street, and his fellow tradesmen would be fully occupied repairing damaged aircraft and other equipment. Rob pondered his mate's whereabouts and whether they would ever meet again. It seemed unlikely, given they came from opposite ends of the country. Rob couldn't imagine moving to the north of England and Alf, for all his talk of Italian liaisons, would most likely slot back into his civilian occupation once war ended, marry a Yorkshire lass and settle down in the village where he'd been born and bred.

A British girl would suit us both, he thought,

flopping back against the pillows as the nurse disappeared from view. *No language barrier, no unpredictable Latin temperament.*

Time passed at snail's pace; he dozed fitfully trying to ignore his pounding head, thick tongue and growling stomach. Nurses bustled around the ward, dressing wounds, writing on clipboards, straightening bedding, exchanging comments on patients' progress or otherwise in low voices. Like Rob, the other men remained silent, as though overwhelmed by the plethora of female activity.

Halfway through what Rob would learn the other patients referred to as 'the morning circus,' Rob watched a cleaner glide down the ward, partnering her mop in a graceful ballet. As she moved closer, he noticed that unlike the nurses in their immaculate uniforms, the young woman wore a faded dress and scuffed shoes. Propping himself on the pillows, he studied her movements with interest and just before she reached his bed called out, 'Hello, I'm Rob.'

The mop slowed; she returned the smile before resuming her task.

Must be a local, he thought, noting her

pinched face and the loose strands of ebony hair fluttering across olive cheeks. 'Roberto,' he added, hoping this was the Italian version of his name.

The mop clattered to the floor. Skinny shoulders shook, she bit her lip to suppress a sob.

'There's no need to get upset. I was just being friendly.'

'Roberto,' she repeated in a shaky voice. 'Bambino Roberto. Sick like you.'

Alarmed, Rob envisaged an injured baby, innocent victim of Allied bombing. 'Your baby has a leg wound?'

She frowned and moved closer to the bed. 'What is leg, please?'

Rob peeled back the bedclothes and pointed to his bandaged leg.

She shook her head, then coughed and mopped her forehead.

'Fever, chest infection, influenza?'

She looked puzzled, so he chose a different approach. 'What does the medico say?'

She sniffed. 'No medico, no dollari.'

'I have some dollars,' he said brightly.

'Susanna, what on earth do you think you're doing?' a Scottish voice called from further down the ward.

Susanna spun around, stood immobile head bowed, hands clasped tightly at her tiny waist.

Pick up the mop and get going, Rob wanted to say, but fearing she wouldn't understand, stayed silent, waiting like Susanna for the inevitable to unfold.

Fleet-footed Nurse McGill soon reached his bed. 'Dovete lavorare,' she said sharply to Susanna before glaring at Rob.

Jolted into action, the cleaner retrieved the mop and flitted away.

Dim lights cast eerie shadows over walls and ceiling when next Rob surfaced from fitful sleep. A murmur of conversation drew his attention to the opposite side of the ward, and as his eyes became accustomed to the gloom, he noticed a man in RAF uniform standing near a window beside a nurse. The man's arms were around her waist, his face close to hers. She seemed relaxed, so Rob presumed they knew one another, although he couldn't imagine why anyone would choose the middle of a hospital ward for a romantic assignation. After a few minutes of whispered conversation interspersed with muted kisses, the pair turned towards the light and Rob saw the outline of a familiar face. 'Alf Simpson, what the hell are you doing here?'

Nurse McGill placed a finger to her lips and hurried away, but Alf appeared unconcerned, sauntered across the room and parked himself on the end of Rob's bed. 'Transferred, mate.'

Rob frowned. 'I thought you'd be at Foggia not Naples.'

'Welding accident. Gammy arm at the moment, burns went deep. Should improve with time they tell me.'

Rob's smile faded. 'Sorry to hear that. When did it happen?

'Weeks back in Malta. Spent a fair time in hospital. Thought I might get home but no such luck.'

'Are you stationed around here?'

'Yep. Been here for a week. Light duties for a while at HQ in the city. Then I suppose they'll send me back into the fray.'

Rob grimaced and decided to change the subject. 'Don't waste any time, do you? How did you meet Nurse McGill?'

'Rosie to me, mate. Met her in a bar down by the harbour.'

'But what brought you to the hospital tonight? You couldn't have known *I* was here.'

'Met a couple of Yanks in a bar. They told

me a tale about picking up an airman who'd collapsed in the street and driving him to hospital. Mentioned it to Rosie this evening. We had a helluva laugh picturing the bloke falling off his crutches, and what do you know, she knew all about it, even your name.'

Stunned, Rob could only shake his head in disbelief.

'So, I thought I'd better come visit my old mate and what better way than to seek permission from a beautiful nurse.'

'I met a beautiful girl this morning,' Rob said wistfully. 'Long black hair, dark eyes, olive skin.'

'Nurse?'

'No, a cleaner, local girl called Susanna. The trouble is I think she's married. At least she's got a baby.'

'Steer clear mate, you don't want a knife in your back. You know what they say about these Latin fellows.'

'It wasn't like that. We talked about her baby. He's sick but she can't take him to the doctor as she hasn't enough money.'

Alf smirked. 'I get it. You want to help so she'll be eternally grateful and throw herself into your arms!'

Rob ignored the banter. 'Nurse McGill

spoke to Susanna in Italian. Do you know if she's picked up much of the language?'

'A fair bit from what I heard in the bar. At least she had no trouble ordering drinks and some of that pasta stuff.'

Rob leant forward. 'In that case, could you ask her to find out what's wrong with Susanna's baby? Then I could try to get medicine for him when I get out of here.'

'Got any money to pay for it?'

'A few pounds. Any idea how the black market's doing here?'

'Thriving from what I've seen so far. American dollars are the preferred currency.'

'No problem. I've still got some dollars from that gambling joint we visited in Cairo.'

'Good, but you'd better leave it to me, mate. You can't do much from a hospital bed. Anyway, Rosie's bound to know the best place to buy black market medicine.'

'Thanks. The dollars are in my trousers, front right pocket. In a bag under the bed.'

Alf bent down, unfastened the brown paper bag and located neatly folded trousers. He resurfaced holding a small roll of banknotes and handed it over.

'Take the lot, you don't know how much medication costs,' Rob said, passing back the roll.

Alf nodded, then raised his head to scan the ward. 'I'd better get going in case the Battle-axe turns up.'

'Do you mean Sister Miles?'

'That's the one. See you soon, mate.'

'Thanks for coming.'

'No problem.' Alf slunk off down the ward and disappeared into shadow.

The following day Alf visited a city market and managed to procure a phial of the new drug penicillin, labelled U.S. Navy, in exchange for three American dollars and two tins of RAF rations, obtained from the cook at HQ in exchange for cigarettes. During a previous visit to the market to buy chocolate for Rosie, Alf had noticed Allied servicemen handing over rations as well as cash, so he went prepared.

In a city still reeling from the dual devastation of allied bombings and the scorched earth policy of retreating Germans, even bully beef and the dry biscuits known as hard tack, were favoured over cash. Broken masonry and abandoned trams still littered the streets and the smell of smashed drains pervaded the air. Beyond the shattered suburbs, women and children searched roadside verges and burnt fields for anything edible, their gaunt faces testimony to long months of deprivation. South of the city, along the coast, children prised limpets off rocks and fishermen looked longingly out to sea, waiting for the day their new military rulers would sanction commercial fishing to begin again.

During a second, legitimate visit to the military hospital during daylight hours, Alf slipped the phial into Rob's hands. 'Let's hope this makes a difference to one little Neapolitan,' he said in a low voice. 'It's a disaster out there. Poor sods.'

'Expensive?' Rob queried as he tucked the phial under the bedclothes.

Alf raised three fingers before retrieving the remaining banknotes from his jacket pocket and handing them over.

Rob nodded. 'I should have asked you to give the medicine to your girl to pass on. Susanna won't be in again until tomorrow morning, so now there'll be an unnecessary delay.'

Alf grinned. 'I thought of that, but on reflection considered you would prefer to give her the present yourself, if you know what I mean.'

Rob sighed and raised his eyes to the painted ceiling.

FEED THY ENEMY

Propped on pillows, his stomach full at last – Sister Miles had removed the 'light diet' sign from behind his bed once his temperature returned to normal -- Rob pretended to doze while listening to the swish of a cloth across the window behind his bed. On the opposite side of the ward, Nurse McGill dressed the wounds of an American soldier, while further down, the Battle-axe, hands on hips, appeared to be lecturing the walking wounded, her right index finger pointing menacingly at one unfortunate's face. Minutes passed, the sister seemed in no hurry to leave. Behind him, Rob heard water pinging against the side of a tin bucket and figured Susanna must be wringing out her cloth. If he didn't speak to her soon, she'd have moved on. He turned slightly, whispered, 'Susanna, come closer.'

'You sick, Roberto? Want nurse?'

'No. I have a present for you.' He smiled and retrieved the phial from under the bedclothes.

'I no wanting regalo,' she answered curtly, reaching for the bucket.

'Look Susanna, medicine for bambino Roberto.' He held up the phial, shielding it from the other patients' view with his left hand.

Susanna straightened up, edged closer and peered at the phial. 'Mamma mia, la penicillina!' Her voice reverberated around the ward and the cleaning cloth fell from her hand onto the freshly laundered sheet as she flung thin arms around Rob's neck, then kissed him on both cheeks.

Surfacing from an unexpected embrace, Rob glanced down the ward, praying the Battle-axe hadn't heard Susanna's exclamation. Fortunately, Sister Miles had terminated her lecture and was leaning over a patient, listening to his chest with her stethoscope.

When Rob turned back to Susanna, she had retrieved her cleaning cloth and was standing by the bed as if uncertain what to do next. 'What I do for grazie?' she asked tentatively, twisting the cloth in her fingers.

'How about showing me around Naples when I get out of hospital?'

She hesitated, trying to make sense of the words. 'Si,' she said at last. 'You finish l'ospedale; I am showing la citta.' A frown creased her smooth forehead. 'But Napoli she is ruin. Molte bombe.'

'We could go to a market,' Rob said quickly before she could change her mind. 'Buy something special for bambino Roberto.'

'Molti good food in mercato,' she said wistfully. 'But is many dollari.'

'No problem, I have dollari. Just let me know when Roberto is well enough to go. I can buy him some sweets.'

'What is sweets, please?'

Rob reached under his pillow to retrieve the chocolate bar Alf had brought him. 'For you.' He held out the bar.

'Candy!' Brown eyes sparkled as she reached for the chocolate. 'Grazie Roberto.'

'Everything all right, over here?' Nurse McGill asked as she approached Rob's bed.

Startled, Susanna blushed, picked up the bucket and hurried away.

'Signed and sealed,' Rob replied in a soft voice. 'I just hope it does the trick for the bambino.'

Nurse McGill looked up from studying his chart. 'Should do, penicillin is a miracle drug. I wish we'd had it before the war. We could have saved so many lives.'

'You've been nursing for a while then?'

'I started my training in thirty-eight, after my....' She glanced up at the painted cherubs cavorting on the ceiling. 'Well, I must be going. Can't risk the Battle-axe catching me wasting time. She'd have my guts for garters.'

As she walked away, Rob's thoughts swung from an Italian baby suffering from pneumonia to a dead Scottish infant, and he wondered whether Nurse McGill had a husband also doing his bit for king and country somewhere in Europe. He should mention this possibility to Alf when, or if they met again. For all his mate's talk of passionate encounters, Rob felt certain a dalliance with a married woman would be off the radar.

SIX

DISCHARGED FROM HOSPITAL FORTY-EIGHT hours later, Rob returned to the Base Personnel Depot. Restricted to light duties for a couple of days, he concentrated on settling in rather than the marital status of a Scottish nurse or the chance, however remote that he would see Susanna again. Light duties involved little more than peeling potatoes in the villa kitchen or washing up, after which he was free to do as he liked until an hour before the officers' next meal. Although the depot officers were housed further down the road in a more sumptuous establishment judging from its exterior, they ate all their meals in the Officers' Mess on the villa's first floor.

Exploring the garden behind the barracks, he discovered a tangled web of overgrown shrubs and grass interspersed with tall pine trees. Regular duties could encompass clearing the mess, he imagined, not that he saw anyone engaged in gardening during his perambulations. Most of the other men spent daylight hours away from the depot, although Rob had no idea where they went. In the evenings they adjourned to the Other Ranks' Mess, a small space divided from their sleeping quarters by thin sheets of ply, where they drank beer and played endless games of cards. They were a pleasant enough crew, but Rob missed the camaraderie experienced with a squadron, especially Alf's cheerful presence. It had been the same during the months spent in Tunis, personnel changing so often he hadn't had the chance to get to know anyone. In the desert, despite the inevitable loss of pilots and aircrew during fierce dogfights, he'd felt the squadron functioned as a cohesive whole. Here in Naples, conversations revealed most of the men were hanging around waiting for a transfer to the real business of war.

Once pronounced fit for regular duties, Rob joined two others engaged in sorting out the equipment piled against corridor walls. Warrant Officer Whitmore, a sallow-faced, forty-something individual whose uniform sagged on his narrow shoulders, directed operations in the manner of a bored schoolteacher dealing with equally bored children. Orders lacked conviction and were prefaced with a series of sighs, while gestures were rarely given as though the energy required would deplete his remaining strength. Office equipment, unless noticeably broken, was re-stacked in the small room where the MO had stitched Rob's leg, to be inspected at a later date before assignment to one of the bedrooms now used as offices by administrative staff. Damaged and miscellaneous items, such as hand tools, were relocated to the cellar, there to languish until someone, presumably Whitmore, organised for the space to be cleaned up.

Sorting continued at a leisurely pace with frequent breaks for what the WO called 'fresh air and exercise.' This involved Whitmore retiring to the Officers' Mess for a cup of substitute coffee while the men strolled over to the barracks to retrieve cigarettes and if desperate for a drink, a tin mug of insipid tea from their cramped and cheerless mess.

The barracks, a lop-sided wooden structure that looked as though it had been built at least a century earlier and never maintained, had inexplicably, a flight of well-built stone steps leading to its entrance. These provided little comfort other than warmth from the day's sunshine, but Rob preferred to remain outside when at all possible. Bunks lined either side of the narrow barracks with barely enough space between them to store a kitbag, and the few windows looked out on piles of rubble from a bombed residence on the adjoining property.

Prior to RAF occupation, British soldiers had shored up the villa's bomb-damaged corner with railway sleepers prised from beneath rails twisted by the heat of post-bomb fires. Breaches in the brick wall surrounding the property had also been repaired to keep the locals, especially the streetwise boys known as Scugnizzi, from helping themselves to food or other items they could sell on the black market.

As far as Rob could tell from his brief forays outside the depot, running, or rather walking errands for WO Whitmore, the surrounding area had been extensively bombed and apart from sections of the main road, piles of rubble remained in situ. Neapolitans took little notice of the debris, walking around large heaps or kicking small pieces of masonry out of their way as they traversed the streets, leading Rob to query why no attempt had been made to clean up the place in the months since the Allied occupation.

Surely someone in authority could have organised the groups of idle youths loitering on every street corner into useful work-gangs? Negotiating narrow, ruined streets at the rear of the villa, he wondered where Susanna lived and whether her home had survived the Allied onslaught of the previous year.

Ten days after leaving hospital, Rob was finishing a late afternoon cup of tea when Alf sauntered into the mess and announced his arrival in a booming voice more suited to a swarthy sailor than a skinny airman.

'Are you pestering me on purpose, Simpson?' Rob called out, lifting his tin mug in greeting.

'I bring good tidings,' Alf replied, 'but I won't share them until you've bought me a beer.'

'Help yourself.' Rob pointed at the makeshift bar, an old wooden table with one short leg supported by pieces of masonry. 'Cardboard box on the left.'

His neighbour, a dour Glaswegian, raised his head. 'Don't forget to put it on your tab, Harper.'

Rob nodded and got to his feet. Mug in hand, he walked over to join his mate. 'Let's go outside. I sense your intelligence has nothing to do with the Italian Campaign.'

Alf grinned. 'You're right there, mate. Lead the way.'

The stone steps were in shadow at this hour of the day, so they stood in a patch of weak sunlight several feet from the barracks, Alf swigging beer, Rob shifting his weight from one foot to the other as he waited for news. A loud burb announced a temporary halt to drinking, then Alf rummaged in his shirt pocket to retrieve a crumpled piece of paper. 'From Susanna,' he said, handing it over. 'Rosie's translation is on the back.'

Rob smoothed the paper and glanced at Susanna's neat script before turning it over.

'You're in with a chance now, mate,' Alf declared when he had drained the bottle.

'I'm not so sure. We're both invited to Susanna's home. I expect her family want to thank us for getting the penicillin that's all.'

'No harm in trying is there? I told you Rosie said Susanna's husband was killed last year while fighting in Sicily. She's free as a bird now, mate.'

Rob frowned. 'Free yes, but available, that's another matter. For all I know there could be a specific mourning period in Italy. I wouldn't want to offend her or her family.'

'Play it safe then. You always do.' Alf glanced at the darkening sky. 'It's time I made a move. I don't fancy walking these streets alone at night. Never know who'll jump you.'

'Don't tell me you walked all the way from HQ?'

Alf shook his head. 'I managed to cadge a lift with a driver charged with delivering a couple of files to your Group Captain. He'll be wanting to leave by now.'

'Let me escort you to your transport, sir,' Rob said, grabbing the beer bottle and holding it high in a mock-salute.

'Give over, you daft bat!'

———

In the living room of a small apartment only walking distance from the depot, Rob and Alf stood either side of Susanna's fifty-something father, in front of an old wooden table dotted with numerous bottles of wine and a solitary plate containing thin slices of dark bread. Before the airmen's arrival, the table had been pushed into a corner so that assorted armchairs and straight-backed wooden chairs could be arranged around the walls, a crowd of relatives expected, all eager to drink the health of the generous British airmen.

Overwhelmed by numbers and the clamour of competing conversations in a language he didn't understand, Rob sipped a glass of wine, wishing he could disappear into the kitchen visible through an open door in the room's rear wall. He hadn't expected a multitude, envisaged only Susanna's immediate family, a father, younger sister and brother having been mentioned during their final conversation on the hospital ward. He'd also hoped for an opportunity to talk to her alone, but after introducing him to her father, she had retreated to the opposite side of the room, where an older woman perched on an upright chair claimed her attention.

Suddenly, Signor Zappetti, a short, broad-shouldered man with a gaunt face, turned and thumped the table with his fist. 'Attenzione, per favore,' he shouted over the din, before stepping away from the table.

Conversations ceased instantly, family members unwilling to risk the patriarch's wrath. All present turned to face him.

'Vorrei fare un brindisi a Rob e Alf, i salvatore di mio nipote.' He raised his glass. 'Rob e Alf.'

'Rob e Alf,' the family chorused, glasses held high.

Thirsty, Alf quaffed the wine as though it were a pint of beer, then slid sideways into the gap left by Signor Zappetti. 'No stalling today, mate,' he advised, elbowing a hesitant Rob in the ribs. 'Down the hatch.'

Rob gulped the effervescent wine, a product of the local region, and tried not to cough when bubbles tickled his throat.

'Not a bad drop, eh?'

Rob nodded and took another swig.

'That's the way, mate.'

Rob blinked rapidly, trying to clear the sudden haze in his brain. 'Christ, it's gone straight to my head!'

Alf grinned. 'Gone straight through me. Won't be a tick. Reckon there's a working lav around here?'

'Probably not. I don't think the water supply has been fixed everywhere yet.'

Alf placed his empty glass on the table. 'Might be a bedpan or something.'

'Good luck,' Rob called as his mate sidled along the wall and disappeared through an open door into what looked like a hallway.

Focused on a second escape route, Rob failed to notice that Signor Zappetti had returned and was opening another bottle of wine.

'Di più?' his host asked, and without waiting for a response, filled Rob's almost empty glass to the brim.

'Grazie, Signor Zappetti.' Rob forced a smile.

'Prego!' A grin split the older man's face and with an exaggerated gesture he signalled for Rob to drink.

Reluctant to appear rude, Rob raised his glass and took several gulps. This satisfied his host, who replaced the bottle on the table and wandered over to an elderly man dozing in a chair nearby. How anyone could fall asleep surrounded by a host of animated conversations, Rob couldn't imagine, and watched attempts to rouse the guest with interest. When a shake of the man's shoulders also failed, Rob experienced a sudden desire to giggle, but instead of taking the sensible option, biting his lips, he suppressed the urge with several more mouthfuls of wine.

Unsteady now, he leant heavily against the table and passed a clammy palm over his damp forehead. If only he could slide to the floor and lean back against the stout table leg. His head spun, and his ears rang, an atmosphere overheated as myriad exchanges reached a crescendo, more the culprit than two large glasses of wine!

A tap on the shoulder roused him and he looked up to see Susanna's young sister, Maria standing beside him, a worried frown creasing her forehead. 'Sì, fa caldo,' she said, motioning him to follow.

FEED THY ENEMY

He nodded and traipsed across the room after her to a small door that led to a balcony.

'Mettiti a sedere, per favore,' she said, indicating a wooden bench in one corner.

'Grazie, Maria.'

'Prego.' She smiled and walking over to the railing, leant folded arms on the rusting ironwork.

After lowering his body carefully, Rob gulped cool air, wishing the older sister had been the one to notice his distress.

Minutes passed, his head began to clear, the sounds of city life in the street below more conducive to sobriety than a crowded living room. Maria continued to stare into space and he wondered what was going through her young mind, if she deliberately avoided looking down at the piles of smashed masonry dotting the street, or across to the partially demolished building opposite. Molte bombe, Susanna had said following her offer of a city tour. It had seemed more like unmitigated destruction as he and Alf picked their way through half a dozen rubble-strewn streets to the apartment building. No wonder so little debris had been cleared away, the scale of the damage was overwhelming. Reconstruction would take years not months. The transport aircraft carrying Rob from Tunis had approached the airfield some miles south of Naples from the sea and during the journey to the Base Personnel Depot he had been more concerned with stemming the flow of blood from his injured leg than looking out the back of the lorry for evidence of bomb damage. He didn't want to think about how the city would appear, viewed from directly above; Alf had said it looked as though Vesuvius had erupted again!

Rob remembered reading about Vesuvius in a library book not long before he joined up. According to the author, AD 79 had been the most catastrophic eruption to date, witnessed by Pliny the Younger and described in two letters to the historian Tacitus. The cities of Pompeii and Herculaneum had been totally destroyed, buried beneath ash, pumice and cinders, their ruins frozen in time for centuries. Musing on the brooding volcano – it rose from the plain of Campania about six miles east of Naples -- Rob wondered if he would have the opportunity to visit Pompeii during his time at the depot.

'She is bella, mia Maria,' said a nearby voice.

Roused from contemplation, Rob twisted around and saw Signor Zappetti standing in the doorway. 'Yes, sir, just like her sister,' he answered, grateful to have understood.

'But she molto sottile,' Signor Zappetti said

sadly, moving towards his daughter. Standing behind her, he caressed the black hair cascading down her back.

Unsure what he meant, Rob could not respond.

'I no have work,' the father explained and began to stroke his daughter's thin arms.

'Perhaps you could get some work at the hospital,' Rob suggested.

'No more work.' Signor Zappetti turned, looked directly into Rob's eyes. 'No work, no eat.'

Light dawned. 'I'll get some food for you from one of the markets,' Rob said quickly, determined to live up to the 'saviour' status recently bestowed by his host.

'Grazie, Roberto.' Signor Zappetti gave a small bow before moving away from his daughter. Leaning towards Rob, he said in a low voice, 'Mia Maria good girl. She no eat big. Uno giorno, uno pasto. She make you good time, you give food from mercato, yes?'

Appalled, Rob leapt from the bench, both hands raised as though he intended to push the older man over the balcony rail. 'No, no, I couldn't, she's only a child!'

Despair clouded the father's face, soulful brown eyes filled with tears.

Rob lowered his hands. 'Don't worry, I'll get

some food for your family. And I don't want anything in return. I'd be happy to help.'

Signor Zappetti stepped forward and much to Rob's embarrassment, embraced him fervently before kissing him on both cheeks. 'Roberto, you good man. Sempre I call you amico mio!'

Discomfort increased when Rob noticed the adolescent son, Luigi, standing in the balcony doorway scrutinising his father, a scowl on his sallow, pinched face.

———

Alf accompanied Rob on the return journey, having arranged a lift back to the city with an officer visiting the depot for the afternoon. As so often occurred when hearing Alf's stories, Rob experienced a tinge of jealousy at his mate's knack of being in the right place at the right time, or perhaps it was the ability to turn a conversation to his advantage. Either way, the gregarious Yorkshireman possessed more self-assurance than his reserved southern friend ever would.

The two airmen exchanged few words as they tramped smashed suburban streets, but when they drew near to the depot's rear entrance – only officers could enter via the villa's front door -- Rob's smouldering anger broke the surface. 'For Christ's sake, a child,' he shouted, kicking out at a broken piece of masonry lying on the dusty road.

'What the hell's the matter?' Alf asked. 'Is your leg playing up again?'

Rob shook his head, wary of repeating a conversation that had sickened him.

'What then, stomach reacting to all that wine? I'm not surprised, you were really going at it with Signor Zappetti out on the balcony.'

So, Luigi hadn't been the only person to witness his father's insistence on additional glasses of wine to celebrate friendship. Rob took a deep breath before saying quietly, 'He offered me his daughter in exchange for food.'

'What you wanted, wasn't it?'

'Maria not Susanna.'

Alf frowned. 'Are you sure you didn't misunderstand?'

'I understood all right.'

'But Maria can't be more than twelve.'

'I know, that's why I refused the offer.'

Alf scuffed at the dirt with the toe of his boot. 'Jesus, I'd heard some Neapolitans were selling their daughters for food, but a twelve-year old? The poor sod must be desperate.'

'I saw empty shelves in the kitchen. They're starving for Christ's sake. I promised to get them some food, but I've only got a few dollars left.'

'Don't panic, you can count me in.'

'Thanks, mate.'

'We can try the market where I brought the medicine. Plenty of food there.'

'Then we'd better buy some quick smart before Signor Zappetti offers Maria to someone else. I hate the thought of her in the clutches of a hulking great Yankee marine.'

'Or a skinny British airman,' Alf said thoughtfully.

They continued walking towards the gate, Rob dragging his feet as he struggled to expunge unwelcome scenarios.

'Stop dawdling,' Alf called out, 'or I'll miss my ride.'

Rob caught up with him. 'We're kidding ourselves thinking we can save Maria. How many weeks' rations do you think our few dollars will buy? One, two? What use is that?'

Alf stopped in his tracks and pointed to a small wooden hut tucked into a corner of the garden a few yards from the gate. 'Latrines in there, mate?'

'No, the other side of the barracks. That's the temporary Officers' Mess store.'

'Temporary?'

FEED THY ENEMY

'Until the cellar's cleared out.'

'No time to waste then.' A wicked grin suffused Alf's face as his eyes focused on the hut's single window. 'I reckon breaking in there would be a pushover.'

'You must be joking! I'd be court martialled if I was caught!'

'We won't get caught, trust me.'

'We? You're going back to HQ in half an hour.'

Alf clutched his stomach and groaned. 'Must have been something I ate at the Zappetti's. Reckon I'd better stick around here for the night. I wouldn't want to make a mess of an officer's jeep.'

'Bloody hell, sure you weren't a burglar in civilian life?'

'Positive, but I'm a dab hand at amateur dramatics. Lead roles in village productions.'

Rob's grin faded as he glanced at the sentry box in front of the gate. 'But what about the sentry?'

Alf shrugged. 'He faces away from the hut.'

———

Night breeze blew cold and a crescent moon hung shrouded in cloud as the two airmen, one wearing an overcoat, emerged from the barracks, turned to the left and sauntered to the end of the building, where a hand-painted sign comprising the word 'latrines' and an arrow was tacked to the wall. Shadow soon swallowed their deliberate change of direction.

'Keep a lookout,' Alf whispered as they approached the hut. 'I'll do the business.'

Rob nodded and took up a position on the corner of a side wall, his body pressed into rough boards.

Meanwhile, Alf slid halfway along the wall and after taking a screwdriver out of his pocket, reached up and prised open the single window. It creaked loudly. 'Sod it,' he muttered, waiting a moment before turning in Rob's direction.

As soon as Rob gave the pre-arranged 'all-clear' signal, Alf raised himself slowly, balanced on the windowsill and slipped into darkness. A match flickered, then his head appeared at the open window. 'You should see the stuff they've got in here,' he announced in a fierce whisper. 'Tinned salmon, pork, fruit, even a selection of puddings. Makes our grub look like pigs' swill.'

Rob rushed to the window. 'Keep your voice down for God's sake.'

'I wouldn't be surprised to find bloody

caviar,' Alf remarked, passing out half a dozen large tins.

'For God's sake shut up.'

'No problem, mate, everyone's pissed tonight. Most likely even the sentry's asleep in his box.'

'I doubt it. MacDonald's on duty tonight. Never seen him with a beer in his hand.'

Alf grinned. 'Even a tight-arsed Scotsman would shell out to celebrate the landing at Anzio.'

'Presbyterian, they don't drink,' Rob muttered, but Alf, preoccupied with climbing out of the window, didn't hear. Once safe on terra firma, he managed to close the window with minimal creaking and after a quick glance in the direction of the sentry box, patted Rob's bulging pockets. 'Take the overcoat off and sling it over your arm. I'm going back to bed. Give it a few minutes before you leave.'

No one noticed any missing supplies the following day. The Allied landing wasn't as successful. At the Anzio beachhead, troops dug in for what would be a protracted battle.

Rob took advantage of a depot recuperating

from a night of heavy drinking to request a few hours leave. 'I'd like to visit the market down by the harbour,' he told his superior officer. 'I want to buy a present for my girl.'

The officer managed a lop-sided grin. 'You boys don't waste any time. Did you meet her at the hospital by any chance?'

'Yes, sir.'

'Good fun those Yankee nurses.' He lay back in the chair, eyes half-closed. 'At least that's what I hear.'

'Yes, sir.' Rob could imagine Nurse McGill's indignation at being referred to as an American. Alf had told him Rosie was on secondment from a hospital in Bari on the other side of the country, her expertise in burns management needed due to a recent influx of sailors badly injured when their ship was torpedoed in the Bay of Naples.

'Report for duty at thirteen hundred hours, Harper.'

'Thank you, sir, much appreciated.'

―――――

Back in the barracks, Rob donned his overcoat and quickly departed, hoping the thin towel he'd wrapped around and between the tins would render them quiet as he walked through the overgrown garden to the gates.

He need not have worried; the sentry barely looked up as he approached, ignored a hearty greeting and shuffled over to open the gate. 'Thanks, mate, see you later,' Rob said cheerily, resisting the urge to clap the bleary-eyed fellow on the back.

SEVEN

When Rob reached the apartment block, exercise and late morning sun had heated his well-wrapped body to such an extent, perspiration was running down his flushed face and pooling at the base of his neck. Before entering the building, he paused to mop neck and forehead with a handkerchief, then unbuttoned his overcoat to allow the breeze to penetrate. Apart from an old woman sitting on a rickety chair opposite, the street seemed deserted, although high above him, clothing flapped on thin wires strung from balcony to balcony across the narrow thoroughfare, evidence of recent activity. The sound was strangely comforting, and he thought of his aunt wrestling with the wooden pole that raised her washing line, her short stature a disadvantage when strong wind invaded the exposed back garden. On the odd occasion when he was at home on a Monday morning, she accepted his help, but firmly rejected his proposal that she alter washing day to Sunday, his day off. He smiled, remembering her rebuke, her astonishment that he would even suggest hanging out washing on the Lord's day.

Fond of his mother's much younger sister and her husband, Rob would be forever grateful for their offer of accommodation when life in the strained atmosphere of his parents' home had become too much for a sensitive young man to bear. His father drank most of his meagre wages from the stables where he tended racehorses owned by wealthy businessmen, while his mother, worn out by poverty and childbearing, Rob the fifth of seven, vented her frustration on whoever was to hand, her shrill voice reverberating through the tiny terraced house. Rob recalled his last visit to his parents' house, autumn nineteen-forty, his mother barely responding to the news he'd enlisted in the RAF, her shoulders drooping as she folded freshly ironed clothes on the kitchen table. His father had been absent, most likely swilling beer in the local pub and for this Rob was grateful, uncertain how he would have reacted to once familiar drunkenness. Since moving out five years earlier, Rob had tried to distance himself from the wretched world of childhood and adolescence, finally acknowledging he felt ashamed of his background. He never spoke of siblings or parents, preferring his few friends, mostly from the local football team -- he played centre-forward -- to assume his aunt, uncle and their two sons were his only living relatives. In later years, he would keep up the pretence, letting his daughters believe their paternal grandparents had died before they were born and making no mention of his two sisters and four brothers.

During those five years, a lingering affection for his mother - he remembered her gentleness before his youngest brother arrived -- had prompted Rob to pay the occasional visit to his former home, visits always carefully timed to ensure he wouldn't come face to face with his father. Saturday afternoon, following an at-home football match was a good time, his father working at either stables or racecourse. After downing a half-pint in the pub opposite the football ground with his team, determined not to metamorphose into his father, Rob rarely drank more than a pint, he would leave his mates to celebrate or commiserate and walk the two miles to

FEED THY ENEMY

a once familiar street of shabby mid-Victorian terraces, one of many in that part of town. Sometimes his mother seemed pleased to see him and would ask about his life while they sat drinking tea by the fire. At other times, she barely acknowledged his presence, continuing with domestic duties and muttering complaints as though he was a small child getting under her feet.

Leaving the house that blustery October day after yet another unsatisfactory visit, Rob had resolved to sever familial ties completely, certain he wouldn't be missed. A new life lay ahead, his mission to help defeat the enemy and restore peace to a fractured world. Past relationships paled into insignificance when he considered the magnitude of this task, the Luftwaffe nightly bombing London to bring Britain to its knees. So far, nineteen-forty had been a horrific year for the Allies, the Axis powers invading Norway and Denmark in April, the Dutch and the Belgians surrendering in May as thousands of British and French troops were evacuated from the beaches of Dunkirk.

Despite the endless drilling, draughty barracks and a coarse uniform that irritated his skin, those first months in the RAF more than fulfilled Rob's expectations. He made friends more easily than he had in civilian life. Perhaps it was the uniform, the sense that for the first time he belonged to a functioning family. No one asked what school he'd attended or what his father did for a living, nobody cared what career he'd interrupted to serve his country. Life on the base was present tense; every raw recruit determined to become a competent airman, clear-headed and knowledgeable, ready to defeat the enemy, the arrogant Germans who were tearing Europe apart.

Some nights, after listening to grim reports on the crackling canteen radio, Rob would lie in his narrow bunk contemplating imminent warfare and whether his life would end in flames somewhere over the dark forests of Bavaria. But when the orders finally came through, there were no forests or even shrubs in sight for his batch of pale-skinned Englishmen, newly graduated from Air Gunner School. Assigned to the Middle East pool, their initial wartime environs encompassed scorching desert days and freezing nights huddled in draughty tents alongside a makeshift runway. Fortunately for some, including Rob, respite came sooner than expected after only a few months. On leave in Cairo prior to joining a squadron based at El Firdan in the Suez Canal Zone, the airmen encountered foul-tempered camels, sulky Arabs and glistening girls that thrust jewelled bellies in their sun-darkened faces. Exploring pyramids and plundered royal tombs, their dusty boots trod paths once walked by barefoot slaves and sandalled overseers. Ancient history resurrected for British airmen taking a break from modern warfare. Taking a break from boredom.

Rob hadn't anticipated boredom; God knows he'd expected more than dragging desert days. Endless forays into a cloudless sky, searching for an elusive enemy, guarding a territory of shifting sand dunes, windswept, empty. His life had contracted to a dorsal turret, a makeshift base, countless card games, monotonous meals and half a cup of drinking water per day.

A rationed existence.

Many months later when the exhilaration, terror and exhaustion of desert warfare had become a daily experience, he longed for a return to those nothing days.

Two weeks into what some officers at the depot were calling 'the lull before the storm,' Rob pondered the incongruity of standing outside a Naples apartment block, weighed down by stolen rations destined for those who until a few months earlier had been the enemy. He had heard the news of Italy's surrender on another crackling radio, cheered along with his mates at the thought war in the Mediterranean might soon be over. *But all of us underestimated the Germans,* he thought, stepping into the apartment block's tiled entrance.

His footsteps reverberated through the stairwell as he climbed bare concrete steps to the second floor and he wondered what to say should residents emerge from apartments doors. 'Buon giorno' seemed the appropriate greeting, but what if someone queried his presence and tried to remove him from the building? Run for it or try to explain his connection

FEED THY ENEMY

to the Zappetti family? Various scenarios presented themselves but on reaching the second landing, he managed to push apprehension aside and crossed confidently to the appropriate door.

Fifteen-year old Luigi answered Rob's knock and without saying a word, ushered him into the living room where Signor Zappetti was sitting in an armchair reading a newspaper. He looked up and smiled as Rob approached. 'Buon giorno, Signor Zappetti,' Rob said politely.

'Luciano, per favore,' the older man replied. 'Siamo amici.'

Rob patted his bulging pockets. 'I have food for you and your family.'

Once more, Rob had to suffer an effusive Italian greeting, Luciano leaping from the chair with the speed of a much younger man to express his gratitude.

Released from unexpectedly strong arms, Rob walked over to the table, now back in its rightful place adjacent to the door leading to the kitchen. It came as no surprise to find the table bare except for a half-eaten loaf and an empty wine bottle. His back to Luciano, Rob extracted the six large tins from his coat pockets and set them on the table, unaware Luigi was watching his every move.

'Where you getting this grossi food?' the boy asked, moving closer to Rob.

'I don't think you want to know.'

Luigi grinned, then pulled out the nearest chair and sat down. 'Is much food. Grazie mille!'

'It's the least I can do.' Rob turned slightly and smiled in Luciano's direction.

'Grazie, amico mio,' came the reply.

Luigi leant forward to examine each tin, frowned as he laboriously translated the English labels. 'La carne, il pesce, la frutta.' He reached for the sixth tin, studied the label without comprehension. 'What is spotted dick?' he asked, looking up at Rob, who stood shifting his weight from one foot to the other, debating whether to ask Luciano if Susanna was at home.

'Pudding,' Rob answered after a lengthy pause. 'Eat it warm. Molto bene.'

'Eat with vegetable?'

'No, after vegetables.'

'Ah, il budino.' Dirty fingers caressed the tin.

'Lascia perdere!' ordered a gruff voice behind him.

Luigi dropped the tin as though the metal was red-hot and leapt to his feet, ducking as his father lashed out. Dancing away from danger, he disappeared into the entrance hall. A door slammed as he fled the apartment.

FEED THY ENEMY

'Vino, amico mio?' Luciano asked in a calm voice.

Rob shook his head. 'No, thank you. I'm on duty soon.' He glanced towards the closed kitchen door. 'Are Susanna and Maria here?'

'Maria in scuola. Susanna in cucina.' Luciano moved closer, said quietly, 'Susanna sad oggi. You make smile, per favore.'

'Is Roberto sick again?' Rob asked, concerned more penicillin would be required. He only had a few dollar bills left and had no idea whether black market traders would accept British currency.

'No, bambino molto bene.' Luciano gave a brief smile, then placed a hand over his heart. 'Il cuore e triste.' He sighed. 'Come, I show.'

Puzzled, Rob followed him over to the dresser, stood at a respectful distance while Luciano picked up a framed photograph of Susanna and her husband on their wedding day.

'Mia cara figlia è vedova,' Luciano explained. 'This day anniversario. Telegramma saying Mario è morto.' He sniffed. 'Da qualche parte in Sicilia.'

Uncertain how to respond, Rob stared at his boots. All he could think of was the Italian soldier he had discovered late one afternoon lying in the ditch running parallel to the improvised runway at the squadron's final Tunisian base. The soldier had looked so young, so intact, fatal injuries hidden until he and Alf moved the body. Under instructions from their superior officer, they buried the smooth-cheeked boy in a shallow grave, the ground too hard to dig deep. A few mumbled words completed the ceremony. 'I'd better go,' Rob said at last. 'It wouldn't be right to disturb Susanna today.' He turned to leave.

'No, no,' Luciano insisted, stepping forward to grab Rob's wrist. 'You go see Susanna. I want see smile.' He propelled Rob to the kitchen door. A flick of the wrist and he had opened the door, pushed Rob inside.

Susanna was standing by the sink, gazing out of a small window. 'Buon giorno, Roberto, 'she said without altering her position.

'Buon giorno, Susanna.' Rob glanced around the narrow room, noticed flower-patterned plates and cups arranged on wooden shelves. There was no sign of anything to eat.

Susanna turned around slowly and wiped her hands on her apron. 'You make visit papà?'

'I brought some food. It's on the table.' He gestured towards the living room.

'Grazie, you help mia famiglia.' She managed a fleeting smile. 'Grosso help.'

'Are you working at the hospital tomorrow?'

Susanna shook her head. 'No, la Domenica. La messa.'

'After messa,' he ventured. 'Would er, would Roberto like to go to a market, so I can buy him some sweets?'

'Sì, sì.' She offered a second small smile.

'Right. I'll call around ten, okay?'

'Ten is dieci, yes?'

Rob held up both hands and spread his fingers wide.

She nodded. 'Now I get vino.'

'No thank you. I have to get back to base.' He smiled. 'A domani,' he added remembering the words for 'see you tomorrow.' And concerned she could change her mind, he beat a hasty retreat.

Smart in his well-pressed uniform and polished boots, Rob stood stiffly in front of the apartment door, a small loaf purchased along the way from a roadside trader tucked under one arm. Obtaining a few more hours' leave hadn't been a problem, his superior officer considering Sunday a day of rest even during wartime, unless an emergency arose. Susanna answered Rob's knock, her face showing none of the previous day's sorrow. 'Buon giorno, Roberto,' she said brightly and ushered him inside.

Bambino Roberto – Rob reckoned he was about two years old, so no longer a baby in his opinion – sat on his grandfather's knee, big brown eyes fixed on the stranger walking beside his mother. 'Buon giorno, Roberto,' Luciano exclaimed, waving an arm in greeting. 'Come sta?'

'Molte bene,' Rob replied, hoping this was the correct response. He held up the loaf.

Luciano beamed. 'Grazie, amico mio.'

'Fra un momento, caro,' Susanna said to her son, trying to escape from his grandfather's arms. Taking the loaf from Rob, she disappeared into the kitchen, returning soon afterwards carrying a small basket.

Roberto slid from his grandfather's knees and looked up at her expectantly.

'Mercato,' Rob told him and, remembering the word for chocolate, added, 'Cioccolato.'

The child beamed and clapped his hands.

Susanna favoured the market down by the harbour some distance away, so they set off at a brisk pace once Rob had swung the boy onto his shoulders. Tiny hands clung either side of his head, reminding him of early adolescence when his brother, John, eleven years younger, would

FEED THY ENEMY

clamber onto his back, tweak his ears and demand a pony ride around their unkempt back yard. Brief periods of pleasure in a young life damaged by frequent abuse from a mother unable to cope with an unwanted seventh baby born eight years after the sixth. A 'change of life' baby who had changed the lives of all those inhabiting the cramped terraced house. Pushing aside bleak memory, Rob began to canter, much to Susanna's amusement, his rider laughing with delight.

When they reached the market, Roberto insisted on remaining atop his perch, but Susanna would have none of it. Prising the child from Rob's shoulders, she placed him firmly on the ground. 'Chiedo scusa,' she said to Rob as Roberto bawled beside her, tears streaking his pinched face.

'Non e problema,' Rob replied, chancing an Italian expression he'd overheard in the street.

One behind two, they walked among the stalls, Rob searching for sweets or chocolate, Susanna focused on more nutritious fare. Halfway along the row she stopped in front of a stall selling tins of fruit, all US Army and Navy supplies Rob noted, no doubt stolen or exchanged for services rendered. The stall keeper, a faded middle-aged woman, gave a toothless smile before addressing Rob. 'Frutta, signore, molto bene.'

Rob pointed to three large tins – pineapple, peaches, pears – at least that was what the labels proclaimed.

The stall keeper held up two fingers. Due dollari ciascuno.'

'Costoso, signora,' Susanna countered, laying a hand on Rob's wrist. 'Un dollaro.'

The stall keeper hesitated, lips pursed. 'Tutti e tre, cinque,' she said at last.'

'Quattro.' Susanna's dark eyes flashed.

Aware his stash of greenbacks was running dangerously low, Rob endeavoured to make sense of the exchange.

'Va bene,' the stall keeper agreed.

Susanna lifted her hand from Rob's wrist and held up four slim fingers.

Relieved, Rob reached into his jacket pocket and pulled out a small roll of notes. He peeled off four one-dollar bills and handed them over.

The woman examined the notes carefully, eyes narrowed. Satisfied they were genuine, she tucked them in her apron pocket before placing the tins in Susanna's basket.

'Cioccolato, mamma?' Roberto asked as they moved away from the stall.

'Presto, caro mio.'

Further along, they noticed a stash of chocolate bars laid out like a fan on a diminutive table wedged between stalls selling tinned meat and fish. Leaving Susanna to barter, Rob studied labels: Hershey's tropical chocolate, Hershey's desert bar made with milk chocolate. His lips curled in a half-smile as he read the directive on one package: 'U.S. Army field ration D, to be eaten slowly in about half an hour.' He couldn't imagine a malnourished child eating chocolate slowly.

Warm fingers tapped his left wrist. 'How much?' he asked Susanna.

'Due cioccolati, un dollaro, per favore.'

Rob smiled, pulled out another dollar note and placed it in the trader's scrawny hand.

EIGHT

SEVEN DAYS AFTER THE HARBOUR MARKET visit, Rob was sunning himself on the barracks' steps, snatching a few minutes respite from the cellar's dank atmosphere, when he noticed WO Whitmore marching towards him. Fearing a reprimand, he was supposed to be clearing out a pile of rubbish, he quickly sprang to attention, but it turned out the officer had more important matters on his mind than a sergeant's idleness.

'I trust you can drive, Harper,' Whitmore said after acknowledging Rob's salute.

'Yes, sir. Learnt during my training.'

'Jolly good. Come with me.'

As they walked towards the villa, Whitmore advised that important papers had to be delivered to an army major in Sorrento and unfortunately, his usual driver had reported sick.

Rob nodded, too busy envisaging a pleasant coastal drive in winter sunshine to respond verbally.

'Take the jeep. Ask Poulton for the key.'

'Yes, sir.' Rob followed him into the building.

'Wait here while I fetch the goodies.' Whitmore disappeared into an office, formerly a sitting room with views over the garden from a large picture window.

Rob resisted the temptation to peer inside, instead stood to one side of the half-open office door, staring at the blank wall opposite. The paintwork had faded, except for a row of squares at average head height, evidence that large paintings had once decorated the narrow corridor. Removed by the owners, Rob presumed, prior to their departure. He wondered why they had left, the damage to the villa's rear corner insufficient to warrant abandonment. Perhaps they were Fascists, who fled when Mussolini had been deposed and imprisoned, not long after the Allies entered Sicily. *Most likely they're in the north now,* he thought, recalling the news of Mussolini's rescue from prison by German forces. Since then, the former dictator had been installed as leader of the Italian Socialist Republic in German-occupied northern Italy, or so the propaganda went. Whitmore's return put paid to further ruminating on the villa's former owners.

'No need to rush back, Sergeant.' He handed Rob a large brown envelope. 'Get yourself some lunch at the hotel.'

'Which hotel, sir?'

'Hotel Minerva, on the cliff top. You can't miss it.' A smile lifted the ends of his drooping moustache. 'We've requisitioned it for the duration. Known as RAF number 2 Rest Camp now.'

'Right, sir.'

'Enjoy the drive, Sergeant. Dismissed.'

———

Rob welcomed the opportunity to leave the ruins of Naples for a few hours. A competent driver, he also relished the thought of a lengthy drive on a road unencumbered by desert sand. Basic training in England had included learning to drive both cars and lorries, a skill he couldn't have acquired otherwise, the cost of a car far beyond the reach of a poorly-paid shop assistant.

When he returned to the barracks to pick up his flying jacket, Rob was surprised to find Bert, an older man with a dicky leg, lying on his bunk smoking. 'Given up on the cellar?'

'Looks like I'm not the only one.'

Rob quickly explained his imminent errand. 'Why don't you ask Whitmore if you could accompany me? I'm sure the cellar can wait; those bottles look as though they've been there for decades.'

Bert raised himself on one elbow. 'Nah, I wouldn't be good company today, too bloody buggered. Leg's giving me jip. Tell you what, I've got a better suggestion for a young bloke like yourself.'

Rob looked puzzled. 'What?'

'Why don't you detour via the home of that Italian girl you told me about, see if she fancies a drive along the coast?'

'Too much of a risk. I could face disciplinary action, if the MPs spotted me.'

'No risk these days, mate. Local girls taking a ride in military vehicles is a common sight around here, no one will raise an eyebrow.'

'You sure about that?'

'Positive.'

Fortunately, Susanna was at home when Rob called in and delighted at the prospect of a drive to Sorrento. Bundling Roberto into a coat, she explained that although the weather was mild, he mustn't catch cold again so soon after the pneumonia. At least that's what Rob thought she said, the combination of Italian and English confusing.

The Willys Jeep had no trouble negotiating the coast road's steep curves, and the views were magnificent, almost vertical cliffs that descended into a turquoise sea, shimmering in bright sunshine. Not that Rob's gaze could linger long on picturesque panoramas, intense concentration required at every turn. Intermittently, he risked a glance at Susanna to admire her long black hair blowing in the wind. The clips she always wore to hold her hair in place had worked free and lay he imagined, somewhere inside her clothing or at her feet. If only he could retrieve them, run his hands over smooth olive skin, lift heavy tresses from her neck, drop kisses on hair-warmed flesh.

Desire, buried for years beneath burning desert sands, had resurfaced since meeting Susanna, but he dared not gamble with their fledgling relationship. Scores of other servicemen, his mate Alf included, might adhere to the premise, 'enjoy yourself today, for tomorrow we die,' but Rob felt reluctant to take advantage of women and girls reeling from the trauma of war. Prostitutes – well, he supposed they were a different matter – not that he had sought their services either before or since joining up. Now and then he queried this reticence, his relationships with all three of his former fiancées hadn't been entirely chaste but concluded years of war had damaged his psyche, made him indifferent to female charms. Relieved to discover his lack of libido had been only temporary, he wondered whether love rather than mere sexual attraction had engineered his change of heart. More than anything, he wanted to care for Susanna, protect her from the swarms of over-sexed soldiers, sailors and airmen swaggering through the streets of Naples looking for a good time. From what he'd observed, Americans were the worst with their rolls of greenbacks and overconfident manner. Money talked in a ruined city, bought not only the necessities of life but luxuries not seen for years or never before. He was well aware that southern Italy had been poverty-stricken for eons, prompting millions to emigrate to the United States during the latter decades of the nineteenth-century and the first thirty-odd years of the twentieth. No wonder the Neapolitans had welcomed Allied troops, especially the Americans with their superior rations that could be exchanged for services rendered.

'Gelati when we get to Sorrento,' Rob

shouted to Susanna, recalling his first taste of the delicious ice-cream, purchased from an Italian immigrant wheeling a cart along the promenade at the base of crumbling cliffs on the perimeter of his hometown. The words were out of his mouth before it occurred to him ice-cream might not be available.

'Gelato delizioso,' she exclaimed, turning her head towards him. 'Is, how you say, regalo for bambino.'

'A treat,' he answered, noting bright eyes and the mien of contentment suffusing her beautiful face. 'But not just for Roberto, you too.'

'Grazie, you are kind man, Roberto.'

They drove on in companionable silence, prolonged conversation impossible in an open-top vehicle buffeted by strong wind. He hoped they could find a sheltered spot for lunch, a picnic on the beach would be preferable to sitting in a café with a wriggling toddler; besides, children loved playing in the sand. Building sandcastles would keep Roberto occupied, leaving space for more intimate adult dialogue. Rob smiled as he envisaged sitting close to Susanna, his arm around her waist. 'I could buy Roberto a bucket and spade if I can find any for sale,' he called out, but his words brought no response, most likely not understood.

As they approached Sorrento, a multi-storey hotel perched on the cliff top overlooking the Gulf of Naples came into view. 'Hotel Minerva,' Rob remarked, lifting one hand from the wheel and pointing as the vehicle slowed.

She nodded. 'Grandioso!

'Yes, it is. 'That's where I have to go first. I'm afraid I'll have to leave you and Roberto in the town. I shouldn't be long with the major.'

'Non problemo,' she answered, smiling up at him. 'Sorrento e bella.'

Rob hoped she wouldn't be disappointed. Minutes earlier, a glance at the opposite side of the road had revealed charred olive groves and a bombed villa, poignant reminders that the consequences of war were never far away. 'Dove I meet you?' he asked.

'Piazza Tasso, vicino la Valle dei Mulini.'

Tasso Square, he translated in his head, wondering what a valley was doing in the middle of a town.

———

Handover of the envelope marked 'Confidential' was accomplished in minutes, the major anxious to peruse its contents. After the meeting, held in the hotel bar, the major's aide escorted Rob to the dining room where several RAF personnel were enjoying an early lunch and a magnificent view of the bay. Rob politely declined the offer of fish and salad followed by trifle, explaining he preferred to eat outside so he could enjoy the sunshine.

The aide frowned, then a grin split his lips. 'Not a problem, sergeant.' He winked at Rob. 'Shall I fetch a packed lunch for two?'

'Yes please.' Rob turned his attention to the view to hide flushed cheeks. Bert had been correct, no one gave a damn about unauthorised passengers riding in military vehicles.

When he drove into Tasso Square, Susanna was standing on the western perimeter, looking down at the long-abandoned mills in the chasm known as the Valley of the Mills, Roberto in her arms. A delightful image that Rob would have photographed had he possessed a camera. Instead, he tooted the horn as he approached, and keeping the engine running, waited for her to join him. 'Did you buy gelati?' he asked when she had settled Roberto on her knee.

She shook her head. 'Fa freddo. I am buying la zuppa.'

He smiled, hoped she wouldn't refuse the packed lunch.

'Gelato, zio Robbi?' Roberto pleaded, huge brown eyes turned to his namesake.

'Presto,' Rob replied. He would try to buy some after the picnic.

This appeared to satisfy the child, so Rob drove back to the Hotel Minerva and parked the jeep a short distance from the entrance. The major's aide had casually mentioned that one could access the beach via a flight of steps to the left of the hotel. The threesome made a slow descent, Roberto insisting on climbing down himself rather than being carried by Rob. The beach was a disappointment. A tiny strip of volcanic sand dotted with rocks, it bore little resemblance to the endless stretch of beach bordering Rob's hometown, but at least the sea, turquoise and sparkling in bright sunshine, looked inviting. Rob knelt on the thin towel Susanna had spread out on the sand and began to share out the food. There were two packets of sandwiches, two pieces of chocolate cake and two bottles of lemonade, the paper bag and waxed paper wrappings proving useful as makeshift plates. As expected, Roberto wanted cake first, but Susanna insisted he eat half a spam sandwich before hoeing into what she called 'torta caprese.' She responded to Rob's questioning look by explaining that the cake had originated on Capri, the rocky island situated a short boat ride from Sorrento.

Rob swallowed the last of his second sandwich and took a swig of lemonade, wanting to erase the taste of cheese and pickle before embarking on cake. As sweet sensations exploded in his mouth – almond, chocolate, icing sugar – he tried to remember when he'd last eaten cake. Never had he tasted anything so delectable! Fruit cake or a Victoria sandwich filled with jam and dusted with icing sugar had been the norm in his aunt's home, not that Rob had cause for complaint, her freshly-baked cakes a treat to one reared on the stale items given away by a local baker.

'Delizioso!' Susanna exclaimed after *her* first mouthful, chocolate crumbs decorating plump red lips.

Rob wanted to lean over and kiss away crumbs, but his usual reticence got in the way and all he could do was part his own lips in a wistful smile.

During the half-hour following lunch there was little opportunity for kisses or close contact of any sort, Susanna up and down like a yo-yo retrieving her child when he strayed too far.

Convinced he had missed his chance, Rob idly watched the child's antics, the remnants of their picnic, screwed up waxed paper, empty bottles and a torn paper bag, lying on the sand in front of him. Eventually, Roberto tired of the game of run, chase and retrieve and relocated to a nearby rock pool where he began tossing in shells and handfuls of sand.

Her son occupied within easy reach, Susanna began to relax, stretching out her bare legs and tilting her face to the sun. Sitting beside her on the small towel, Rob searched his mind for appropriate words with which to begin a more intimate conversation. 'What a beautiful day,' he ventured, edging even closer. 'I haven't had such a good time in years.'

'Sì, sì is beautiful,' Susanna replied, shifting her gaze from son to airman. 'Grazie from my heart. Bambino contento play spiaggia and he love torta you are buying from hotel.'

'Roberto is a beautiful bambino,' Rob remarked, adding quickly, 'his mother is also beautiful.'

Susanna blushed and looked down at the sand. Encouraged, Rob reached over and took her hand. Several minutes passed before he realised that she was crying, her tears falling silently onto dry sand.

'I just wanted to show I care about you,' he explained, releasing her hand.

'Is no good,' she said sadly, looking up and staring straight ahead. 'I am old vedova.'

'Old, don't be silly! I'm the one who's old. I'm thirty!'

She frowned, obviously not understanding, so he leant forward and drew the number thirty in the sand with a finger sticky from torta caprese.

'Trenta,' she murmured before tracing the number twenty-five with the tip of her index finger.

They both looked up and laughed.

'Now we've got that out of the way,' Rob continued, confidence returning, 'how would you like to go out for a meal...' he hesitated, wishing he'd brought along the Italian/English dictionary bought at a market close to the depot. 'One evening la prossima settimana?'

She smiled. 'Grazie, Roberto.'

'Mercoledì?' he asked, counting off the Italian days of the week on his fingers.

'Sì but.' She frowned. 'La sera non possibile,' she said, adding by way of explanation, 'Il coprifucco.'

Deflated, he looked down at the sand, then remembered the seven o'clock curfew for civilians. He'd have to take a punt, trust he could get away early. 'What time?' He pointed to his watch. '

'Mercoledi, I work late. Finisco cinque.'

'Five it is then. I'll pick you up outside the hospital.' But before Rob could lean over to kiss her cheek, little Roberto had arrived and was tipping a handful of shells into his mother's lap. Impulsively, Rob got to his feet, scooped up the child and began to twirl him around and around.

Roberto squealed with delight. 'Di più, di più, zio Robbi,' he demanded, while his mother sat back on her heels, her smile wide as the blue horizon.

———

On the return journey, Rob pushed thoughts of time alone with Susanna to the back of his mind and concentrated on driving, both hands on the steering wheel as he negotiated the sharp bends. Beside him, Roberto slept in Susanna's arms, his curly head resting against her breast, a lock of her hair wrapped around a tiny finger. Rob envisaged a 'Madonna and child' photograph, an image to cherish during restless nights or tedious days. Despite his relief at being 'grounded' since before Tunis, cleaning out a cellar or sorting out paperwork for Whitmore seemed a poor contribution to the war effort and during quiet moments, guilt often pervaded his mind.

A smile began to play around the corners of his mouth; he attempted a complimentary remark, but strong wind and engine noise eclipsed his words, leaving Susanna oblivious to an airman's whimsy.

They were approaching the outskirts of Naples when Rob broke the comfortable silence. 'Look, Susanna, they're planting crops over there,' he said, taking one hand from the wheel and gesturing towards the denuded fields on his right where groups of women and children were scraping the soil. 'That's a good sign. A few months and there'll be plenty of fresh food in the markets.'

Susanna turned her head to observe the stooped figures. 'No, Roberto, you see wrong. Nothing for plant. Look for old patate, old cipolle. Everyday le gente come from city look in field for food.' She shifted her gaze back to Rob. 'Is same in all Napoli, same as girl we are seeing on beach in Sorrento.'

'You mean the girl with a basket near the rocks.'

'Sì, she looking for fish with shell.'

'I thought she was collecting shells like Roberto,' he said, half to himself.

A hand shot out and slapped his wrist. 'Tedesco bomb, americano bomb, inglese bomb. Mia patria ruin. What you no understand?'

Acutely embarrassed by his naivety, Rob gripped the steering wheel and stared at the road ahead. Roberto, woken by his mother's loud retort, began to whimper and despite Susanna's attempts to pacify him with promises of stories from Nonno on their return home and kisses planted on flushed cheeks, the sound intensified as though they were trapped in a sealed vehicle not an open-top jeep. Unable to bear cries that were *his* fault, Rob reached into his shirt pocket and fished out the bar of chocolate he'd intended to give Susanna when they pulled up outside the apartment block. Leaning towards her, he tucked the chocolate bar in the crook of her elbow.

'Grazie, Roberto,' she said without turning her head.

———

Back at the depot, Rob was waylaid in the mess by an inquisitive Bert, determined to hear every detail of the Sorrento outing. Unwilling to share his story with all and sundry, Rob suggested they have a walk and a smoke in the garden, even though he'd left his pipe and tobacco in the barracks. For some time, he had favoured the long drawn out ritual of pipe smoking to the quick roll and light of cigarettes; it gave him time to gather his thoughts. Bert offered him a cigarette as they wandered towards the perimeter wall, but Rob declined, preferring to regale the older man with descriptions of the grand Minerva Hotel and the beach picnic. He also made sure to mention that Susanna had agreed to another date.

'Well done, mate,' Bert replied, cigarette balanced precariously on his lower lip.

They walked on in silence, Bert puffing contentedly, Rob considering whether to mention the humiliating exchange during the return journey. 'The trouble is, I nearly blew it on the way home,' he admitted when they reached the depot gates and were staring at the piles of rubble still littering the far side of the road.

'What the hell did you do? Put your hand up her skirt or something?'

'I'm not that stupid,' Rob countered, annoyed by the inane question. 'I made a daft remark and she took offence.'

'Is that all? Cheer up, she'll have forgotten all about it by now.' Removing the cigarette from his mouth, Bert ground the butt into the gravel.

'You've got to try and understand the Italians, mate. They're an emotional lot, fly into a rage one minute, all smiles the next.'

'The Latin temperament,' Rob muttered.

'So, enjoy yourself while you can,' Bert advised, punching Rob's arm playfully. 'We'll all be on the move again soon, I reckon.'

'You've heard something?'

'Only that it's not going well up at Anzio. That bloody Field Marshall of theirs, Kesselring, has managed to surround the beachhead. He's throwing everything at us.'

Rob kicked out at the gate. 'Bloody war. At this rate, I'll be an old man before it's over.'

'Look on the bright side, mate. You've got a date with a beautiful woman. Anything could happen.'

Rob managed a fleeting smile.

They turned and sauntered back to the barracks.

NINE

The wine bar was crowded with raucous soldiers, despite the early hour and that the only tables, outside on the pavement, were subject to the blasts of cold air that funnelled between four-storey buildings on either side of the narrow street. Much to Rob's relief, Susanna appeared immune to both Neapolitan wind and American merriment, her attention focused on the plate of what she called 'la salsa.' Rob had heard one of the Americans ask for 'spaghetti Napoli,' so used the term when ordering to the apparent amusement of the barman. Nonetheless, the plates had contained spaghetti and a tomato sauce when practically thrown on the table by a harassed waiter. During the long wait for food, Rob and

Susanna had consumed two-thirds of a bottle of wine, the alcohol generating an attractive flush on her normally pale cheeks and an atypical flood of conversation from both parties. Their odd amalgam of language – Susanna's sentences a combination of Italian and English words, Rob's attempt at simple vocabulary in either idiom – had given rise to the odd misunderstanding, but overall, nods, smiles and shared laughter.

As he struggled to manoeuvre slippery spaghetti onto his fork and thence to his mouth, Rob couldn't help reflecting on how his use of a single pronoun, the Italian version of his own name, had led to not only this moment, but also to an illicit act he would never have undertaken in pre-war life. War and its aftermath had altered the moral code, witness the variety of stolen goods blatantly displayed in Neapolitan markets, while his primary concern in recent days had been how to obtain further RAF rations for the Zappetti family without being caught.

The warming weather was his major concern. A thick wool overcoat with deep pockets provided excellent cover but wouldn't be needed soon. Spring in southern Italy bore no resemblance to the season experienced in southern Britain, where weak sunlight and cold winds, ensuring heavy coats, were worn well into May. He would have to devise another method to carry tins or else take only small packets when next he paid a nocturnal visit to the temporary Officers' Mess Store.

Susanna pushed her plate, empty except for a smear of tomato sauce, into the centre of the table and reached for her glass. 'Grazie for beautiful sera, Roberto. I contenta.'

Grateful for an excuse to give up on the spaghetti, Rob looked up and smiled. 'My pleasure. I've really enjoyed hearing about your family.'

'I like talk you.' She raised her glass. 'Salute.'

'Salute,' Rob echoed, lifting his own glass. 'Perhaps we could go out again some time?' he asked a few minutes later, when both glasses and bottle were empty.

Susanna nodded, then asked, 'What is 'some time?'

'Next week, er prossima settimana.'

She smiled. 'Sì, sì.'

'Una sera next settimana,' he said, adopting her hybrid speech. 'Una problema. I don't know which giorno I can get some leave.'

She shrugged. 'Non problemo. You give messaggio amico Alf, he give Nurse McGill, she give me.'

'How did you know Alf and Nurse McGill

were going out?' he asked, forgetting to mention that he and Alf were stationed miles apart.

Susanna leant towards him as though the other patrons were intent on eavesdropping. 'I am seeing kiss fuori hospital.'

'Kissing, er, oh yes.' Courage faded as Rob fiddled with his glass. He glanced at his watch. 'I'd better be seeing you home, curfew in half an hour.' Getting to his feet, he walked to the other side of the table and waited for her to stand before pulling out the chair.

'Grazie, Roberto.' She bent to retrieve her bag.

When they had passed the bar and were heading into a narrow street flanked by half-demolished buildings, she slipped her arm through his and he felt fingers tighten around his wrist. *A step in the right direction,* he thought, regretting the wasted opportunity for a kiss. But his natural pessimism couldn't help adding, *unless she just feels concerned about tripping in the rubble.*

―――

A second raid on the Officers' Mess Store was accomplished without difficulty, the night sky thick with cloud and cold rain keeping visits to the latrines to a minimum. Early next morning, the weather remained overcast and cool, so the wearing of a thick coat didn't attract undue attention as Rob walked from barracks to rear gate, the sentry waving him through without a word.

Anxious to offload tins and packets at the earliest possible moment, Rob almost collided with a jeep as he crossed the main thoroughfare to access the street leading to the Zappetti's apartment block. Stumbling over the kerb in his haste to reach safety, tins rattled as he struggled to keep his balance. A screech of brakes followed by a string of English expletives drew his attention back to the road; inexplicably, the jeep was reversing towards him! *Shit,* he thought, *the last thing I need is an argument with a couple of cranky Yanks.*

'You should watch where you're going, stupid bugger,' a familiar voice sang out as the jeep pulled up to the kerb. After a quick word to the driver, Alf climbed out and clapped his old mate the shoulder. 'Where are you off to at this ungodly hour?'

'Susanna's. I've got a few presents.' He patted his pockets.

'Christ almighty, I never thought you'd have the guts!'

'Like you said, a pushover.'

'No talk of converting the cellar into a more permanent store any time soon then?'

Rob shook his head. 'If there is, I haven't heard about it.'

Alf nodded. 'Mind if I join you, I've got a little something in *my* pocket that would interest the little lad?'

'Non problemo.'

Alf grinned. 'Getting the gist of the lingo, eh?'

'It helps.'

'So, how's it going with the lovely Susanna?'

'Slow but sure.'

Alf poked him in the ribs. 'You want to up your game, mate, time isn't exactly on your side.'

'What have you heard, I thought it was stalemate up at Anzio?'

'It is but Anzio isn't the only location on the generals' minds.'

'Keep me posted, will you?'

'Course, mate.'

Deflated by this second warning about imminent transfer, Rob made no further attempt at conversation, preferring for once to listen to Alf prattle on about Rosie McGill. As rain began to fall, they walked briskly along the street, taking care to avoid large potholes and bomb debris.

Luigi ushered them into the apartment, his usual adolescent scowl momentarily absent. As he opened the door leading to the living room, Roberto came toddling towards them, arms outstretched.

'I think he knows why we're here,' Rob remarked to Alf.

Alf grinned. 'I'm sure he does, the smart little bugger.'

'Cioccolato, zio Robbi,' came the response as though the child had understood every word.

'That child's developing gourmet tastes.' Alf extracted a small package from an inside jacket pocket and placed it in the boy's tiny hand. 'It'll be bloody caviar next time!'

'Bloody caviar, zio…' The child's voice trailed off as he looked to Rob for assistance.

'Alfredo,' said Rob before Alf could enlighten the boy.

Roberto grinned and clapping his hands, repeated the words 'bloody caviar' in a loud voice.

The airmen's laughter proved contagious, Roberto squealing with delight and even moody Luigi managing a brief chuckle.

'Buon giorno,' Susanna called from the kitchen when laughter subsided.

'Buon giorno, Susanna,' Rob answered, 'Come stai?'

'Sto bene, grazie.'

'Go on then, kiss her buon giorno,' Alf said, pushing his hesitant mate towards the open door.

They collided in the doorway, Susanna stepping back before apologising for treading on Rob's foot.

'Non problemo,' he murmured, reaching out to squeeze her shoulders. 'I didn't feel a thing. Stout boots.'

She frowned. 'Non capisco, Roberto.'

Reluctantly, Rob lifted one hand from her shoulder and pointed to his dusty boots.

'I stivali,' she murmured, then smiled up at him.

'I stivali,' he repeated like an obedient student, hoping to prolong the moment of closeness.

In response, she stroked his wrist, her hand warm and soft. Encouraged, Rob was about to kiss her upturned face when Roberto pushed past him and held up chocolate-covered hands for his mother to see. 'Buono cioccolato,' the boy announced, parting chocolate-coated lips.

'Mamma mia!' Susanna exclaimed, grabbing Roberto by the waist and steering him towards the kitchen sink.

Rob stood in the doorway watching the

struggle between mother and son: Susanna wielding a cloth with one hand, the other holding a flailing Roberto over the sink. Water, collected earlier from a street vendor and stored in a bucket, splashed onto the floor, a cloth muffled screams, small hands and mouth emerged shiny pink. Smiling to himself, Rob turned to see Luigi standing close to the table, his dark eyes fixed on Alf's coat pockets. 'I'm the one with the bene cibo, Luigi,' Rob remarked, hoping to induce a smile, but the boy made no response. Delving into his coat pockets, Rob began to retrieve his stash of RAF rations.

'Uno, due, tre, quattro,' Luigi muttered, as Rob placed three large tins and a packet of dried fruit on the table. 'Cinque!' he exclaimed as a second packet appeared, unaware that Susanna had emerged from the kitchen and was standing behind him.

A hand shot out and slapped his cheek. 'Ragazzaccio!'

Luigi swung around, the curse dying in his mouth when he noticed the ire in his sister's eyes.

'Caffè per i nostri amici,' she ordered, her right hand still raised as if challenging him to refuse.

Head bowed to hide his smarting cheek,

Luigi hurriedly got to his feet and slunk into the kitchen.

There was no sign of Luigi when next Rob called for Susanna, the apartment unusually quiet with Luciano also absent and Roberto having a nap. Maria had agreed to tend to her nephew's needs should he wake before his mother returned. After Rob had exchanged the usual pleasantries with the two sisters - his Italian dictionary contained several pages of useful phrases – he escorted Susanna to a wine bar he'd made a note of while running an errand for Whitmore the previous afternoon. Access to the bar was via a set of dilapidated, narrow doors resembling an apartment block entrance, and, but for the few patrons lounging in the open doorway sipping wine, Rob would have walked past without a second glance. For the evening trade, small round tables with seating for at least twenty had been arranged haphazardly on the cracked pavement either side of the doors. A lop-sided board tacked to the wall caught his eye as they approached, its scrawled chalk menu offering pasta and risotto as well as vino. 'Over there ok, Susanna?' He gestured towards a vacant table with two chairs positioned close together, tucked between a tree and the corner of the street.

'Sì, sì' She stepped off the pavement and headed for the table, the worn metal tips of her shoes pinging on the rough road surface.

Behind her, Rob focused on the sway of slim hips and the smooth curve of buttocks beneath a faded blue skirt. If only he could buy her a new outfit, but to date he hadn't noticed any clothing for sale in the markets. He watched her slide into the seat nearest the tree, a graceful movement designed he imagined, to keep 'above the knees' out of sight. 'I'll fetch some vino,' he said, leaning across the table. 'La cena?' he added, hoping she hadn't already eaten dinner. A meal, however meagre, would prolong their time together.

'Grazie, Robbi.' She smiled up at him.

He returned the smile, her use of 'Robbi' rather than the usual 'Roberto' convincing him the warm smiles and tender touch of their previous meeting had been more than good manners.

He reappeared a few minutes later, carrying a bottle and two glasses and noticed she had made no move to separate the chairs. *Another good sign,* he thought, setting his wares on the table before moving around to the vacant seat. Behind the chairs, bricks from a partially demolished wall had been stacked in a pile and he doubted whether he would fit in the narrow space remaining between table and chair. He needn't have worried; years of RAF rations had trimmed his already slim torso.

Wine poured, they raised their glasses and murmured 'Salute' before taking several sips. Sheltered by wall and tree, neither felt cold when a blast of wind blew ribbons of dust along the road, prompting nearby patrons to complain and express a yearning for warmer weather. Spring growth above their heads promised renewal, although Rob doubted the tree's few spindly branches would provide much shade for bar patrons come summer.

Two hours passed, they remained seated side by side, toying with a last glass of wine as though deliberately avoiding the impending curfew. Earlier, they had consumed a simple but tasty meal of pasta and sauce topped with a sprinkling of herbs, washed down with two glasses of the local effervescent wine. Conversation had seemed easier than on previous occasions, Rob managing without once referring to the dictionary tucked in his jacket pocket, although he couldn't decide whether wine or Susanna's arm brushing his throughout the meal had dissolved his habitual reserve. 'I must be getting used to this vino,' he remarked, holding up his almost empty glass. 'It doesn't knock me about so much now.' He patted his stomach in case she hadn't understood.

'Vino is buono, Robbi. It warm the heart.'

Rob stroked her arm with his free hand. 'I don't need vino to warm my heart. Just being with you makes me contento.'

Susanna leant closer. 'I molto contenta, caro.'

Seizing the moment, Rob put down his glass and cradling her beautiful face in his hands, kissed wine-reddened lips.

———

'Success or failure?' Bert asked later that night the moment Rob climbed into the adjacent bunk.

Rob ignored the question and turned on his side.

'So, how was your date?' Bert persisted, reaching out to poke Rob in the ribs.

'Give it a rest will you.'

'Failure then.'

Irritated by this slur on his manhood, Rob rolled onto his back and began to whistle Glen Miller's Moonlight Serenade.

'Well done, mate.'

A pillow launched from the bunk opposite struck Rob on the chest. 'Call it a day, Harper,' said a weary mechanic who had spent the day fixing a broken-down lorry. He had been transferred to the depot temporarily on account of his skill with engines that had seen better days and resented this interruption to a well-earned sleep. 'Some of us aren't sitting around this bloody depot doing sweet bugger all, you know.'

'Sorry, mate.' Grabbing the pillow, Rob slipped out of bed and padded across the narrow gap between the two rows of bunks. 'You might need this.'

'Thanks.' Oil-stained hands accepted the pillow and tucked it behind his head.

'Sweet dreams,' Rob murmured and was about to turn around when the mechanic propped himself up on one elbow.

'Fat chance of anything sweet for us ground crew at Foggia, mate.'

Rob tensed. 'Are the squadrons heading north soon?'

'No firm orders yet, but rumour has it the stalemate up at Anzio will be broken before long.'

Rob recalled the tree near the wine bar, fresh foliage unsullied by street dust. 'So, what are we talking, a couple of weeks, a month?'

The mechanic shrugged. 'All I know is we've been told to have every aircraft ready to go at a moment's notice. Even the old crates that barely made it over from Tunisia.'

'Thanks for telling me. Night, mate.'

'Night.'

Lying in his narrow bunk, Rob listened to the sounds of sleep: snuffles, snores, the creak of wooden bedframes as men shifted position. Torn between his wish for a swift conclusion to a campaign that had cost thousands of lives on both sides and his longing to spend time with Susanna, he lay rigid, fingers clutching the thin blanket. Why couldn't he be like Alf, just enjoy a girl's company without dreaming of a future? It was always the same, a desire, some would say an obsession, to secure long-term love by buying a ring. Since the age of twenty-one, he'd been engaged three times, all to unsuitable girls as it turned out, but only once had he plucked up the courage to end the relationship, the outbreak of war prompting that decision. Unlike some of his friends at the football club, he'd had no wish for a hasty marriage that could be short-lived. Leaving a girl behind dreading a telegram from the War Office seemed cruel, something his last fiancée had failed to comprehend when she urged him to think of the benefits instead. He'd heard her out but wouldn't change his mind. What use would a miserly war widow's pension be, especially if she had a child to support?

His thoughts turned to little Roberto growing up without a father, a father he had barely known and would not remember. What chance would the boy have of rising above the poverty that afflicted the whole of southern Italy? *I could be a father to him,* Rob mused, jumping ahead of himself as usual. *I could build a better future for him at home.*

Fingers of sunlight filtered through the barracks' dusty windows, waking Rob from fitful sleep and dreams of a cottage garden where a dark-haired child with olive skin kicked a football to his English step-father. Blinking, he slowly surfaced into early morning, the roomful of sleeping men proof of his current reality. Nothing he desired or dreamed could alter the progress of this interminable war already well into its fifth year. Generals and politicians safely ensconced in faraway offices would determine the immediate course of his life, an individual's longing for home of no consequence. Focusing on the Italian sunlight, he reflected that 'home' for Roberto was here, in this broken city, surrounded by a loving family.

Gifts of food from a former enemy were received with gratitude but removing a child and his mother from the bosom of their family would be viewed as an outrage. He recalled Luigi's surly smile, the half-broken voice carefully counting RAF rations, the grubby fingers curled around a tin.

Then, as he tried to dismiss negative images of a sulky adolescent, a niggling doubt crept into his tired mind. Susanna's friendly smiles and gentle kisses might be no more than thankfulness for generosity, a ploy to ensure the food kept coming. It was common knowledge that young women were playing the same game throughout the city, although Rob imagined that most would have to offer more than kisses to keep *their* foreign benefactors' content. Susanna must welcome the snail's pace of their relationship with its emphasis on sharing food and hybrid conversation.

Around him bodies stirred, and yawns punctured stale night air. Grateful for the forced conclusion of an internal monologue going nowhere, Rob turned his attention to the day's mundane activities.

TEN

THE DAY BROUGHT A FLURRY OF UNEXPECTED activity. The initial surprise came early, the appearance of Whitmore as they ate breakfast in the mess, causing several men to almost choke on the slabs of coarse toasted bread and slices of lukewarm bully beef that passed for a cooked meal. Atypically, the Warrant Officer appeared uneasy, prompting whispered speculations from those not chewing that the depot was about to be vacated and all hands relocated to distant airfields. When the coughing subsided, the men rose from their wooden benches and stood to attention.

'At ease, men.' Whitmore waited a few moments before advising the purpose of his visit.

Listening to the WO drone on about Group Captain Clarkson's plans for the cellar, Rob's emotions swung from relief to irritation and back again. Relief that he wasn't returning to air crew duties somewhere further north, irritation that the opportunity to nick rations from the Officer's Mess Store would soon be eliminated, relief for extra time to spend with Susanna. Deep down he knew a permanent relationship was nothing more than a pipe dream, but nevertheless remained determined to make the most of future dates.

Ten men spent the day, apart from a short break for lunch, labouring in the dusty confines of the cellar, their task: The removal of hundreds of empty wine bottles to a designated spot behind a stand of trees close to the rear gate. Whitmore had arranged for a lorry to transport the bottles to a municipal rubbish dump on the city outskirts, but despite several telephone calls, the lorry failed to show. A shortage of wheelbarrows, only two had been found on the property, slowed the process to a trickle until Bert suggested constructing several large containers from the pile of old floorboards propped in a corner. A coil of rope discovered behind the floorboards served as handles, two men were required to carry each container.

FEED THY ENEMY

Rob would have willingly opted to transport bottles down the gravel path that meandered through tall trees to the gate, anything to get away from the dust swirling around the cellar. However, he wasn't given a choice, taller, more robust men chosen for the task. A handkerchief tied around nose and mouth reduced the spates of coughing, but his irritated eyes watered constantly, moisture merging with perspiration and dust to form dark streaks on exposed skin. Catching sight of himself in a window during lunch, he remembered the boot polish applied to his face during a basic training exercise. Despite endless scrubbing that threatened to remove several layers of skin, it had taken days to get rid of the caked camouflage.

Nightfall saw Rob lying in his bunk soon after dinner, too weary to join his fellow 'bottle shifters' in the mess to celebrate the removal of the last dusty relic. Sound asleep within minutes, physical exhaustion ensuring a night free of dreams either fanciful or horrific, Rob missed the new arrival's appearance mid-evening and the subsequent allocation of a bunk at the far end of the barracks. Waking early, he lay back on the thin pillow, hands behind his head to support his neck and surveyed the familiar scene. Jumbled blankets suggested that despite a full day of physical activity, some of those opposite had tossed and turned throughout the night, or perhaps they had drunk too much in the mess, so were forced to make numerous visits to the latrines. His eyes flicked to other bunks further down the barracks, noted Bert lying on his back, blankets tucked tightly. *Nothing ever disturbs that old bugger,* he thought, wishing Bert would turn on his side, a manoeuvre that should terminate the strident snores emerging from his gaping mouth with monotonous regularity.

A shape in the bunk nearest the door caught his eye and he stared hard, certain it had been vacant the previous night. He was thinking that someone had decided to move on account of Bert's snoring, when the occupant sat up and yawned. 'Alf Simpson, what the hell are you doing here?' he called, forgetting the early hour.

Several men stirred but fortunately didn't wake, while sensible Alf propped himself on one elbow and crooked a finger in Rob's direction rather than risk disturbing others.

Out of bed in seconds and padding down the narrow aisle, Rob couldn't help smiling at this unexpected arrival. If his old mate stayed at the depot for a few days, there might be an opportunity for a third nocturnal visit to the Officer's Mess Store before the provisions were transferred to the cellar. One to look out and one to do the business, as Alf had put it, would be far easier than working alone. 'What brings you here this time?' he asked, sitting on the end of the bunk.

'Your depot commander requested a tradesman with welding experience.'

Rob looked puzzled. 'Has the boiler in the officers' billet down the road gone bung?' There were no such luxuries as hot showers for other ranks; they had to make do with a metal bowl, boil a kettle if they wanted warm water for washing either themselves or their clothes.

'No, I'm needed for work in the cellar.'

'The cellar? But we haven't finished clearing it out yet.'

Alf shrugged. 'That's as maybe, but I was told to pack my kit and get over here quick smart. Got a lift in Group Captain Clarkson's car. He was going further south, Gragnano I think he said, so he dropped me off here last night. Funny old geezer didn't stop talking the whole way. Kept calling me old chap.'

Rob nodded, recalling the station commander's plummy voice. 'I don't think he's that old though.'

'Over fifty at least.'

'Ancient then.' He gave Alf a friendly shove that saw him fall back on the pillow.

'Take it easy, mate, you don't want to injure the tradesman.'

'Christ, I didn't mean to hurt you.'

Alf grinned. 'Joke, Robert, lighten up.'

Relieved, Rob got to his feet. 'Shall I escort you to the mess, old chap?'

Alf twisted around, swung skinny legs over the edge of the bunk. He'd gone to bed in his underwear, too pissed to bother undressing. 'Pass me my boots and trousers, old chap. Need a slash before I drink anything.'

Rob saluted. 'Yes, sir, right away, sir.'

The cellar conversion occupied daylight hours and evening leave was cancelled for an unspecified period, WO Whitmore saying he needed his workers fresh as daisies early each morning. The new Officers' Mess store comprised only part of the construction, Group Captain Clarkson having decided the 'chaps' needed a workshop to keep them fully occupied until they were needed elsewhere. Repairs to office furniture and equipment, building bookshelves, benches and stools, were some of the activities he had in mind.

Clarkson had expounded his plan a few days earlier, appearing one morning with a large sheet of butcher's paper on which he had drawn a neat rectangle divided into three. The left-hand section was labelled 'Workshop,' the middle, 'Officers' Mess Store,' the right-hand side Miscellaneous Storage.' In answer to a question from Mac, the dour Scot, Clarkson explained that excess furniture, wheelbarrows and anything else lying around the property would be stored there.

Discussing the plan later in their mess, the men concluded that the siting of the Officers' Mess Store in the middle section didn't make much sense when a door in the outside wall led directly to the set of steps connecting the cellar with the kitchen on the ground floor.

'Less damp in the middle,' Whitmore maintained when Bert questioned the layout the following morning.

The cellar ran under the entire villa and already comprised three large spaces, separated by brick walls. that stopped short of the rear stone wall, thus avoiding the need for doors. From the look of the brickwork, the dividing walls had been standing for decades if not a century, but they appeared sound and according to an airman who had worked on house renovation in civvy street, would stand the addition of doorways. Using a pile of old bricks discovered behind the shed housing the latrines, the men extended the two walls, leaving spaces for a single door in each. Old timber gathered from other cellars – the RAF had appropriated several abandoned villas in the area – proved useful for door frames and a few shelves.

One morning, a small amount of scrap metal was brought in the back of an Army lorry and dumped in a corner. Unfortunately, the lorry driver refused to remove the piles of wine bottles still languishing at the bottom of the garden, maintaining his orders were to deliver scrap metal, not pick up the RAF's rubbish.

Initially, Alf was instructed to use the smaller pieces of scrap metal to make free-standing shelves, but he soon discovered why his boilermaker skills were needed, his primary task was to make metal cladding for the new doors. 'Security,' Whitmore said when someone asked why the old floorboards weren't sufficient. No mention was made of stolen supplies, but Rob, fixing wooden shelves nearby, couldn't help feeling guilty and swore Whitmore had noticed the flush creeping up his neck and over his cheeks.

'Don't be so bloody stupid, mate,' Alf told

him as they walked to the mess for dinner. 'You're not the only one with a red face. It's bloody airless in that cellar.'

'All the same, I'm not sure we should chance another raid.'

'Oh, I think we could manage it at an appropriate time.'

'Any thoughts on when?'

'After the relocation of stores.'

'Don't you mean before?'

Alf shook his head. 'Just remember who's responsible for the Fort Knox doors.'

'What have you in mind?'

'Nothing you need to know about.' Alf extracted a cigarette and matches from his shirt pocket and stopped to light up. 'I suggest you volunteer to help transfer supplies, though.'

'Will do. May I ask why?'

'A little sleight of hand should ensure a few packets reach deep pockets rather than shelves.'

'You're enjoying this, aren't you?'

Alf gave a lop-sided grin, releasing smoke from one corner of his mouth.

After seven days, WO Whitmore announced the resumption of evening leave, a few men at a time, maximum three hours. As expected, Alf was included in the first batch and wrangled leave for Rob by appealing to Whitmore's patriotism, telling him they were both dating girls who worked at the military hospital and if neglected much longer by their RAF boyfriends, the girls might resort to Yankee servicemen.

Somehow, Alf had discovered Rosie would be on duty that evening, so he headed for the hospital, Rob tagging along to see if she knew details of Susanna's next shift. He didn't expect to see Susanna. Cleaning usually took place during the morning, so he'd written a note to explain his recent absence for Rosie to pass on. Alf could have delivered the note, but after a week spent in the close confines of a dusty cellar, Rob needed a break from the depot. He could have paid a visit to the Zappetti apartment but like Alf before him, didn't relish the thought of tramping dark streets alone. Beyond the main road heading north, the streetscape altered radically, narrow streets lined with shabby apartment buildings replacing the grand villas surrounded by gardens found on the other side.

On arrival at the hospital, the two airmen headed for a room off the foyer allocated for staff meals, hoping to find a nurse who could be persuaded to go to the ward and fetch Rosie. The door was half-open, and Alf knocked several times to attract someone's attention, but when this failed, he shoved the door back against the wall and called out a greeting.

'Alf!' Rosie exclaimed, making a move towards him. 'This is a surprise.'

He grinned. 'Is it safe to come in?'

She nodded.

'Sister Miles has the day off,' a younger nurse with an American accent advised as Alf stepped into the room. 'And who have we here?' she added, noticing a second airman.

'Sergeant Rob Harper,' Rosie answered. 'Rear gunner par excellence.'

Rob coloured at the, to him, unwarranted appellation. He hadn't even held a gun for months. 'Pleased to meet all of you.'

Turquoise eyes scrutinised him from his dark blue peaked cap to his shiny black boots. 'Delighted to meet you,' the nurse purred in a soft southern drawl. 'Perhaps we could get better acquainted?'

Embarrassed, Rob stood still as a statue, eyes fixed on his boots.

'He's already taken, Nurse Beaumont,' a Glaswegian voice rang out. 'So back off.'

Plump red lips pouted and with a toss of blond curls the girl flounced over to the table, where she picked up a half-eaten sandwich, tore strips from the coarse bread with strong white teeth.

Thankful for Rosie's intervention, Rob pulled the note from his pocket and moved towards her. 'Could you deliver this?' he asked, deciding not to mention Susanna by name. Alf had told him that Americans considered the local population low-life predisposed to criminal activity and treated them accordingly.

'No problem, Rob, but our shifts won't coincide for a couple of days. Why don't you try her at home?'

Rob looked at his watch. Nineteen hundred hours. Just enough time left for a quick visit, it had taken less than half an hour to walk from depot to hospital. 'Good idea,' he answered, dismissing previous safety concerns. He turned to Alf. 'See you back at base, mate.'

'Stick to the main roads as much as you can,' Alf advised and turned back to his girl.

―――

Luigi answered Rob's knock on the apartment door, his scowl and lack of a greeting a sure sign he wasn't pleased to see the visitor. The boy looked even more scruffy than usual, his patched shirt in need of a wash, his over-large trousers, probably an old pair of Luciano's, held in place with a length of frayed string tied tight around his thin waist.

Rob followed Luigi into the living room, expecting at this hour, to see Luciano sitting in his usual chair near the balcony door, but there was no sign of him or any other family members.

Luigi stepped up beside him. 'You 'ave the grossi tin?'

'Not tonight.'

'You 'ave the piccoli tin?'

Rob shook his head.

'Perche you here?'

'To see Susanna. Where is she?'

'Cucina,' the boy answered curtly.

'Grazie.' Rob headed for the kitchen, but Luigi quickly stepped in front of him blocking the doorway. 'I just want to talk to her, Luigi.'

'No, you want fuck her!' Dark eyes bored into blue.

'Certainly not. I respect your sister.'

'Liar! You Americano all same. Mangiare per sex.'

'No, you've got it all wrong. And I'm British not American.'

A thin finger poked Rob in the chest. 'No,

you wrong. She is dating perche you bring food per la famiglia.'

Crestfallen, Rob said half to himself, 'I have wondered whether that explained her continued interest.'

Luigi took his time digesting the foreign words. 'What you say?'

'Nothing important. Get out of my way, Luigi.'

The boy turned to open the door. 'You will see I am knowing la verita. No tins, no kiss.' Darting behind Rob, he opened the door and pushed him into the kitchen. 'Non ha barattoli,' he shouted as though his sister stood at the far end of the apartment, not wiping her hands on her apron three feet away.

Steps faltered and a bright smile slipped, prompting thoughts of a swift retreat. But as Rob turned on his heel, a damp hand reached out to clutch his right arm. Determined to salvage a scrap of self-respect, he said firmly, 'please let me go, Susanna,' adding more for his own benefit than hers, 'it's better this way.' Pressure eased, he squared his shoulders, glanced at the doorway where Luigi stood smirking, arms folded against his skinny chest. 'Move, Luigi,' he hissed through clenched teeth.

Arms shifted, grubby fingers grasped either side of the doorframe.

'I said move.'

The boy grinned. 'You have make me, stupid English.'

The slap took them both by surprise: Luigi, the imprint of his sister's hand stinging his cheek, pinned to the doorframe unable to move, Rob, halted mid-step by the proximity of heaving breasts. 'La guerra è finita,' Susanna declared, although it remained unclear whether she meant the Italian surrender or immediate conflict, further speech obstructed by subsequent actions.

Trapped by her fierce embrace, Rob surrendered to moist kisses, his only thought how to keep his balance. At last she released him, twisted around and grabbing the door handle, slammed the door in Luigi's face.

Footsteps pounded across the living room; a second door slammed.

In the silence that followed Luigi's departure, he heard repeated exhalations, felt the air between them quiver. She seemed deflated, her thin shoulders sagging, her mouth slightly open to ease respiration. Despite fervent kisses and an embrace that had threatened to squeeze the breath out of him, he felt compelled to seek verbal confirmation, so searched his mind for a suitable way to begin what promised to be a testing conversation. 'Can I ask you something, Susanna?' he managed after a lengthy silence.

Her expression altered from grateful respite to concern. 'Sì,' she answered warily.

'It's very important I ask this question you understand.' Reaching forward, he took her hand.

'Sì.' She blinked, then looked directly into his eyes.

'Now I don't want you to take offence; it's just that I have this little doubt and I er...' He hesitated, tried to translate the words in his head, failed miserably, emotion clouding rational thought. 'I do not think I can carry on dating you until it is sorted out,' he continued, pronouncing each word like a student at an elocution class. 'You see er, I need to know if there is any future in our relationship, er I need to know the truth.'

Susanna snatched her hand away. 'Truth! I always tell truth!'

'Per favore, let me finish. I just need to know if you really like me or...'

'Or what?' she interrupted, hands on hips, eyes flashing fury.

Rob decided on a different tack. 'I want you to know how I feel. I like you so much, Susanna, not just for your smile or because we have good times together. You are very special.' He moved towards, slipped an arm around tense shoulders. 'And I hope you like me for more than talk and meals, and not just because I bring food for your family.'

She raised both hands and cradling his face, kissed him passionately.

ELEVEN

Raids on the new Officers' Mess Store began soon after its completion, Alf insisting on taking part despite Rob assuring him it wasn't necessary. Having a larger space for supplies meant everything was neatly displayed, so the two mates changed tactics to ensure no one noticed missing items. Small, more frequent raids were the order of the day, or rather night, large tins left on the shelves.

Contrary to expectations, Alf had remained at the depot, Group Captain Clarkson, impressed by his excellent workmanship and determined to hang on to a tradesman for as long as possible.

Opening the steel-clad door that divided the

workshop from the store, proved a simple task once smears of grease had silenced its creaking hinges. Whitmore and the cook held the only keys, so Alf had fashioned a special tool that resembled a screwdriver without a handle.

'Are you sure you didn't moonlight as a burglar in civvy street?' Rob asked following the initial raid.

'No way. I just relish helping myself to superior officers' superior rations.'

'Your personal protest against the class system, eh?'

'Got it in one, mate. Reckon we should all be equal, especially during wartime.'

'Fat chance of that.'

'That's what my father said. Mind you, from what he told me when I joined up, it was worse in the last show. Working-class men like him were nothing but cannon fodder in the army. That's why I picked the RAF.'

'What passing-bells for these who die as cattle?' Rob murmured, recalling the poet Wilfred Owen, killed in 1918 a week before the Armistice was signed.

'What's that, mate?'

'Just a line from a poem.'

Alf shook his head. 'I'll never understand the way your mind works.'

Beyond the depot walls, city markets burgeoned with what seemed an endless supply of stolen goods, mostly American, as the populace became more daring. Anything left unattended for more than a few minutes vanished. Near the docks, horse-drawn hearses moved sedately through the streets, their coffins filled with goods from American supply ships. Stiff sentences were imposed for Neapolitans caught stealing -- at least for those with no means to bribe officials -- but this failed to deter the majority.

Encouraged by all this local activity, Rob and Alf became a little careless: a packet left unsealed, a potato dropped on the floor, dusty handprints left on the metal-clad door.

Late one night, Rob was standing near the cellar's back door, scanning the immediate area prior to giving Alf the all-clear signal, when he heard footsteps and a familiar public- school accent. 'Evening Sergeant Harper.'

'Evening, sir,' Rob replied in a loud voice as Group Captain Clarkson materialised from the side of the villa.

'And what might you be doing loitering near the cellar at this hour of the night?'

'Nothing, sir. I couldn't sleep so decided to stretch my legs.'

'Strange place to choose for a moonlight stroll.'

'I was just walking, sir. No particular destination in mind.' Rob gestured towards the cigarette butt at his feet, silently blessed whoever had dropped it. 'Stopped for a smoke.' He bent to pick up the litter before Clarkson could issue a rebuke.

'Not planning a little pilfering by any chance?'

'Certainly not, sir. I wouldn't dream of it.'

'I'm pleased to hear it, Harper. A fair few rations have gone missing from the Officers' Mess Store in the last few weeks. Must be someone with a sweet tooth, the thief favours chocolate and tinned puddings.'

Rob looked up, stuffed the cigarette butt in his pocket. 'That seems a bit odd, sir. Chocolate I can understand, but tinned puddings?'

'Several varieties according to the kitchen staff.'

'Perhaps it's those boys you see hanging around everywhere. From what I hear, they're up for stealing anything from anywhere.'

Clarkson shook his head. 'Unlikely, Whitmore says there's no sign of interference with the lock.'

Rob nodded, thankful he was standing in shadow.

'Could be the kitchen staff, I suppose,' Clarkson continued. 'I realise they might prefer officers' rations to their own.'

Guilt rose like bile in Rob's throat. He swallowed hard and decided to risk contradicting his superior. 'Doubtful, sir. I haven't heard any talk of pilfering or seen anything suspicious. I'd put money on it that locals are involved.'

Clarkson sighed. 'You may be right.' Looking into the distance, he said wistfully, 'my wife does a splendid spotted dick. Actually, it's my favourite pudding. The tinned variety we get here isn't a patch on hers. What's your opinion, Harper?'

'I wouldn't know, sir,' Rob replied confidently. 'I've never tasted spotted dick from a tin.'

'Right you are then. Think I'll turn in now.'

'Me too, sir.'

Lying in his bunk anxiously awaiting Alf's return, Rob remembered that despite some initial apprehension, Luciano Zappetti shared the Group Captain's fondness for spotted dick. He pictured the swarthy Italian tucking in to what some considered 'stodgy' British fare, a smile replacing the sombre expression present ever since the night's near exposure. Movement near the door drew his attention away from steamed puddings, and he watched with growing relief as a familiar figure crept between the rows of sleeping men towards him.

'Christ, that was a close one,' Alf whispered. 'I thought we were done for.'

'Me too. Lucky escape.'

'My wife does a splendid spotted dick,' said Alf, giving a fair imitation of Clarkson, albeit with a Yorkshire accent. 'Actually, it's my favourite pudding.'

Rob suppressed a laugh. 'We'd better go easy on the tinned puddings next time.'

'If there is a next time. Surely they'll break out of that beachhead soon.'

On one level, Rob didn't mind how long the troops at Anzio took to break out, but he knew better than to express such an unpatriotic and selfish opinion. 'We'd best get some sleep,' he muttered instead and turned on his side.

Muffled snores from the end of the row soon told him Alf had taken his advice.

A subsequent raid on the Officers' Mess Store two nights later, proved successful, the loot including half a dozen tins of sardines and pilchards. Tucked in a corner behind sacks of potatoes, the fish had been overlooked on previous occasions. Keen to deflect attention from their nefarious activities, the two mates left tinned puddings of any variety on the shelf. Let the Group Captain enjoy his spotted dick.

Sardines and pilchards were greeted with unforeseen delight the following afternoon, Luciano revealing surprising athleticism as he danced around the living room clutching a tin in both hands. 'Magnifico, magnifico, amici miei,' he cried repeatedly, his melodious voice reverberating through the apartment like a La Scala tenor.

Caught up in the moment, Rob grabbed Roberto, standing nearby clapping his hands, lifted him level with his chest and danced the child back and forth between the chairs.

Alf shook his head at such uninhibited behaviour, no Yorkshireman would ever make an exhibition of himself in this way and began to pile the contents of his pockets onto the table.

Alerted by the revelry, Susanna ran in from

the kitchen, her expression a mixture of joy and astonishment at the sight of grown men prancing around the furniture. 'Cosa stai facendo?'

A red-faced Luciano skipped towards her, and with an extravagant gesture, laid the tins at her feet. 'Finalmente, mia bella figlia, le sardine!'

'Meraviglioso, papà.' She bent to retrieve the tins.

'Buon giorno, Susanna,' Rob called as he swept past.

Looking up, she flashed him a brilliant smile. 'Buon giorno, Robbi. Grazie mille per le sardine.'

'There are pilchards as well,' Alf remarked to no one in particular.

Susanna straightened up, a worried look replacing the smile as Luciano continued his energetic antics. 'Sederti, papà,' she pleaded to no avail.

'Vino should stop them,' Alf muttered, stepping towards her.

'Vino,' she repeated and rushed into the kitchen.

As if on cue, Luciano, who couldn't have heard Alf's suggestion, headed for the table and collapsed in the nearest chair, breathing heavily.

'You okay, mate?' Alf asked.

'Nonno, you okay mate?' Roberto echoed, wriggling in Rob's arms.

Breathless, Luciano could only nod.

A welcome calm descended, Roberto scrambling onto his grandfather's knee to lean against the heaving chest, thumb in his mouth; Alf and Rob taking a seat either side of the table. Susanna brought water as well as wine for the weary dancers, a welcome relief for thirsty Rob who had no wish to gulp alcohol.

Thirst assuaged, conversation began, Luciano waxing lyrical about the meals Susanna would create from sardines and pilchards, Alf responding by saying he preferred cod and chips to bony little fish and pasta. There followed a loud but friendly argument about the merits of their native cuisines, both men trying to outdo the other by describing ever more elaborate dishes. Bouncing on his grandfather's knee, Roberto added to the mix by calling out for chocolate and cod! On the opposite side of the table, Rob took no part in the discussion, his attention focused on stroking the hand resting on his knee.

Alf had just finished a description of the luscious strawberries and cream served to parishioners in his village church hall following the harvest festival service, when Luciano's demeanour altered as though someone had said rancid meat would be on the menu for the foreseeable future. Broad shoulders tensed, and a hand shot out to clasp the empty wine bottle. Even the child stopped wriggling, his pink mouth a circle of surprise, while beneath the table, his mother's fingernails dug into Rob's wrist. 'Distruzione, inutile distruzione,' Luciano hissed, saliva and syllables colliding mid-flight.

The two airmen exchanged glances, both at a loss to understand what had triggered the outburst. Then Rob remembered the news from Monte Cassino two weeks earlier, wave after wave of American bombers unleashing their deadly cargo until the famous Abbey had been destroyed. Founded in 526 by Saint Benedict, the abbey had been described as the most beautiful monastery in the world. Its destruction had created a furore among the Italian population.

Tears welled in Luciano's eyes. 'Perche you are bombing nostro bello monastero?' he said in a low voice, his lips barely moving.

Alf opened his mouth to speak, closed it before uttering a single word.

Frivolity eclipsed by obliteration, Rob thought, wondering whether the Allied servicemen walking the streets of Naples were merely tolerated now, rather than welcomed by the local inhabitants as they had been on the day the city was liberated. The Italian government might have surrendered months earlier, but he knew there remained pockets of resistance, not all citizens willing to abandon fascism. Unable to either defend the destruction of the ancient abbey or offer condolences, he remained silent, wishing he could leap up and run from the apartment. Fingers stroked his wrist, he felt the warmth of a slim thigh. How could he leave her to deal with a widowed father's profound distress? In recent weeks, Susanna had told him her mother had succumbed to pneumonia the previous winter, poor nutrition and lack of money for medicine contributing factors.

The allied airmen exhaled as Luciano's fingers loosened their grip on the bottle. Tears slid down a weathered cheek, shoulders shook, lips quivered. An overt display of raw emotion engendering acute embarrassment for Englishmen schooled in keeping feelings buried deep.

The arrival of Maria, carrying a bunch of wildflowers, provided an opportune distraction, seized upon immediately by Alf. 'Buon giorno, Maria,' he called, as she walked into the living room. 'What beautiful flowers. Where did you find them?'

Maria smiled. 'Buon giorno, zio Alfredo, buon giorno, zio Roberto. I find fiori near scuola.

I molta contenta la primavera come again.' She headed for the kitchen.

Rob envisaged fields dotted with tiny shoots. 'Now primavera is here, the farmers can plant vegetables,' he remarked to Luciano, hoping to break the pall of tension still hanging over the table. 'Fresh food in the markets before you know it. You won't have to eat tinned food anymore.'

'I no think i agricoltori have seed for plant,' Luciano answered, his speech liberally peppered with loud sniffs.

'Don't worry, there are plenty more tins where these come from,' Alf reassured him.

Luciano managed a small smile. 'Oggi, I am seeing much food in mercato. Mio amico Georgio he is selling at porto. He is saying business good. Many grossi tin: frutti, torte, carne.'

Alf leant towards Rob. 'Navy rations from those Yankee ships anchored in the bay, I reckon. The word's going around market traders are doing deals with the marines.' He glanced at Susanna, and seeing she was looking towards the kitchen, added quietly, 'Girls for food.'

'Proprio così,' said a loud voice and Rob looked up to see Luigi standing by the door leading to hallway and bedrooms. Earlier, the boy had fled from the living room, probably embarrassed by the adult's antics. After glaring at the visitors, he ambled across the room and stood behind his father, hands resting lightly on Luciano's shoulders.

'Yankee pudding good, Alfredo?' Luciano asked.

Alf shrugged. 'I've no idea.'

'Otterrò del budino per te, papà,' Luigi offered. 'Il mio amico Francesco ha un amico americano.'

Luciano smiled broadly and reached up to pat his son's hand, but Susanna's expression altered to one of displeasure. Leaning forward, she waved her hands over the tins and packets stacked in the middle of the table. 'Non necessario, Luigi. Abbiamo sufficienza.'

Luigi responded with a tirade that further upset his sister.

'They say the Yanks have great rations,' Rob remarked innocently, the rapid-fire dialect beyond his understanding.

Luigi grinned. 'Buono, buono. Il cibo inglese…'

'Niente scatolette americane, Luigi,' Susanna cried, leaping from her seat. 'Ho visto la polizia al porto.' And sweeping the rations into her arms, she stormed off into the kitchen.

Silence descended, a thick blanket smothering the likelihood of subsequent light-hearted conversation. The three men lifted almost empty glasses but kept their eyes fixed on the table, while a second innocent stuck his thumb in his mouth and began to suck noisily. No one observed a defiant adolescent leave the apartment, the entry door, for once closed with care.

Luciano broke the silence, his empty glass striking the table with such force, Rob and Alf almost jumped out of their seats. 'You have English pudding oggi?' he asked, his expression showing no sign of recent animosity.

'Not today, I'm afraid,' Rob answered.

'Triste, triste,' Luciano murmured. 'I am loving Inglese pudding.' Leaning back in his chair, he patted his stomach. 'Spotted dick magnifico!'

'What is spotted, zio Alfredo?' Maria asked, returning from the kitchen with her flowers arranged in a small vase.

'It means the dried fruit in the pudding.'

Maria looked puzzled.

'Sultana, er frutta dried in the sun.'

Maria nodded. 'Sì, sultanine.' She walked over to the dresser and placed the vase next to her sister's wedding photograph. 'What is dick?' she asked, turning to Rob.

Alf winked across the table at his host before

pointing to his trousers. Roaring with laughter, Luciano failed to see his elder daughter standing in the kitchen doorway, arms folded tight against her chest, her expression grim. 'Maria, vieni qui,' Susanna called in a tone reminiscent of their late mother, known for her sharp tongue.

Maria obeyed at once, rushing from living room to kitchen in record time.

———

In a narrow street, some distance from the Zappetti's apartment, the two airmen picked their way through piles of rubble, convinced they must have taken a wrong turn. Half the buildings had collapsed, while the remainder appeared to be boarded up shops with the apartments above also showing signs of bomb damage. 'I think we must be closer to the waterfront than usual,' Rob remarked, wishing they had left earlier when twilight would have guided their footsteps.

'Reckon you're right, mate. Look over there.' Alf indicated a group of American marines loitering further up the street. From their extravagant gestures and discordant voices, the men appeared to be looking for something or someone.

'Up to no good,' Alf muttered, slowing his

pace. 'Best we make ourselves scarce, don't fancy a fight with that lot.'

'Me neither.'

British airmen retreated rapidly but were forced to take cover in a dark doorway when they heard masonry fragments crunch beneath heavy boots.

'So, where the hell are these damn girls?' they heard a marine ask, his drawling voice reverberating from building to building. 'If you've led us on a wild goose chase, I'm gonna tan your skinny Neapolitan arse.'

British airmen peered from their hideout, saw only well-built Americans.

Then, a familiar voice rang out. 'Girls up there in appartamento,' Luigi called, pointing to a light above a battered door opposite, where the silhouette of a woman with long hair could be clearly seen, even by airmen sheltering in shadows. 'Girls bella, bella. Give americani molti good time.'

Rob stared at Luigi, standing in front of the group, one ill-shod foot tapping a piece of fallen masonry as though about to kick it towards substantial American boots. What was the boy playing at? Outnumbered, he could easily become a target should the marines turn nasty. Rob risked a step forward. White uniforms and glowing cigarettes provided a modicum of light, enabling him to observe the subsequent transaction between scrawny boy and massive marine. Thick fingers parted, revealing a roll of notes; the marine peeled off a few and handed them to Luigi. 'Nice doing business with you, kid.'

'Grazie, signore.' Luigi ran off down the street.

'Time to leave,' Alf whispered.

'Let's wait till they're inside,' Rob replied, curious as to the outcome.

'Ok.'

They watched the marine approach the door, heard a sturdy fist whack flimsy wood. The other five stood at a respectful distance.

The door remained closed, but the silhouette disappeared from the window. Impatient, the marine raised his fist and gave a series of loud raps. The sound of a large bolt being drawn back drifted across the street. The door creaked open, disclosing an old woman holding a broom. Long hair streamed over thin shoulders like silver moonbeams.

The marine touched his hat. 'Good evening, signora. Girls here I believe.' Reaching into his pockets, he pulled out the roll of greenbacks.

A series of what Rob presumed from the pitch were Neapolitan curses, erupted from the doorway as the broom struck a broad chest, sending five marines racing down the street. Their self-appointed leader – when he'd recovered from the indignity of repeated assaults – turned on his heel and ran after his mates.

In the doorway of an abandoned shop, British airmen clutched one another to smother unmitigated mirth.

―――

A subsequent encounter with American marines proved far from amusing and could have led to serious repercussions had Rob not intervened. Two hours of unexpected free time had seen Rob and Alf set off for the waterfront market, where it was rumoured a greater variety of goods was now available.

The stall keepers were doing a brisk trade, customers crowding around, pushing and shoving their way to the front. Rob headed straight for the stall where American chocolate and sweets, some still packed in wooden crates labelled 'US Army Field ration, C 8 rations' were openly displayed despite the presence of several military policemen. Naples was proving a challenge for the U.S. Army, the continual theft of supplies creating huge problems for those tasked with feeding thousands of troops. Adolescent boys known as 'scugnizzi' were the major source of trouble, climbing into the backs of slow-moving supply trucks as they wended their way through rubble-littered streets to the American bases beyond the city limits. After slitting boxes with pocket knives or prising open wooden crates, the boys would wait a few moments for their friends to appear, then toss goods into outstretched hands before climbing down and disappearing down narrow side streets. The boys' ability to move quickly and quietly, meant their crimes often went undetected until the driver arrived at his destination and discovered his truck half-empty.

When Rob pulled out a ten-shilling note -- the Cairo greenbacks were long gone -- the elderly stall keeper hesitated, but soon acceded with a toothless grin, Rob's basic Italian, including mention of a beautiful girlfriend who loved sweet things, smoothing the way. Fudge, caramels and Hershey chocolate bars safely secured, Rob made his way to the stall selling American cigarettes where he'd left his mate.

He was waiting for Alf to finish his purchase, when he caught sight of Luigi and two other boys swaggering along the promenade, their feet kicking out at small shards of stonework, all that remained of bomb damage in this locale, popular with Neapolitans and servicemen alike. A wave and a shouted 'buon giorno' failed to attract the boy's attention, instead, Luigi and his friends veered closer to the stalls, pausing now and then to peer through the slight gaps between customers. A few yards away from Rob, the three stopped altogether, but he made no move to approach them, more interested now in discovering what they were up to, than engaging in a brief and most likely unwelcome conversation. Heads bowed, the boys stood in a huddle for a few minutes, then Luigi left the others and walked over to the neighbouring stall, where an elderly woman was the only customer. She appeared to be chatting with the stall keeper but moved away when Luigi made his presence known.

Edging towards the stall, Rob observed Luigi gesture towards a small packet and several tins, all that remained to be sold. What seemed to be bartering followed, a combination of excessive gesticulation and Neapolitan dialect that ended when Luigi pulled two notes from his shirt pocket and held them out. The stall keeper leant across his table, but before he could take the money, a military policeman appeared from nowhere. 'Right, kid, where did you get those dollars?'

'A friend he is giving for buy food,' Luigi answered confidently. 'Per mia familia.'

'A likely story.' The MP seized Luigi's outstretched arm and dragged him away from the stall.

'Is there a problem here, sir?' Rob asked as the pair passed him.

'And who the hell are you?'

'Sergeant Harper, RAF, sir. I'm a friend of this young man.'

The MP snorted and looked from man to boy. 'Friend eh?'

Both Rob and Luigi nodded.

'Gave him the dollars, did you?'

'Yes, sir, to buy food for his family.'

'So where did *you* get American dollars?'

'A gambling joint in Cairo.' Rob smiled, grateful for a plausible half-truth.

'All yours then, buddy.' The MP's lips curled in a sneer as he released Luigi and pushed him towards Rob. 'There's no accounting for taste,' he added before marching away.

Rob waited until the MP was out of earshot before asking, 'Right, Luigi, what do you want to buy?'

'Budino americano.'

'For your papà?'

'Sì. Uno jam, uno syrup. It is saying on tin.'

Rob hesitated, recalling Susanna's agitation at the mention of American rations. What did Luigi hope to achieve by playing off one family member against another? As the patriarch, Luciano might have the last word, but Susanna would be the one to heat up the pudding. Rob could envisage her tossing the tin out of the kitchen window. 'I will buy the budino,' he said, fixing Luigi with a cold stare. 'Uno regalo from me, you tell your papà. Comprendi?'

'Sì, amico mio, e grazie'

'Non problemo,' Rob held out his hand to receive the dollar bills.

TWELVE

A week later, the theft and/or purchase of U.S. Army and Navy supplies paled into insignificance, the vagaries of a legendary volcano determining the immediate course of nefarious activity for both Neapolitans and two British airmen stationed at Portici. On the seventeenth of March, Mount Vesuvius began to erupt, eyewitnesses, including British and American troops stationed nearby, reporting molten lava spewing from the caldera. Vineyards on the mountain slopes were quickly destroyed by the lava stream, which continued to flow onto the plain for many days. Villages on the western side were evacuated, the U.S. military, in the absence of Italian officials, taking control of public safety.

Only one village, San Sebastiano, was annihilated, but on the eastern side, U.S. Army Air Force 340th Bombardment Group lost eighty-eight aircraft, having left it too late to relocate them.

Eight miles away on the outskirts of Naples, Alf cursed the volcano and the station commander as he stood beside Rob's bunk waiting for him to finish packing his kit. Group Captain Clarkson had decided to relocate the depot to the airfield near Gragnano, a hill town cited between the mountains and the Amalfi Coast. 'It was only a few inches of bloody ash here,' Alf remarked. 'It's not as though the villa was destroyed or anything. Trust Clarkson to turn tail at the first inconvenience. I hear the officers are going to be billeted in some posh villa once again. I suppose we'll be stuck in bloody cowsheds or something.'

'More than likely. Plus, it's at least twenty miles from the city, so God knows how I'm going to get to see Susanna. And just when things were starting to warm up.'

Alf punched Rob lightly on the arm. 'It took you long enough.'

'We don't all work at your speed.'

'Well, nothing's going to stop me seeing my girl. I'll hitch a lift when the supply lorry's going to the port. Rosie's worth any amount of loading and unloading.'

'Think of everything don't you?'

Alf grinned.

'At least we're staying around Naples. We could've been sent north to help those poor buggers trapped at Anzio. Over two months since they landed, who'd have thought it would take so long to break out of a beachhead? They should have been in Rome by now. It's only forty miles away.'

'It looks like Jerry's determined to hang on to Rome. He's chucking everything at Anzio. Heavy casualties on both sides from all accounts.'

'Bastards! They must know we're going to win this bloody war,' Rob shouted, his atypical outburst reverberating through the barracks. Several airmen looked in his direction, their heads nodding in agreement. Others ignored him and carried on packing.

'Easy, mate,' Alf murmured, reaching out to touch Rob's shoulder.

His eruption over as fast as it had begun, Rob muttered, 'Why don't they just give up and go home?'

Alf lifted his arm and slung his kitbag over one shoulder. 'Would you?' he asked, and without waiting for an answer, headed for the door.

Still focused on enemy tactics, it took Rob a few moments to register his mate's departure. Earlier that morning, when Clarkson had ordered all personnel to assemble on the makeshift parade ground, a tiled courtyard to one side of the villa, Rob had expected news of an Allied victory not relocation. After three and a half years, he'd had enough of war and its associated itinerant life. Draughty tents, barracks that smelt of sweat and oil, tasteless rations eaten in a cramped and noisy mess, all were anathema to him now. He wanted a room of his own, preferably in a quiet neighbourhood, somewhere he could spend winter evenings reading or doing crosswords. In summer, he would take a bus to the woods on the edge of town, or to the river meandering through meadows, sandwiches and a flask of tea in a backpack, a book in his pocket. Glancing down at his kitbag, he thought of the dictionary purchased in a Cairo bookshop much to Alf's amusement, buried now beneath worn underwear. It had proven useful when reading the copies of Shakespeare's sonnets, he'd also bought and doing crosswords during those uneventful days and nights in the Egyptian desert before the pace of war intensified and all he could think of was surviving the next dogfight.

Pensive, his thoughts turned to the immediate future: a different camp, a different environment far from the city. Whatever the news from Anzio, the move promised to be short-term, it was inevitable Rome would fall soon and he and his fellow Aircraft Hands be relocated to northern Italy. What then for his new-found friends eking out a living in a shattered city? Would Luigi continue to con American marines? Would Susanna attract another British airman? The previous evening, just before they kissed goodnight, she had given him a photograph taken a few years earlier he imagined, its corners bearing evidence of extensive handling. A sudden desire to gaze at her beautiful face, saw him reach into his shirt pocket to retrieve the gift. Her smiling countenance bore no trace of grief, hunger or despair; this was a photograph taken for another man, the Italian soldier standing proudly beside his wife in the wedding portrait displayed on the dresser in the apartment living room.

Unexpected silence returned his attention to the present moment and he realised that everyone else had vacated the barracks. With a sigh that was half regret for the second-hand gift and half thankfulness for the time he had spent with Susanna, he pocketed the photograph and picked up his kitbag.

———

In a cleared space behind the rear gate, depot staff stood waiting in a neat line for the order to board the lorry and jeeps parked one behind the other in the road outside. Rob soon located Alf, and ignoring hostile looks from those at the end of the line, walked halfway down and stepped in front of his mate.

'You took your time,' Alf remarked.

'Nearly forgot my dictionary,' Rob lied.

Alf raised his eyes to the morning sky, still hazy with remnants of volcanic ash. 'That bloody thing. Hardly worth worrying about.'

Disregarding the comments, Rob stood at ease, the kitbag at his feet.

Minutes passed, a knot of officers appeared but no order was given.

'Want to hear the latest bad news about the new base?' Alf asked, leaning forward.

Rob gave a slight nod.

'I overheard Clarkson talking to Whitmore just now,' Alf said quietly, his chin almost touching Rob's right shoulder. 'We're not going to be stationed close to the airfield.'

'So,' Rob countered, turning his head slightly.

'Whitmore said the farm was a good location, as it's too far from the town to attract any local lads intent on pilfering.'

'More for others then.'

'No mate. He went on to say the Officers' Mess store is going to be located in the farmhouse cellar. Thick stone walls and only one entrance, a massive wooden door with a heavy padlock.'

'I don't like our chances.'

'Neither do I.'

'We'll have to try nicking supplies from our own store.' Rob hesitated before adding, 'That's if you want to continue?'

'Why not, I'm sure I can make another useful tool.'

'Let's hope our own store is less fortified.'

One of the officers barked out an order, preventing further conversation. The line began to shuffle towards open gates.

―

A wooden barn situated in an overgrown field had been chosen as barracks for the new arrivals. Although the smell of hay and its former bovine inhabitants still permeated the building, it proved warm and dry during the spring of forty-four. A short distance away up a slight incline, a large farmhouse provided more salubrious quarters, the Portici officers joining those already in situ. The first floor comprised the Officers' Mess, kitchen and a couple of offices, the second, spacious bedrooms with marble floors. As anticipated, the Officer's Mess Store occupied the centuries-old stone cellar.

By contrast, the Other Ranks' Mess store was a newish structure located adjacent to the barn barracks. More of a shed than anything else, it had a single door, flimsy but padlocked unless catering staff were fetching supplies, and no windows. Inside, shelves that looked as though they'd been thrown up in minutes lined three walls, while beside the door stood an empty barrel.

Unimpressed, and surprised by the disorder – rations appeared to be housed at random -- Rob grabbed a few small tins from a bottom shelf, shoved them in his pockets and backed out of the store, making sure to avoid knocking into the barrel. Alf was leaning against a nearby tree, smoking a cigarette and gave no indication he had seen his mate. After checking no one else was in sight, Rob closed the padlock and sauntered over to the tree.

'I don't suppose there was anything decent?' Alf remarked.

Rob shook his head. 'Little Roberto won't like it one bit,' he said, already picturing the scene at the Zappetti dining table, the child's grimaces as he endeavoured to swallow unpalatable rations.

'Waste of time then.' Alf stubbed out the cigarette, leaving a black smudge on the tree's pale trunk. 'I've had second thoughts about pilfering. It's not worth risking a court martial for a few tins of bully beef and hard tack. You should stick to the markets, mate.'

'Where will I find a market out here?'

'Bound to be one in Gragnano. Might even be some of those Hershey chocolate bars on sale.' Alf licked his lips. 'Good tucker, as the Australians say.'

'Not a patch on Cadbury's,' Rob replied.

THIRTEEN

The tourist coach slows as it approaches the outskirts of Naples, heavy traffic impeding its progress to the night's accommodation. Shops line either side of the road, mostly family-owned businesses selling a range of foodstuffs, both fresh and factory produced. Slivers of late afternoon sunlight protrude from the narrow gaps between shop awnings, giving the pavement a striped appearance. Curious British tourists peer from coach windows, eager to digest their first sight of ordinary Neapolitan life, some remarking on the unusual produce piled on the pavement beside open doors, vegetables and fruit rarely seen at home. Others note two middle-aged women engaged in conversation, loud voices and extravagant gestures implying disagreement, while those in the front seats watch a group of small children sucking ice lollies, as their basket-toting mothers barter with shopkeepers. One small boy begins to jump on and off the kerb like a Jack in the box, a sight that brings smiles to weary travellers' faces until he drops his icy treat and steps into the road to retrieve it, prompting the coach driver to brake hard.

Halfway down the coach, slouching in an aisle seat, Rob Harper blinks rapidly and stares at the seat in front, confused by the swirl of chatter around him. Jolted from a dream of half-chewed bully beef and hard tack spewing from a small boy's mouth, he feels unsure of his location, or where he has been during the long summer afternoon.

'Biscuit, love?' the woman beside him asks, holding out an open packet.

'Bloody tasteless tack,' he answers without turning his head. 'I wouldn't feed them to a dog.'

'But they're your favourites, lemon cream.'

She sounds offended, so he reaches out to take several biscuits. 'Sorry, love,' he says, remembering the holiday begun days earlier in Rome as well as their twenty-seven-year relationship. 'I was dreaming.'

'About biscuits?'

'No, Naples.'

Ivy squeezes his arm. 'It's going to be wonderful. According to the brochure there's plenty to see. The Royal palace, a thirteenth-century castle and an ornate eighteenth-century opera house among other things. Dawn says the cathedral is well worth a visit, it's full of frescoes. She also recommended a visit to the Isle of Capri. I wonder if we'll get the chance to go there while we're in Sorrento?'

His mouth full of lemon cream biscuit, Rob can only nod, a response that must satisfy, because Ivy immediately releases his wrist and turns back to the window. He chews slowly, oblivious to tangy cream sandwiched between crisp latticed biscuit, his thoughts swirling through the light and shade of post-war decades as the coach resumes its languorous journey.

Victory in Europe, newsreels showing Londoners dancing in the streets, girls embracing strangers in uniform; his own return to England and discharge from the RAF, late June forty-five, cause of discharge: *Ceasing to fulfil Royal Air Force physical requirements although fit for employment in civil life.* Not that Rob had any desire to remain in the RAF; after nearly four years' war service, he'd had more than enough of a regimented life spent in the company of men. At thirty-two, he wanted to settle down, make a decent peacetime life with a woman he loved, have a couple of children.

I'm getting ahead of myself, he muses, turning back memory pages to job interviews and eventual employment in the Goods Office at the central railway station, where he'd met Ivy. The Air Ministry had been right; at that time, he *was* fit for employment in civil life, debilitating mental illness yet to surface. The clerical position didn't pay well, but the men and women in the office were friendly, the work undemanding. Three of the women were already close friends when he arrived, and remained so throughout the decades since, despite in Edna's case the distance between them. Licking his dry lips, Rob recalls numerous afternoon teas whenever the friends met, Ivy's homemade butterfly cakes, cream horns and chocolate cream biscuits.

Memories of sweet delights – he hadn't eaten much at the lunch stop – remind him of a holiday in Dublin during the summer of forty-seven. Separate rooms as befitted an unmarried couple, but how he and Ivy had relished the scones and jam served with lashings of fresh cream, a luxury unavailable in still-rationed England, the generous servings of crisp bacon and eggs dished up daily at their modest hotel. The following year, a summer wedding, his aunt and uncle beaming their delight, his cousin Colin pleased to be best man. Honeymoon in a smart north Devon hotel, post-war worries cast aside as they lay in one another's arms.

Eighteen months later, a welcome pregnancy convinced him peacetime life held great promise, but a threatened miscarriage at five months saw Ivy confined to a hospital bed for weeks. Then, on Easter Sunday morning, as bells pealed the Christian message of resurrection, a baby girl arrived eight weeks prematurely, her tiny body placed in an incubator moments after birth; no time to weigh or wipe her clean. He shudders, remembering Ivy's distress on seeing the baby's malformed right hand, the first three doll-sized fingers fused, one so underdeveloped it even lacked a nail. Only the doctor's reassurance that the webbed fingers could be separated when the child was older and his comment, 'Don't worry, Mrs Harper, the wedding ring goes on the left hand,' brought a brief smile to Ivy's tear-streaked face.

Visiting the hospital later that day, Rob peered at his daughter through thick plate glass – only medical staff were permitted in the room reserved for premature babies – wondering how on earth such a tiny baby could survive. Her skin, a sickly yellow by then, jaundice, a passing nurse explained, which added to his concerns. Baby Frances remained in the incubator for five weeks. Day after day he trailed up and down the steep hill from their flat to the hospital, sometimes carrying a tiny bottle of breast milk if Ivy felt too tired to make the twice-a-day journey. A difficult beginning.

Three years later, another daughter, a few weeks early but no problems, brown-haired Frances delighted with her blond baby sister. He remembered the day Ivy brought Sally home, Frances sitting in the child-sized armchair made by her grandfather, her arms outstretched to receive the baby.

All of a sudden, thick clouds shadow sun-bright memory.

Soon after Sally's birth, the severe depression that had resulted in a two-week stay in hospital back in forty-nine, reared its ugly head again. He spent five weeks as an in-patient, followed by fortnightly out-patient visits for the next two years.

Unwilling to dwell on troubled times – throughout the fifties and sixties, there were numerous stays in psychiatric hospitals – Rob dismisses reminiscence and twists around to speak to Alf. 'Let's hope the traffic improves soon. I'd love a cup of tea. How about you?'

Alf looks up but merely nods, a worried expression tightening his thin lips, the eyes behind his glasses half-closed.

'What's up, you look a bit pale? Are you feeling sick?'

'Nothing wrong with my stomach, mate. Too many wartime memories that's the trouble. They're doing my head in.'

'I know what you mean,' Rob replies in a low voice. 'I can't stop thinking about the Zappetti family. If only I'd had the opportunity to stock them up with rations before I was posted home. I hope to God they survived.'

Alf hesitates before responding, a glance at

his wife Dawn essential to ensure she remains asleep. 'Rosie didn't survive. A stray bomb hit the field hospital she was working in somewhere north of Naples. July forty-four if I remember correctly. A fellow nurse sent me what turned out to be Rosie's last letter along with a note saying she'd been badly injured. I was stationed at Pescara by then, so there was no possibility of visiting her in hospital.'

Rob blanches. 'Oh God, I didn't know. I thought you'd fallen out with her. Why on earth didn't you write and tell me?'

'What was the point? By the time I found out for certain that she'd died, the war had ended and all I wanted to do was forget.'

'You never forget,' Rob murmurs.

Alf leans forward. 'Before we left home, I tracked down the war cemetery where she's buried.'

'How did you manage that?'

'I wrote to the Queen Alexandra's Imperial Military Nursing Service, explained I would be spending time in Italy and wanted to visit her grave.'

'Why, after all this time?'

Alf gives a wry smile. 'Simple really. A few months ago, I watched a television programme about nurses during wartime. It got me thinking about Rosie.'

'Understandable. Is the cemetery far from Naples?'

Alf shook his head.

'Are you really going to visit?'

Alf looks sideways at his wife. 'If I get the opportunity.'

'You'll think of something, you always were inventive.'

The coach lurches forward, forcing Rob to grab the back of his seat to prevent a fall into the aisle. 'Talk later, mate.'

———

Rosie McGill dead only weeks after her departure from Naples; a genial Glaswegian voice silenced forever. Rob recalls their last meeting in the street near the hospital entrance, a fleeting conversation as he waited for Susanna to finish work. News of Alf exchanged in minutes, Rosie's face shining, his own damp with perspiration from the midday heat. A brief touch of hands as they parted, a promise to keep in touch. Thirty years on, the news of her death is still a shock, Rob once convinced his mate would marry the lively, fun-loving nurse after the war. He had been baffled by Alf's post-war choice, Dawn a nervy woman prone to headaches and stomach upsets. She also chain-smoked, a habit that Rob, having given up the pipe, had found difficult to deal with during the Simpsons' summer visits, especially when the children were young. Elder daughter, Frances suffered from bronchial asthma, but despite pointed suggestions from both Rob and Ivy, Dawn couldn't be persuaded to smoke in the garden. Given the pair lived in a Yorkshire mining town, Rob thought they would enjoy spending time on the beach or exploring the town, but they spent most of the day inside, reading, drinking innumerable cups of tea and filling ashtrays, Alf also a heavy smoker. Sometimes they ventured to the local shops to buy a newspaper, returning within the hour grumbling about how long it had taken to cross the road or how the café on the corner was full of tourists. What do you expect, Rob wanted to say, this is a seaside town?

Despite these shortcomings, Rob had to admit his friends were good with the girls, displaying no sign of irritation when pestered to play a board game or read a story. Although they had no children of their own, Alf and Dawn had always taken an interest in Frances and Sally, even when they were very young, and often took them around the corner to the sweet shop while Ivy cooked dinner. Generous presents every time they visited delighted the girls: board games, dolls, a folding easel with an extensive set of paints. Rob smiles at the memory of garish paintings adorning the walls of the cubby-house he'd built among fruit trees at the end of the garden: stick figures representing the family; an uncle's sailing boat bobbing on blue waves, golden sun shining in one corner. The only painting he found difficult to praise depicted the spinster neighbour's troublesome cats, spoilt overweight pets that insisted on doing their business in his vegetable patch.

'Cats,' he says under his breath, reminded of another painting, decades old. Buried beneath holiday clothing, the six by five-inch watercolour and ink portrait, lies in a tatty envelope at the bottom of his suitcase. At the last minute – the taxi already pulled up outside the house – he'd rushed into the shed to retrieve the painting, convinced he ought to return it to Italy.

Ivy turns her head. 'Did you say something, dear?'

'Nothing important. Just wishing for a cup of tea to go with these biscuits.'

'You're as bad as you know who,' she says, leaning towards him.

'Never,' he counters, as she turns back to the window.

Two cats, one black and white, a green bow tied around its neck, the other white with a yellow bow, sitting on a wooden seat, a tiled floor beneath, its pattern resembling the one in the Zappetti living room. An unexpected gift for a British airman, painted as a token of friendship by an adolescent boy grateful his rescue from a suspicious military policeman hadn't been divulged to his father or older sister. A painting signed and dated by the artist but handed over by his sister, the boy probably too embarrassed, during a summer evening at a favourite wine bar.

Rob and Susanna were sitting at a small table, one of six arranged haphazardly on cracked pavement either side of a doorway, sharing a bottle of wine. She was wearing the sleeveless dress he had purchased at a shop near a city market, polka dot cotton clinging to her shapely breasts and tiny waist. Despite her remark there would be nothing new for sale, he had insisted they enter the shop, and it was true a layer of dust clung to the dress displayed on a battered mannequin near the door. 'Dust from the road,' he'd said when Susanna wrinkled her nose after fingering the fabric. The shopkeeper, a middle-aged woman wearing a faded and clearly pre-war outfit, soon noticed their interest and approached smiling. 'Un bel vestito, signora,' she'd remarked, running her hands over the dress.

'Nuovo?' Rob asked, earlier optimism waning.

'Naturalmente, signore.'

———

After complimenting Susanna on how much the dress suited her, Rob couldn't help asking if she thought the shopkeeper had been telling the truth about its vintage.

'Is true, Robbi,' she replied, placing her empty glass on the table. 'La negoziante say she make vestito for daughter but...' She looked down, smoothed red polka dots over her knees.

'But what?' he persisted, regretting the question as soon as the words were out of his mouth. How many more years of war would it take to dislodge embedded naivety?

'Figlia she is dying from bombe.'

'I'm sorry,' he said and was reaching out to take her hand when Susanna twisted around to retrieve the bag hanging over the back of the chair.

Damn, I've blown it again, he thought, recalling the drive from Sorrento. *She wants to leave now.*

But Susanna made no attempt to stand and appeared instead to be searching for something in her bag. Curiously, he watched her extract first a hairbrush, then a handkerchief, followed by a small brown envelope. 'Luigi give me for you,' she explained, slipping it into his hand.

Rob turned the blank envelope over in his hands, trying to imagine why Luigi would be writing to him. The envelope was unsealed and appeared to contain a single piece of paper.

'Attento,' Susanna advised as he extracted a diminutive painting.

'That's kind of him.' He wondered what had prompted a present that despite its dimensions, must have taken some time to produce given the meticulous detail. Luigi rarely seemed pleased to see him and even after the incident with the military policeman hadn't said more than a muttered 'grazie' before re-joining his friends.

'Is more, Robbi, look on back.' Susanna reached out to pat his arm.

It took a minute or two for Rob to read and digest the inscription, translation still a slow process, but when he raised his head to smile at her, his blue eyes were moist. 'My beautiful family,' he said, his voice wavering.

A beautiful family that had welcomed him throughout what months later, freezing in draughty barracks on a Lincolnshire airbase, Rob would call his 'summer of love,' more than two decades before the term was coined to describe events occurring in hippie San Francisco. The joy of being in love – the real thing this time, he believed – helped deflect the sordid reality of life in a ruined city where locals and Allied servicemen alike disregarded the basic principles of civilised society. Law and order had ceased to exist, murder and rape so commonplace as to be hardly worth reporting, the incidence of venereal disease on the rise and the black market blossoming as though the arrival of summer had engendered an unprecedented growth spurt.

Eight weeks after the move south, Rob returned to Portici, leaving behind not only his mate Alf, but the other men with whom he had shared both city and cow-shed barracks. Unwittingly, he had become indispensable by stepping into the breach when two administrative staff were carted off to hospital following a drunken altercation involving broken bottles. Group Captain Clarkson, impressed by the new Sergeant Clerk's efficiency and pleasant manner, had requested Rob accompany him back to Naples.

Clerical work suited Rob, the click-clack of typewriter keys or the concentration required to accurately file innumerable reports and personnel files, generating a protective layer that suppressed conflicting emotions, at least for the hours he spent in the former sitting room of a Neapolitan villa.

Once outside in the street, making his way to Susanna's home in soft evening light, he tried to focus his thoughts on their imminent meeting, rather than the gaping wounds of bomb-damaged homes or the old women sitting in doorways trying to hawk their pitiful possessions. Sometimes, he was accosted by a younger woman or two, promised a good time in return for a tin of corned beef and had to increase his pace to escape from wandering hands intent on emptying pockets. Not that the women would have found much of interest, food gifts for the Zappetti family restricted by then to what he could purchase in city markets or the occasional tin handed over by the cook in exchange for cigarettes.

There were several reasons for Rob's decision to stop stealing rations, not least an unwillingness to jeopardise his liberty and thus his relationship with Susanna. Despite Allied officials often turning a blind eye to the black market, it was well known that some individuals, mostly Neapolitan, had been charged with dealing in stolen goods and imprisoned. Apart from the odd day's pay forfeited for returning late from leave, Rob possessed an exemplary service record, which would surely help when seeking post-war employment. Alf's absence was also a contributing factor in the cessation of raids, his supreme confidence and gung-ho attitude impossible for Rob to replicate. Meanwhile, the Zappetti family's fortunes had taken a turn for the better with Luciano finding employment. In return for food and a little money, he assisted an elderly baker who had managed to restart his business with a little help from American flour supplies, no doubt.

The return to Naples in the first week of May, marked the arrival of summer, hot days and warm evenings perfect for walks by the harbour or sipping wine at bar tables located on the shady side of the street. Further north, the warmer weather saw new offensives against the Gustav line and by the end of the month Allied troops finally broke out of the beachhead at Anzio. By early June, the Allies had liberated Rome, a victory that sparked raucous celebration among the servicemen stationed in Naples. Even Rob had a sore head on that occasion!

As summer wore on and other Italian towns and cities fell to the Allies, Rob felt confident he could begin to focus on a life beyond war. Most of his planning took place in the barracks just after dawn, when day after day, slivers of sunlight streamed through the window behind his bunk. Eyes wide-open, he would direct his gaze to dust motes hovering in the languid air, while his mind indulged in post-war possibilities. The administrative skills he was acquiring in the depot office should enable him to obtain a clerical position instead of returning to work as a shop assistant, a poorly paid occupation with few opportunities for promotion. Government departments might be the best place to start, or the council offices housed in an impressive Victorian building that had served as a hotel and hospital prior to becoming the town hall.

Despite estrangement from most of his family, Rob intended to return to the southern coastal town, nestled between a ridge of low hills and a wide bay. Developed during the eighteen-thirties and forties as a seaside resort for the well-to-do, a century later the town still attracted the more affluent visitor to its grand hotels perched along the cliff top and possessed many advantages for permanent residents, such as extensive beaches, lovely municipal gardens and a mild climate. The town also lacked the slums still prevalent in the area around the neighbouring port, home to the Harper family for many years. Rob's birthplace, a dilapidated terraced house backing onto a filthy yard, the street number recorded in heavy black ink on a red-edged certificate, marking forever a disadvantaged beginning. In young adulthood, he had visited the street out of curiosity but never returned, too ashamed to acknowledge the link with his past. Years later, asked by his twelve-year-old daughter where he'd been born, he had plucked another, less seedy street name from his memory. By the time Frances learnt the truth, unfolding the birth certificate found among Ivy's papers after *her* death, the port slums were a distant memory and the yard no longer mentioned on maps of the town.

Lying in his narrow bunk in the garden of a Portici villa, Rob felt thankful that Susanna and her family, although suffering from the deprivations of war, did not inhabit the appalling slums clustered around the port. These centuries-old buildings where many families lived in single rooms known as 'bassi' located in cellars or at street level, had been repeatedly bombed by Allied forces prior to the liberation of Naples, making life even more precarious for the inhabitants. He thought of the knots of barefoot children dressed in rags hanging around the markets, thin arms clutching at Allied servicemen in the hope of a handout. At least he had made a difference to one family and would continue to do so for as long as possible. A sergeant's pay couldn't buy luxuries, but the purchase of basic foodstuffs remained within his means and meals at cafes and wine bars, while not particularly nutritious, were ridiculously cheap.

Caught up in traffic, the coach lurches to a halt only a few streets from the hotel where participants in the '14-day Italian Delight tour' will spend the next few nights.

'Not again! At this rate, we'll miss dinner as well as afternoon tea,' Dawn remarks, her complaint so loud it stirs more than one weary traveller from welcome rest.

'It's only five o'clock, dear,' Rob hears Alf say in response.

Warm breath tickles Rob's ear. 'Impatient as usual.'

'I don't know why she's so worried about missing meals,' he whispers back. 'She doesn't eat much at the best of times.'

Ivy nods and settles back in her seat.

FOURTEEN

As expected, the coach party arrive too late for afternoon tea, but Rob and Ivy enjoy the evening meal of soup, local fish and vegetables, followed by a slice of chocolate torta, served in a cavernous dining room located in the centre of the hotel's first floor. A tiled floor, chipped in places, its garish red and gold pattern uneasy on the eye, forces diners' attention upwards to the dusty chandeliers hanging above round tables covered with white tablecloths. Each table has seating for twelve, the heavy wooden chairs painted gold with worn red brocade inserts. Curved windowless walls have been painted with images of local land and seascapes, faded like the frescoes seen in Rome. Among them are a benign Mount Vesuvius, its slopes green with vines, the ancient streets of Pompeii and the Isle of Capri with its steep cliffs descending to a turquoise Mediterranean. Each mural is separated by plaster pillars decorated with trailing vines. The room reminds Rob of nineteen-fifties films, ostentatious décor attempting to depict the lifestyle of the rich and famous. Weathered now like the film stars themselves, and poor recompense for windows revealing genuine panoramas.

Alf is unusually quiet during the meal, his conversation limited to echoing his wife's complaints about the food – fish with too many bones, no parsley or tomato sauce, over-rich dessert. Glancing at the drawn face opposite, Rob imagines Alf is still pondering how to grab a few hours alone the following day. Despite his explanation, the decision to visit Rosie McGill's grave seems incongruous to Rob, given Alf's unwillingness to dig up the past, expressed only twenty-four hours earlier.

The scrape of chair legs on tiles alerts Rob to an imminent departure. 'Not staying for coffee?'

Alf shakes his head.

'Says he needs his beauty sleep,' Dawn replies with a hint of sarcasm.

Ivy looks up. 'Why don't you stay here with

us, Dawn? There's no need for you to miss out on coffee.'

'Thanks, but I'd better not.' She leans towards Ivy. 'He had a nightmare last night, woke me at two shouting about stray bombs. I can't think why, it hasn't happened for years.'

Ivy nods her understanding. 'See you at breakfast then.'

Dawn gives a quick smile and hurries after Alf, her stiletto heels clicking on the tiled floor.

———

The Harpers don't linger over coffee, so are soon back in their room – more gaudy tiles, wooden furniture past its prime – and preparing for bed. Already changed into her nightdress, Ivy returns from the bathroom to find Rob still fully clothed, kneeling in front of his suitcase. 'I put your pyjamas on the bed,' she says, as he lifts a pile of shirts and begins to rummage in the bottom of the case.

'Thanks,' he murmurs without looking up.

Puzzled, Ivy perches on the edge of the bed, watches his continuing search with interest.

'Ah, here it is.' Rob holds up an envelope spattered with brown marks and torn in places. Neatly folded shirts fall to the floor as he gets to his feet. He joins her on the bed. 'I don't suppose you remember my talking about the Zappetti children?'

'Zappetti?'

'The family I befriended when I was stationed here.'

She smiles. 'Sorry, I'd forgotten their name.' She peers at the envelope and frowns. 'What's Gabriel Choueri, Pyramid's official photographer got to do with Italian children?'

'Nothing. Originally the envelope held photographs I had developed while on leave in Cairo. Remember that one of me and some of my squadron sitting on camels in front of the Giza pyramid?

'Yes, it's in our old black photo album along with others of you taken in Cairo.'

He nods. 'Well, ever since you put those photos in an album, I've used the envelope to keep this safe.' Carefully he removes his thirty-year-old gift and, reluctant to hand it over, holds it towards her. 'Fifteen-year-old Luigi Zappetti painted this for me.'

Ivy studies the well-defined images of a domestic animal Rob has always detested. 'What a sweet gesture.

'He wrote on the back as well.' Turning the painting over, Rob points to Luigi's greeting. 'What does it mean?'

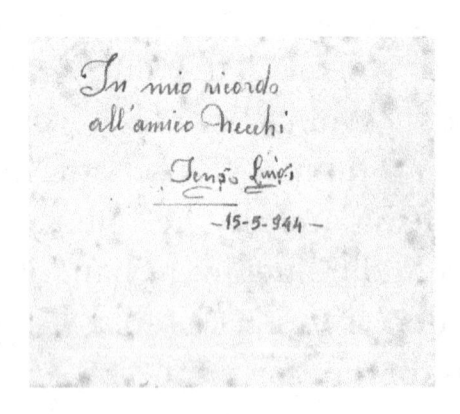

'My memento to our friend.' He feels the warmth of her bare arm around his shoulders, the press of lips against his cheek.

'May forty-four,' she murmurs, her breath

soft as silk on his face. 'Wasn't that about the time Rome fell?'

'It was June the fifth,' he corrects automatically.

'That's right, I remember seeing a Pathé News bulletin of Allied troops entering Rome. Crowds lining the streets, cheering.' She sighs. 'What a blessing the city wasn't destroyed during the war.'

Unlike Naples, he thinks, but instead says, 'Yes, all those antiquities we saw would have been reduced to rubble.'

'Did the Zappettis have any other children?' Ivy asks, *her* thoughts focused on family matters.

'Luigi had a younger sister and an older married sister who lived in the apartment with them.' He looks down at Luigi's words to hide the blush creeping over his cheeks. 'She had a two-year-old son.'

'Must have been a bit of a squash, seven people in an apartment.'

'Seven?'

'Mother, father, three children, a son-in-law and a grandchild.'

'The son-in-law was away fighting in the north,' he lies, struggling to keep his voice even. 'And sadly, the mother had died the previous year.'

'A bomb?'

'No, pneumonia, complicated by lack of food.'

'How tragic.' Ivy fiddles with a lock of her curly hair. 'Didn't they have penicillin in Italy then?'

'Allied troops did. Not sure about civilians, probably too expensive.' He pulls up his right trouser leg and points to the scar below the knee. 'Good thing that American military hospital had penicillin, or I might have lost my leg.' Keen to terminate a conversation which is proving more difficult by the moment, he rolls down his trouser leg and unbuckles his belt. 'Time to get some sleep, love. We've got a busy day tomorrow.'

'Do you still want to try and find the family?'

'Of course. As I said before, I don't have a choice.'

'I just hope you won't be too upset if it proves a futile exercise.'

He looks up and smiles. 'I just want to know if they survived. If I can't locate the apartment block quickly, we'll visit the town hall and ask someone there. It's in the historic centre, so there's plenty to see.'

'I wish my memory was as good as yours,' she remarks wistfully. 'Anyone would think you were here last week not thirty years ago.'

'Teatro di San Carlo, Sansvero Chapel, Santa Chiara, to name but a few landmarks,' he says to prove her point.

'Show off,' she retorts, poking him in the ribs.

When the Harpers arrive in the dining room the following morning, Dawn is sitting alone at the table.

'I wonder where Alf is?' Ivy asks.

'Slept late most likely, he looked tired last night.'

'I just hope he isn't coming down with a cold or the flu, it would really spoil his holiday.'

'Spoil ours too, if we caught it,' Rob mutters as they approach the table. 'Morning, Dawn, what's up with Alf?'

'Stomach upset,' she answers without a hint of empathy. 'He's worried about being caught short, so has decided to spend the morning in bed.'

'Oh, what a shame, he'll miss the museum,' Ivy commiserates, pulling out the chair on Dawn's right and sitting down.

'And he was so looking forward to it,' Rob adds to support his friend. Glancing at the Mount Vesuvius mural opposite their table, he reflects that Dawn couldn't have chosen a more appropriate seat, given the eruption that will occur if she discovers her husband has lied about his illness in order to visit the grave of a wartime girlfriend.

'I told him he probably just needed something to eat.' Dawn sighs. 'Stomach cramps don't necessarily mean you're going to vomit or,' she hesitates and glances around. 'Or the other end. We ate the same food last night and I'm fine. Have you two had any problems?'

Both Rob and Ivy shake their heads.

'Orange juice, love?' Rob asks, anxious to distance himself from further comments about Alf's pseudo-illness. He gestures towards the jugs lined up on a long narrow table positioned between two pillars.

'Yes, thanks.'

Rob scurries away, pleased Alf has engineered a plausible reason to spend several hours by himself. Dawn will soon find others from the tour to tag along with at the National Archaeological Museum, their guide, Patrizia highly recommended a visit. A smile dusts his lips as he envisages Alf watching for Dawn's departure from their bedroom window, his bony frame concealed by heavy curtains. Slight stature and agility had been such a boon when climbing in and out of a small window, whereas he'd had great difficulty manoeuvring himself over the windowsill, short stocky legs and long body a distinct disadvantage. Still smiling, Rob pours juice into glasses, but as he walks towards the table a sombre image supplants the cheerful: sixty-two-year old Alf bending arthritic knees to kneel in front of a white cross, place fresh flowers on well-tended grass.

'It's too bad you have to go with Rob on that wild goose chase,' he hears Dawn remark to Ivy as he nears the table. 'You would have enjoyed the museum.'

Affronted by the implication that Ivy will be wasting precious sight-seeing hours, Rob almost retorts that people are more important than Roman antiquities, but his reluctance to provoke an argument keeps him silent.

'I didn't have to go, I offered,' Ivy answers curtly. 'Rob had already asked Alf, but he declined.'

'Very wise of him. I'm sorry to say it, Ivy, but I think Rob's a fool to rake up the past.'

Behind her, Rob suppresses the urge to tip orange juice over coiffured curls.

'Well I don't.' Ivy unfolds her napkin and spreads it across her knees. 'Who knows, it might even help put all that war trauma behind him.'

'Rob's not having nightmares too, is he?'

Ivy shakes her head.

'Juice, my love,' Rob announces, stepping sideways to deposit the glass.

'Thanks. Just what I need.'

Dawn shunts her empty plate into the centre of the table. 'I'll be off then.' She pushes back her chair and gets to her feet.

'Enjoy the museum,' Ivy calls after her.

———

Breakfast over, Rob seeks advice on public transport from the reception desk, while Ivy returns to their room to collect hats and sunglasses. The receptionist speaks excellent English and soon provides Rob with a map of the inner suburbs marked with tram stops, pointing out a stop only a few steps from the hotel. Their journey will entail taking a tram into the city centre, then changing to one heading for Portici. 'It is an interesting area,' the receptionist explains. 'In Portici you will see Santo Ciro Church built in 1633, the beautiful Town Park and Royal Wood. There are people selling fresh fruit and vegetables from stalls in the streets, also many small shops that sell everything a tourist could want. Good for your wife, I think.'

Rob smiles before folding his map. It seems pointless to explain to a girl who looks no more than eighteen, that he has no interest in local churches, parks or shopping. He doubts she would understand his quest to reconnect with a family not seen for thirty years. 'Grazie, Maria,' he says instead, reading the name badge clipped to her smart jacket. 'Your help is much appreciated.'

'Prego, signore.'

As he steps away from the counter, he catches sight of Ivy entering the foyer, waves and hurries towards her.

'I've got a map and details of the tram route,' he informs, but Ivy appears more interested in ensuring he puts on the panama hat she bought for him in Rome. 'The sun's hot here and you are getting a bit thin on top,' she explained when he objected to the cost. 'Besides, you'll need it for our next trip to Australia.'

The six weeks visit to their daughter and her husband in Brisbane the previous year, had been a wonderful holiday, but one that seems unlikely to be repeated for years, given Rob's current lack of employment, not that he said as much to Ivy in Rome. She has hopes of visiting every few years, especially now Frances is pregnant. The baby is due in November and although Ivy has no plans to visit then – Sally will be there in her stead – already she has mentioned September seventy-five as a tentative date for a second Australian holiday. 'The baby will be ten months old then and much more fun,' she explained when Rob asked why September. 'Plus, the weather will be cooler, it's spring over there then, remember?'

Converse seasons and an imminent arrival remain far from Rob's thoughts as he helps Ivy step down from the tram on the northern edge of Portici. He has decided to begin the search in the upper streets, figuring it will be easier to walk downhill. If he's honest, the name of the road where the Zappetti family lived and hopefully still lives, eludes him at present. All he can remember is the apartment number and that Via is followed by a personal name. Considering he can recall whole chunks of the Macbeth and Hamlet learnt at school, this sudden amnesia is a concern. Has his mind deliberately engineered the lapse, a protective mechanism to prevent a subsequent depressive episode once the joy of reunion has evaporated? It has been some years since his last stay in a psychiatric hospital;

modern medication keeps the 'black dog' more or less under control these days.

Yet despite memory loss and an unlikely, or at least unproven hypothesis, Rob feels duty bound to discover what has happened to the Zappetti family in the decades since the end of the war. On his return to England in January forty-five, he contemplated writing to Susanna on many occasions, but intention didn't lead to action. Something stayed his hand; perhaps it was the struggle to adapt to civilian life or the guilt he felt as a survivor, or the difficulty accepting he was considered one of the lucky ones. In those days, 'lucky' meant surviving the war with only a slight health problem, in his case, the ulcers that erupted frequently in his mouth and on the back of his neck. The Ministry of Pensions rejected his claim that the onset of severe depression was also the result of war service.

Once he became part of a convivial office environment, Rob decided nothing would be gained by trying to rekindle a fleeting wartime relationship. Despite his musing when alone in the Portici barracks, the subject of love or a future together hadn't been raised during their intermittent dates, the present all they had in those desperate days. Mid-forties newspapers and magazines often reported stories of 'GI brides' setting sail for a new life across the Atlantic, but Rob could not envisage transplanting Susanna. Two years after war's end, he was still living with his aunt and uncle, rental accommodation scarce in the town and what there was he couldn't afford. He had little to offer a woman and child surrounded by a loving family and friends. Besides, Susanna could have remarried; it was doubtful a beautiful young widow would remain single for long.

So, unlike other aspects of his war, Rob consigned his nine-month Neapolitan interlude to memory and endeavoured to concentrate on his job, football and the occasional girlfriend. Less than a year after starting work in the railway goods office, a promising relationship with Ivy proved he had made the right decision. Caring and non-judgmental, she accepted him for who he was and seemed unfazed by the prospect of marriage to a damaged man. Rob might have made vague responses to Ivy's questions about his family, but he had never concealed his mental instability, convinced that honesty was essential when contemplating a life-long relationship.

Ivy's parents had welcomed him into their home, offering a spare bedroom for the first year of their marriage, accommodation of any sort still in short supply three years after VE day. Although the seaside town lacked the factories and other industrial targets of the neighbouring port, German fighters returning from raids on inland cities had dropped any remaining bombs on the coast before heading home across the Channel. In the street where Ivy and her family lived, less than a mile from the cliffs that ringed a wide bay, gaps remained where houses had been demolished due to bomb damage. Ivy told him she and her sister had slept under the dining room table for much of the war as protection against flying glass and other debris.

The solid Edwardian house, its shattered front windows finally reglazed, rather than patched with ply, was crowded during the latter half of forty-eight with parents, two daughters, their husbands and a three-year old granddaughter occupying the three double bedrooms. Ivy's other sibling, a younger brother who had served in the Navy, slept in what was known as 'the box room,' a narrow space just wide enough for a single bed and little else. When Rob asked why one bedroom was so small, his mother-in-law explained it would have been a maid's room in the days before the Great War when even ordinary folk had a servant. Downstairs in the large kitchen, a servants' bell box hung above the sideboard, another mystery to a man raised in a cramped terraced house. Father-in-law, Will, often troubled by stomach upsets and pain – he'd had to retire early due to an ulcer -- used the bell in his bedroom to alert wife and daughters to his intention to remain in bed past breakfast time. One of the three, usually Ivy's sister, would prepare watery porridge and a cup of milky tea, and carry them upstairs for the invalid.

At other times, his father-in-law worked tirelessly, gardening, maintaining the house and making furniture. A master carpenter before enforced retirement, his work was always beautifully constructed and finished, French polishing a speciality. The writing bureau he had made for Ivy's twenty-first birthday was exquisite, finely turned drawer handles and legs plus numerous slots for envelopes or letters.

Evenings were often spent around the piano in the dining room, Will pumping out music hall tunes from his youth, the rest of the family singing along. On Sundays, a short walk to the local Congregational chapel for morning service was followed by a hot meal comprising generous helpings of home-grown vegetables, a slice of rationed meat and a fruit pudding also made from garden produce. After lunch had been cleared away, grandparents and small granddaughter retired for a nap, leaving Rob and Ivy free to take a walk to the nearby beach if the weather remained fine, where they would stroll arm in arm along the promenade. Rolls of barbed wire no longer separated promenade from beach, as they had done during the war, so Ivy could indulge her love of swimming on warm days. Seated on a towel, watching his beloved wife dive into waves or swim between concrete groynes, Rob felt intense gratitude to be part of her delightful family, and apart from the occasional visit to his aunt and uncle, exorcised the memory of his own kin.

FIFTEEN

Far from a seaside town that even by nineteen-seventy-four only came to life during the brief English summer, Rob stands on a sunlit strip of pavement marvelling at the vibrant street life around him. A row of small shops occupies the ground floor of the apartment block opposite the tram stop, striped awnings shading the produce displayed in windows and either side of open doorways. A colourful canvas of fruit, vegetables, bread and pasta tempt pedestrians to pause, while aproned vendors call out enticements in melodious dialect. Further along the row, he can see garments strung on wires beneath awnings, flapping in the light breeze, multihued fabric rivalling harvest brilliance. A complete contrast to the lacklustre vistas of wartime streetscapes: Bomb damaged buildings supported with rough timber scaffolds, crumbling cement and pieces of masonry littering cracked pavements, grey-faced inhabitants sitting in doorways trying to sell tattered belongings. *Or their daughters*, he thinks, blinking to dislodge the memory of an appalling proposition.

He glances at Ivy, standing in a patch of shade beneath an awning. She appears to be rummaging in what she refers to as '*my holiday bag,*' a capacious handbag with numerous pockets both inside and out. 'Lost something, dear?' he calls, moving towards her.

'Ah, here it is.' She holds up a small book. 'An Italian/English dictionary, plus useful phrases,' she advises in response to his questioning look. 'I bought it in Rome, remember?'

'A tiny bookshop not far from our hotel.'

She smiles. 'So, now we're in Bellavista, do you recognise this street?' She indicates shops and apartment block with her free hand.

'Can't say I do. A street name would help.'

'Why don't we ask in the shops?'

'Good idea.' He heads for the nearest shop, where a swarthy middle-aged man, an apron taut around a generous stomach, lounges in the doorway. 'Scusi, signore.'

The man looks up and smiles. 'Buon giorno, signore e signora.' He gestures towards his colourful display of fruit. 'Frutta, signora?' Bella e a buon prezzo!'

Ivy points to a pile of oranges and holds up two fingers.

'Ah, turista,' the fruiterer murmurs. 'Inglese?'

Ivy nods, tries in vain to remember the Italian for how much.

'Quanta costa?' Rob asks, reaching into his trouser pocket for small change.

Smiling, the vendor takes several coins from Rob's outstretched palm. 'Grazie, signore.' After slipping the coins into his apron pocket, he extracts three large oranges from the pile.

'Due,' Rob reminds him.

'One for luck as you English say. No charge.'

Ivy smiles and unfastening her holiday bag, proffers it to receive the fruit. 'Grazie, signore.'

'Prego.'

'Questa strada, nome, per favore?' Rob asks, before the fruiterer can turn away.

'Via della Libertà.'

The name is vaguely familiar, although Rob can't remember where it was in relation to the Zappetti apartment. 'Grazie, signore.'

'You are looking hotel, la Chiesa?'

Rob shakes his head. 'Cerchiamo amici. La

famiglia Zappetti. Roberto, Luigi, Susanna, Maria.'

The fruiterer frowns. 'Non questa strada.'

Ivy tugs at Rob's wrist. 'Let's try the other shops.'

'Ok.' He smiles at the fruiterer. 'Grazie, signore. Arrivederci.'

Six small shops, six conversations conducted in a mixture of half-remembered Italian and dictionary vocabulary, with a sprinkling of English thrown in for good measure. Six negative responses the disappointing result.

'We're getting nowhere fast,' Rob remarks pointlessly, as they emerge from the last shop in the row.

'That woman selling underwear looked at us as though we were mad.' Giving the shop a last look, Ivy notices a board propped against the window. 'Fancy hanging bras on a board outside your shop. Whatever next!' She attempts to suppress a giggle.

'What's so funny?' he asks, irritated by her levity.

'Nothing, dear.'

'It's probably my accent,' he says half to himself, oblivious to lace panties swaying in the breeze on the wire above his head. 'I never could master it and found it difficult to communicate even after living here for months.'

'I think you're doing well, considering it's been thirty years since you spoke Italian.' She looks up at him. 'If only we'd known back in the winter that we were going to Italy, we could have enrolled in one of those language classes they run in the evenings at the local school.'

If two weeks in Italy had been on the agenda months ago, I wouldn't have agreed to go,' he thinks, recalling the phone call that altered their holiday itinerary only weeks earlier. 'Let's cross the road, it's shadier on the other side. There are bound to be more shops further down; this is a main road.' He peers at the burgeoning traffic. 'We'd better cross at traffic lights. Safer.'

'I just hope the traffic stops.' Ivy points to several Lambretta scooters zigzagging between cars, their youthful drivers paying no heed to danger or road rules.

'If it doesn't, just keep walking once you've stepped off the kerb. They'll go around you.'

Shaking her head in disbelief, Ivy grabs his hand.

———

Safe on the opposite pavement, they follow the Via della Libertà for at least a mile, passing small and large businesses, which seem either closed, or their occupants unwilling to answer a knock on the door, before detouring into a side street to see if anyone is around. Four-storey apartment buildings dotted with small balconies stand either side of the narrow street, paint peeling from entrance doors and windows. Above their heads, washing hangs from wood and wire clotheslines attached to outside balcony rails. The street is deserted and a dead end.

'Back to the main road or do you want to try knocking on doors?' Ivy queries.

'Main road,' Rob answers, his face heavy with disappointment.

After retracing their steps, they continue the downhill trek, grateful for a wide pavement. They try to ignore the persistent honk of car horns, the screech of brakes, the shouts of frustrated drivers. Trams rattle past on their way to the waterfront, but no one alights at the frequent stops. Before long, commercial premises give way to more apartment blocks, some with shops at street level. Risking further incomprehension, Rob enters each shop to pose his questions. Overall, the shopkeepers are friendly and appear to understand his mangled Italian. Only one dismisses him with a curt response on learning he doesn't want to purchase anything. But the results remain the same: a shake of the head and a shrug of the shoulders at the mention of the Zappetti family. One shopkeeper suggests asking at the post office and gives directions, but after the first sentence, Rob fails to follow dialect-peppered speech. On reflection, he should have asked the man to draw a map, Ivy always carries a notebook, but this option doesn't occur to him until they are some distance from the shop.

Another aberration, he thinks, half-convinced the day's cerebral impediments – the name of the Zappetti's street continues to elude him – are signs he should discontinue the search. A simple premise prompted the slog through suburban streets, he has no desire to rekindle romance or even friendship, only wishes to discover whether the people, briefly considered 'family', survived the deprivations of war and hopefully, prospered in the years since. Surely there's no harm in that?

The stench of petrol fumes assaults his nostrils and the uproar of undisciplined traffic bruises ears accustomed to obedient small-town transport. For a few moments, he regrets abandoning the phone call to Aeroporto Fiumicino Roma.

Moist fingers touch his wrist. 'Why don't we

try some more side-streets?' Ivy asks, tired of waiting for a decision.

'Why not,' he answers, placing his sweating palm over her sun-browned hand. Ivy tans easily even in weak English sunlight, while the almost translucent skin of part-Irish ancestry, condemns *him* to burn and peel. He never accompanies Ivy to the beach less than a mile from their home, or out on the sailing boats owned by her brother and brother-in-law. Last year in Australia, daughter Frances persuaded him to buy a pair of tailored knee-length shorts, then laughed at the whiteness of hitherto concealed calves and knees. Determined never to wear shorts again, he left them behind, figuring his son-in-law could pass them on to a similar-sized friend. Most of the time, James wore the brief shorts known by the odd name of 'stubbies,' his long limbs so tanned by the Queensland sun, he could easily be mistaken for Greek or Indian. Jet-black hair and an olive complexion only served to compound nationality confusion.

For the next hour, Rob and Ivy trudge the back streets of Bellavista turning at random: left, first right, straight ahead, second left, second right. There's no one about, no one to ask, no one else foolish enough to venture out in scorching noonday sun. *Mad dogs and Englishmen,* Rob thinks, as perspiration escapes from beneath the rim of his panama hat and trickles down glowing cheeks. He glances at Ivy. 'I need a break, love to wipe my face.'

She turns towards him, cheeks scarlet despite her broad-brimmed hat. 'Wish I perspired like you, instead of just getting hotter and hotter until I feel like an over-ripe tomato about to burst.'

'Strange phenomenon that,' he murmurs, pulling out his handkerchief, already damp from previous mopping. Absorbed in his task, he fails to notice an elderly woman enter the street or hear her walking stick tap the pavement as she walks slowly in their direction.

'At last someone to ask.' Ivy exclaims, tugging at his arm.

Rob raises his head. 'One last attempt then. After that I really must find somewhere to sit down. I'm worn out.'

'I could with a break too.' Ivy retrieves the dictionary from her handbag as the
old woman draws nearer. 'Oh no, she's turning into that doorway.'

'Scusi, Signora,' Rob calls, an unexpected burst of energy propelling him along the street.

The old woman peers at the stranger bearing

down on her, raises her walking stick and brandishes it menacingly.

Undeterred, Rob steps towards her. 'Buon giorno, Signora.'

The old woman looks him up and down before lowering the stick.

'Sono Inglese, turista.'

'Sì.'

'Cerchiamo amici. Luigi Zappetti, Maria, Susanna.'

The old woman smiles. 'Sì sì, Luigi e Anna.'

Rob wants to hug her, asks instead, 'Dove Luigi e Anna?'

The old woman points with her stick to a building opposite. 'Numero tre.'

'Grazie mille, Signora.'

'Prego.'

Despite heat and fatigue, Rob sprints back to Ivy. 'Success at last!' He bends forward to grasp Ivy's shoulders, kisses her on both cheeks in the Continental manner. 'Luigi and Anna Zappetti, number three.'

'Marvellous! Ivy exclaims.

They link arms and cross the road.

Double doors, one propped open with a piece of wood, lead into the apartment building foyer. The tiled floor is bare except for scraps of litter blown in from the street. Rubbish rustles as

Rob and Ivy step inside, gulp mouthfuls of cool air before ascending bare concrete stairs edged with rusting railings. Three doors face the first landing, each marked above the handle with a badly painted numeral. Rob soon locates number three but there's no sign of a doorbell or knocker. 'No bell,' he says, turning to Ivy.

'Go on then, knock,' she urges as he tentatively raises a hand.

Knuckles rap tarnished timber.

Silence from within prompts a second and third attempt with the same result. Bitterly disappointed, Rob and Ivy are about to descend the first step when the sound of a key turning in the lock stays their steps. Twisting around, they see a young woman leaning against the doorframe, tousled black hair tumbling over narrow shoulders, cleavage showing above an incorrectly fastened summer dress. Bare toes dig into a coir doormat.

'Cosa c'è?' she asks, lipstick-smudged lips pursed, dark eyes glaring.

'Anna Zappetti?' Rob queries, blushing as it occurs to him, he may have interrupted midday intimacy.

'Sì.'

'Buon giorno Signora.' Rob moves towards the open door. 'Cerco amico Luigi Zappetti.'

Now it's Anna's turn to blush. 'Luigi non è a casa.' She steps back into the apartment, reaches for the door handle as a man flits across a half-open doorway behind her.

'Buon giorno, Luigi,' Rob calls.

Eyes wide, Anna freezes, then slams the door in Rob's face.

'How rude,' Ivy remarks from the top of the stairs.

Rob hurries to her side. 'Caught her at a bad moment by the look of it. She said Luigi wasn't at home, but I'm sure someone else was there.'

Ivy raises a hand to stifle a giggle. 'Most likely her lover. Her husband would be at work this time of the day.'

Shared laughter reverberates around the stairwell as they make their descent.

In the foyer's cool shade, they stand close together, heads almost touching. 'Should we make a second attempt?' Rob whispers, half-hoping Ivy will answer in the negative.

'Of course, we can't give up now.' Mischief dances in her sparkling green eyes. 'We just give lover boy sufficient time to vacate the premises. Hopefully, Anna will be more receptive by then.'

Rob nods.

'Let's go back to the main road,' Ivy continues, moving towards the door. 'We need to find a shop, buy some cold drinks and something to eat besides oranges.'

'Good idea, I'm dying of thirst.'

'Me too. It seems a long time since breakfast.'

Rob peers at his watch. 'It is. Four hours to be exact.'

During the convoluted walk back to the Via della Libertà, Rob's memory functions as usual, and before long they're heading for the row of shops where he purchased the oranges. Anticipation spurs them on, they can almost feel ice cold liquid tumble down parched throats, but when they reached their destination, disappointment delivers a huge blow, each shop window is covered with a blind, each door closed.

Furious, Rob kicks out at the stonework beneath a shop window. 'Bloody siesta, I suppose. That puts paid to cold drinks.'

'At least we can have a sit down to eat the oranges.' Ivy points to a lopsided bench positioned against a blank wall further up the road. 'And there's some shade.'

They stagger to the bench, collapse onto timber worn smooth by countless backsides.

'That's better.' Ivy opens her handbag to extract oranges and a clean handkerchief.

A familiar aroma wafts past Rob's nose, but he manages to ignore the memory of Israeli oranges crushed beneath a loaded trolley.

'They're nice and juicy,' Ivy remarks. Drops land on the handkerchief spread over her knees.

'Good.' Rob takes the proffered segments, chews slowly, savouring taste and welcome moisture.

Beside him, Ivy struggles to stay awake, her head drooping as she lifts each segment to her mouth. Finishing her share, she wraps discarded peel in the handkerchief and shoves it into her bag. In minutes, her head is slumped on her chest, muffled snores emerging from a half-open mouth.

Suddenly incapable of sleep or even a doze, Rob sits staring into space, an uninvited montage passing before his tired eyes. A young woman stands by a hospital bed sobbing; a middle-aged man offers his twelve-year-old daughter to a British airman; an RAF transport flies over the Bay of Naples. Then, as the ruined city of Naples recedes from view, he hears something metallic hit a hard surface over and over again. Jolted into action, he leaps from the bench to take cover in the nearest shop doorway. The sound intensifies; he presses his body against the shop door and holds his breath.

After what seems an agonising wait, three boys aged about ten, appear from around the side of an adjacent apartment block, their scruffy shoes kicking empty drink cans along the pavement.

Rob laughs with relief, startling the trio. Cans roll into the gutter; the boys remain at a safe distance staring at the weird stranger crouched in the doorway.

On the bench, Ivy stirs. 'What's going on, Rob?'

'Nothing,' He straightens up, steps out of the doorway. 'Buon giorno,' he calls to the boys. 'Sono turisto Inglese.'

Two of the boys run off down the street but the third, bolder than his friends, stands his ground.

'Cerchiamo amici Zappetti,' Rob sidles towards the bench, sits beside Ivy.

'Zappetti?' the boy repeats, his voice high-pitched.

'Si. Luigi, Mari...'

'Mario?' the boy interrupts, shuffling forward.

Rob smiles. 'Buon giorno, Mario.'

The boy shakes his head, then points to himself. 'Mi chiamo Pietro. Mario è il mio amico.'

'Mario Zappetti?'

'Sì.'

'Dove la casa di Mario?'

Pietro steps back a pace.

'Dove la casa di Mario,' Rob repeats slowly, but Pietro's attention is fixed on Ivy, busy rummaging in her holiday bag.

'Sherbet lemons,' she declares, extracting a brown paper bag and holding it towards the boy.

Curiosity quickly replaces apprehension. Running over to the bench, Pietro dips his hand into a sticky mess and pulls out a clump of sweets before retreating to the kerb.

'Offer him more,' Rob says, eager to ply the boy with further questions.

'Wait a minute, we don't want to scare him. He'll have been told not to speak to strangers.'

Impatient, Rob grabs the bag. 'Pietro, sapete Anna Zappetti?'

The boy nods and moves towards the bench, his eyes fixed on the crumpled paper bag. 'Anna e la matrigna di Mario.' Extending one hand, he seizes the bag, then backs away.

Rob taps Ivy's knee. 'Quick, look up matrigna, I'm not sure what it means.'

Ivy retrieves the dictionary. 'I'll just look for my glasses.'

'Give it here.' Rob makes a grab for the book and quickly thumbs through wafer-thin pages. 'Step-mother.'

'Luigi, the cat artist,' Ivy murmurs.

'Could be.' Rob leans towards her, whispers, 'I'll ask him the address.' He glances at the boy sucking contentedly, one hand grasping the paper bag, the other coiled around a street sign. 'Vivere, er abitare,' Rob begins, trying to remember which verb is correct. 'Anna e Luigi abitano numero tre,' he calls in what he hopes is a confident tone. 'Via...' he hesitates, the street name floating just beyond his reach.

'Via della Libertà,' the boy says, swinging around the pole.

'Non questa strada, piccola strada.' Rob points up the hill.

'Piccola strada,' Pietro repeats. 'Piccolo cervello.' Grubby sneakers land on the pavement and with a wave of the hand, he races off down the hill.

'Scugnizzo!' Rob shouts after him. His command of the Italian language might be limited but he is not pea-brained.

'What does that mean?'

'Street urchin.' Rob sags on the bench, debating whether to revisit the home of Anna and Luigi or follow Pietro. The boy can't have gone far, no doubt his friends are waiting for him nearby. 'We search for the boys,' he announces decisively, rising from the bench.

'Don't you want to try Anna again?'

'Later.' Arms swinging, he strides away, leaving Ivy staring after him, a resigned expression on her face.

Husband and wife reconnect halfway down the hill. 'Why don't we do this logically?' Ivy suggests, grasping his arm to prevent a second swift departure. She points down the hill with her free hand. 'I'll check any side streets to the left, you check the right. Meet me at the bottom of the hill.'

'Fine by me,' he answers through taut lips, wishing he had been the one to propose such a sensible approach. What the hell's the matter with him? First memory loss, now jealousy; his emotions are scrambled. 'Seen you soon, my dear,' he adds by way of penance and tosses her a smile.

She releases his arm, mutters something about red herrings before setting off down the hill.

―

There are three side streets on the right, one leading to a school, one to an intersection, one a dead end. No one walks the streets or lounges in doorways. Rob considers entering the school to ask for Mario Zappetti, then changes his mind, acknowledging how such a question coming from an older, obviously foreign man, will seem to a teacher. Reaching the intersection, he surveys each street in turn, peering into the distance so hard it makes his eyes water. Identical four-storey apartment blocks line both sides of the street, shuttered windows creating an impenetrable barrier. Most entrance doors are open but sudden agitation prevents him entering a single foyer. Stranger in a foreign land, he cannot claim right of entry.

Dejected, he makes his way back to the main road, cries out for joy when he spots Ivy waiting in the meagre shade of a stunted tree on the opposite pavement. Cars and scooters zoom past him, but ignoring the pedestrian crossing less than twenty yards away, he steps into the road.

'You took a chance,' Ivy comments, having observed his reckless dash through traffic to the accompaniment of blaring horns and angry voices.

Rob shrugs. 'They're used to it, I imagine.'

'All the same, I would like to celebrate our wedding anniversary together.'

'Sorry,' he mutters, feeling foolish now. How can he explain the compulsion to reach her side without delay, the complete absence of fear as vehicles wove around him? In the minute or two it took to cross the road Ivy was his only focus.

'No sign of any of the boys, I'm afraid,' she says.

'Same here. It's as though they've vanished into thin air.' He gestures towards a tram a few hundred yards away. 'There's no point in continuing. We'll take a tram back to the city centre and visit the town hall or the post office.'

'Are you certain? What about Anna?'

He shakes his head. 'I don't have the energy for another altercation.'

'I'm so sorry it didn't work out, love.' She slips her arm through his and they begin a second descent of the Via della Libertà.

SIXTEEN

Each engrossed in their own thoughts, neither Rob nor Ivy pay any attention to the middle-aged man emerging from a side street further down the road. Dressed in working gear - boots, thick cotton trousers and short-sleeved shirt -- he hesitates at the corner as though uncertain whether to turn left or right, then begins to walk in their direction. Short and stocky, like many southern Italian men, he possesses the sun-darkened complexion typical of someone who spends his working life out of doors. Hands in his pockets, he saunters towards the tram stop, aware no doubt that ample time remains before the next tram is due.

Opposite the centre barrier separating traffic

lanes and tram tracks, he steps towards the kerb, but not before noticing a couple making their way down the hill. As he waits for a stream of vehicles to pass, he glances now and then at the rapidly approaching pair, noting the floppy sunhat shielding the woman's face, the stiff panama hat perched on the man's head. No one he knows, that's for sure, tourists by the look of it. He twists around to check the traffic. Cars and scooters continue their relentless onslaught; sighing, he refocuses on the couple, now about three metres away.

Suddenly his expression alters from one of mild irritation at uninterrupted traffic to undisguised astonishment. 'Il nostro salvatore,' he cries, breaking into a trot. 'Robbi, Robbi, salvatore!' And pushing the woman aside, he flings his arms around Rob before kissing him on both cheeks.

Every muscle tensed, Rob anticipates the stranger's hands foraging in trouser pockets for wallet and small change. Beneath his shirt, he wears a light cotton money belt containing traveller's cheques and a wad of notes, but will he have the strength to prevent a much younger man ripping it from his waist? The question remains unanswered as the stranger relinquishes his hold, although he remains close enough to touch. Still wary, Rob steps back a pace to study the man from a safe distance. Hands clasped to a broad chest, a foolish grin suffuses the swarthy face, and dark eyes sweep over Rob's flushed face as though trying to absorb every feature.

Memory flies to the surface, hangs in the air like a bright balloon. 'Luigi Zappetti?' Rob asks tentatively.

'Sì, sì, il tuo amico Luigi!'

'It's all right, dear, he's a friend,' Rob informs Ivy, standing nearby, the holiday bag pressed tight against her chest.

Still apprehensive, she shuffles forward.

'Luigi, la mia moglie, Ivy.'

A beaming Luigi moves towards her. 'Molto lieto, signora Ivy. Mi chiamo Luigi Zappetti.'

Ivy returns the smile. 'Buon giorno, Luigi. I'm so pleased you found us.'

'You are losing way?'

'No, we were looking for you!'

Luigi looks puzzled, so Rob explains they were taking advantage of a few spare hours to search for old friends.

'You no remember address of casa?'

Rob is forced to confess the street name slipped his mind.

'Non importa, I have find you!' Luigi exclaims, stepping between husband and wife.

'Venite con me a casa.' He gestures towards a side street directly opposite. 'Non much walk. We have the vino and molto talking.'

'Like we did long ago,' Rob murmurs.

Luigi makes no comment. Instead, placing an arm around each of their shoulders, he leads them to the crossing, waits patiently for a break in the traffic before escorting them across the road. Safe on the other side, he shifts his position, moving to Rob's right.

The three make slow progress along the lengthy street, Luigi talking non-stop in a spirited combination of Italian and English that Rob finds difficult to follow, let alone answer. However, he does manage to deduce the gist of Luigi's words, learning he works as a gardener, finished early today and was on his way home when he recognised Rob. Periodically, Luigi clasps his hands to his chest exclaims, 'Dio mio, zio Robbi!' followed by a glance at Rob that speaks volumes, so by the time they reach the next intersection, Ivy is dabbing at her eyes with an orange-scented handkerchief.

'Casa no far now,' Luigi announces, halting at the pavement's edge, even though this intersection is empty of traffic.

Automatically, Rob looks left, right, left, then remembers it should be the other way around in

Italy. Taking Ivy's arm, he ushers her across the road, Luigi so close behind, Rob swears he can feel warm breath on the back of his neck.

After crossing the street, Luigi resumes both his position closest to the gutter and his hybrid monologue, accompanied by the extravagant gesticulations' characteristic of his Latin heritage. For his part, Rob offers the occasional comment, hoping his responses are pertinent, while Ivy remains atypically silent.

They proceed in this fashion for several hundred yards, then Luigi points to an apartment block opposite. 'Casa della famiglia Zappetti. Ti ricordi?'

Rob peers at a four-storey building no different from any of the others he has observed during hours spent in a once familiar neighbourhood. 'Naturalmente, Luigi.' The white lie comes easily, fully justified he decides, considering he hasn't visited the apartment for thirty years. He reaches for Ivy's hand to give it a squeeze.

'Do you recognise the place?' she asks quietly.

He leans towards her. 'Can't say that I do, but it's definitely not that Anna's place.'

'That's a relief, a second encounter would be embarrassing.'

'Andiamo, amici miei,' says Luigi, hurrying them across the road, a hand firm between Rob's shoulder blades.

As expected, the foyer resembles the one they entered earlier, tiled floor and concrete stairs with wrought-iron railings. *Second floor*, Rob thinks but doesn't say in case memory proves unreliable.

'Secondo.' Luigi heads for the stairs. Grabbing the railing, he ascends the first flight with the speed of an agile adolescent, then stands looking down at Rob and Ivy climbing slowly. 'Va bene?'

Rob nods, adding by way of explanation, 'Sono sfinito.'

Luigi grins. 'Ancora una rampa.'

Rob manages a brief smile, wishes weary legs would move faster.

'Is ok, take plenty time,' Luigi urges when they join him on the small landing.

'It must be the heat.' Ivy struggles to catch her breath. 'Stairs don't usually bother me.'

'Oggi fa caldo,' Luigi agrees.

Beside her, Rob clings to the railing with both hands, his heart pounding. The pain in the middle of his chest is proving difficult to ignore.

'Andiamo?' Luigi queries after several minutes.

Ivy smiles. 'Sì, Luigi.' She touches Rob's arm. 'All right now, love?'

Releasing his grip, Rob turns around. 'Yes, I'm good to go.'

Concern etches Ivy's face. 'Are you sure, you're very flushed?'

'So are you.'

'Yes, but my cheeks are always red.'

Unwilling to argue the point, he pushes past her and climbs the second flight, taking care to inhale deeply after every step. Much to his relief, chest pain eases to a dull ache.

Husband and wife reconvene on a landing leading to four apartments, they hang back, waiting for Luigi to knock on one of two doors on the right.

Instead, he pushes the door open with the flat of his hand and steps inside. 'Sono io,' he calls, addressing a door at the rear of a small entrance hall before turning back to his guests. 'Come, come, we are arriving.'

The living room door opens, revealing a petite, fifty-something woman wearing a short-sleeved button-through summer dress and sandals. Her short curly black hair is streaked with grey and laughter lines crease the skin around her wide brown eyes. 'Ciao, Lui...' she begins, the greeting arrested as she notices the couple standing beside her brother. A frown creases her forehead, she stares at Rob with unconcealed perplexity. After what seems an age to Rob, her expression alters to one of delight. 'Non ci posso crederci!'

Italian vocabulary vaporises in the heat of reunion. 'Yes, it's true, Susanna. I'm Rob Harper, the RAF airman who befriended your family thirty years ago.' Arms extended, he covers the short distance between them in record time, holds her tight for a few moments before kissing her on both cheeks. Then, as though conscious of Ivy's knowing smile, he steps back to resume his rightful place beside her.

Flustered, Susanna's hands fly to kissed cheeks. 'You here miracolo, this, how you say in English?' She hesitates, looking to her brother for assistance, but he can only smile. 'La volontà di Dio,' she cries, raising her hands heavenward.

'The will of God,' Rob repeats for Ivy's benefit.

Alerted by raised voices, a man of about thirty appears in the doorway and stands behind Susanna, hands resting lightly on her shoulders. 'Che cosa c'è mamma?'

Susanna turns her head. 'Rob Harper, buono amico di familgia durante la guerra.'

'Zio Robbi!' he exclaims, pushing past his

mother and almost knocking Rob over with an enthusiastic embrace.

'Mio figlio, Roberto,' Susanna informs the petite woman still standing on the doorstep.

Ivy smiles and steps forward. 'I am Rob's wife, Ivy.'

'Benvenuto, signora Ivy. Please to enter my home.'

'Grazie.' Ivy glances at Rob still crushed to Roberto's chest, before following Susanna into the living room.

In the far corner of the room, a young woman sits in an armchair set against the wall. She smiles in Ivy's direction before getting to her feet.

'La signora Ivy,' Susanna declares.

'Piacere, signora. Mi chiamo Isabella.'

'Pleased to meet you, Isabella.'

Isabella moves towards Ivy. 'You are English?'

'Yes.' Ivy accepts the hastily proffered hand. 'We're on a coach tour of Italy, visiting Naples for a few days.'

Isabella nods. 'I am Roberto's wife. How do you know my mother-in-law?'

'I don't. It's my husband who knows the family.'

Loud male voices preclude further explanation, as Luigi and Roberto stride into the room, quickly followed by Rob. Engaged in animated discussion, the elder Zappetti is refuting the younger's insistence he remembers being taken out by zio Robbi during the war.

'Non posso, Roberto,' Rob interrupts, understanding the gist of their disagreement. 'Tu eri un bambino.' He holds up two fingers. 'Due anni.'

Roberto opens his mouth to speak but his mother calls a halt to argument, her displeasure at their bad manners requiring no translation. Embarrassed, nephew and uncle hang their heads and creep to the relative sanctuary of a sofa, where they sit side-by-side, studying their shoes.

Taking advantage of rare silence, Isabella approaches Rob to shake his hand. 'Welcome. I'm Roberto's wife Isabella.'

'Pleased to meet you. I'm Rob Harper, an old friend. Many years ago, I lived in Portici for a while and often visited this apartment,' he adds, unwilling to mention the circumstances that brought him to Naples.

Isabella nods. 'You were stationed here with the RAF during the war. Nineteen-forty-four wasn't it?'

'That's right,' Rob replies, surprised she can

recall details of his long-ago deployment. 'Did Roberto tell you about my friendship with the family?'

'Roberto, Luigi, everyone. I have heard the story of your great kindness on many occasions. It is part of Zappetti family lore, so I am delighted to be meeting you at last.'

Rob gestures towards Luigi. 'It's thanks to Luigi I'm here. If he hadn't come up the road and recognised me, Ivy and I would have gone back to the hotel.'

Isabella looks puzzled. 'Your hotel is near here?'

'No, but I decided to take advantage of our stay in Naples to look for my old friends. I thought I remembered this address, but we searched the streets around here for hours without any luck. No one I spoke to seemed to understand my questions even when I mentioned the Zappetti name.' He looks sheepish. 'My Italian is pretty bad, not like your English, Isabella.'

She smiles at the compliment. 'I studied English at school and university. Now please sit down and tell us about your Italian holiday.' She indicates the armchair behind her. 'But first let me get you some drinks. Homemade lemonade with ice ok?'

'That would be lovely thank you.' Rob walks over to join Ivy, now sitting in the adjacent chair watching proceedings with interest, her green eyes flicking from one Zappetti to the other, her expression a mixture of curiosity and gratitude. 'Isabella's gone to fetch us some lemonade,' he says, sinking into soft upholstery.

'Just what we need.' Ivy reaches out to squeeze Rob's knee. 'Susanna was right, it is a miracle. I can't believe Luigi recognised you after thirty years. You must have made a big impression on him.'

Rob gives a wry smile and leans towards her. 'I got him out of trouble with the military police down by the harbour. He was a bit of a devil back then. Understandable given the circumstances.'

'A vulnerable adolescent,' Ivy murmurs.

Rob resists the urge to contradict. Luigi was reckless, rude, moody but vulnerable, never. He recalls a sister's slap, a father's harsh words, a military policeman's towering presence. Maybe Ivy's right, God knows what would have happened if Luigi had fallen into the hands of a recent enemy: months behind bars, beatings, worse? He shudders at the thought of physical or sexual abuse.

'Everything ok, Rob?'

Mercifully returned to the present, Rob nods and pats Ivy's hand.

On the opposite side of the room, Susanna sits on the sofa next to Roberto, one hand clutching the other. She appears dazed, as though she can't quite believe what's happening.

Suddenly, the outer door slams shut and a boy about ten years old races into the room. 'Ciao, nonna,' he calls, skipping towards her.

Susanna blinks. 'Ciao, mio caro Mario.'

Leaning over her, the boy kisses his grandmother on both cheeks before flopping on the floor at her feet. He ignores both father and uncle.

Roberto taps Mario's shoulder, then whispers in his ear.

'Sì, papà.' Mario gets to his feet, approaches the strangers shyly. 'Benvenuti signore e signora Harper,' he says without raising his eyes from the floor.

'Grazie, Mario.' Rob fishes in his trouser pocket. 'Caramella?' he asks, holding out a toffee.

Mario raises his head, studies the sweet lying in the stranger's pink palm. 'Grazie, signore.' He grabs the toffee and immediately steps back, almost colliding with his mother returning from the kitchen with a tray of drinks.

'Attento, Mario.'

'Scusa, mamma.'

'They're the same the world over,' Rob muses, watching Mario beat a hasty retreat to the safety of his doting grandmother.

'Just what I was thinking,' Ivy replies. 'Won't it be wonderful when we've got a grandchild?'

'Wonderful,' he murmurs, pushing aside negative thoughts of a child seen only in photographs, English grandparents unable to afford a visit to the other side of the world. 'Oh, thank you Isabella.' He takes a glass and passes it to Ivy before taking one for himself.

'Prego.' Isabella crosses the room to distribute the remaining drinks.

Adults sip and swallow, a child gulps and crunches ice-cubes between his teeth; familiar sounds, familiar actions observed in homes around the globe on hot summer afternoons. Outside in the street, children dawdle on their way home from school, shouting to one another in high-pitched voices, while high above them, women call to neighbours from sun-heated balconies as they haul in washing lines to gather dry clothes in strong brown arms. Roused from siesta, old men and women yawn, urge unwilling bodies to rise from bed or armchair.

At last, Susanna places her empty glass on

the floor and turns to her guests. 'So, you visit mio Napoli. Is una vacanza?'

'Sì,' Rob answers, thankful she has overcome her reticence. 'We're on a two-week coach tour of Italy. We arrived yesterday from Rome.'

'You are liking Roma?'

'Very much,' Ivy responds. 'This is one of the best holidays I've ever had. I can't believe I've seen the Sistine Chapel, St Peter's Square, the Trevi fountain, the Spanish steps.'

Susanna beams. 'Roma is beautiful city. What you have see in Napoli?'

'Not much yet, we only arrived late yesterday afternoon. Today we were supposed to go to the Museum of Antiquities with our friends Alf and Dawn, but...'

Luigi jerks as though he has just woken from siesta. 'Alf? Is amico from war?'

'Sì, we're still good amici,' Rob replies quickly, grateful Luigi has interrupted what could be a lengthy monologue. Ivy loves to talk. 'Alf and his wife often have a vacanza at our casa.'

Luigi's face darkens. 'Zio Alf no wanting look for family Zappetti?'

'His wife insisted on going to the museum,' Rob explains.

'I understand.' Luigi sits back in his seat.

An uncomfortable silence ensues, even the boy remains still, his curly head resting against Susanna's legs.

Anxious to restore harmony, Rob struggles to think of reassuring words, but images kept intruding, not his mate kneeling before Rosie McGill's grave, but row upon row of white headstones, thousands of young lives lost in an ill-conceived battle for a single mountain. He'd wanted to remain in the coach while fellow passengers toured the war cemetery at Monte Cassino, but Patrizia insisted he alight, the driver wishing to lock the vehicle so he too could pay his respects to the war dead. Despite having seen footage of war cemeteries on television, the actual experience proved deeply distressing, Rob overwhelmed by sheer numbers and the realisation that most of those buried in that foreign field, were men barely out of their teens. Only Ivy's constant vigilance prevented him from falling to his knees and sobbing uncontrollably. Noticing his ashen face, she murmured something about the heat and steered him into the shade of a nearby tree.

Headstones fade as Susanna breaks the silence. 'You have bambini?' she asks, addressing her question to Ivy rather than Rob.

'Yes, but they are grown up now. We have

two daughters. Frances is twenty-four and Sally twenty-one.'

Susanna claps her hands. 'Meraviglioso!'

'I heard you mention daughters,' Isabella remarks from her seat at the dining table. 'Are they in Naples with you?'

'Oh no,' Rob says before Ivy can embark on a lengthy explanation. 'Frances is married and lives in Australia. Sally is a nurse in a town not far from London.' He decides not to mention that Sally will be heading to the southern hemisphere within months.

Isabella smiles, unaware her mother-in-law's expression has altered from one of pleasure to compassion.

'Australie is very long way from la Inghilterra.' Susanna's voice is tinged with sadness. 'Making visit difficile for you.'

'We visited Australia last year,' Rob says cheerfully. 'Six weeks. It was a wonderful holiday.'

'Hopefully we'll be able to go again soon,' Ivy adds. 'Frances is expecting a baby in November.'

Susanna beams. 'Nipote, meraviglioso!'

Lengthy unemployment looms, erasing the bright afternoon atmosphere. Determined to shield both Ivy and Susanna from the grim expression shadowing his face, Rob looks down at his feet.

Susanna ruffles Mario's hair. 'Daughter she come home soon, forse.'

'I don't think that's likely, they seem pretty settled out there.' Ivy manages a small smile. 'James has a good job and they've just bought their first house.'

'Triste, molto triste, Susanna murmurs, reaching out to stroke her son's wrist.

Amicable conversation stalls once more, as all except eleven-year-old Mario ponder the negative consequences of offspring leaving the land of their birth to settle twelve thousand miles from parents and other family members. Rob recalls a book on migration perused in his daughter's local library while waiting for her and Ivy to finish shopping. Hundreds of thousands of Italians had settled in Australia during the post-war decades, many coming from rural towns in the south where poverty prevailed. Some of these migrants went to work on farms, others worked in market gardens on the fringes of major cities, their vegetables and fruit much sought after by those inhabiting the new outer suburbs. Later that day, he accompanied Frances to buy what she referred to as 'vegies' from a covered stall built at the front of a market garden owned by an

Italian family. Hanging on nails above the tubs of produce he noticed framed black and white photographs of pre- and post-war Italy, including one of Naples. A brief conversation with the stall keeper, a Mrs Martelli, followed vegie purchases and Rob learnt the family had migrated from a town south of Naples twenty years earlier. Delighted Rob could understand Australian-English liberally peppered with Italian, Mrs Martelli proudly pointed out her 'marito' busy harvesting 'our zucchini molti beautiful' in the adjacent field.

Despite qualms it may be years before he can afford a second Australian visit, Rob smiles to himself. Who would have thought he'd be sitting in a Neapolitan apartment less than a year after that encounter with successful migrants, judging by the substantial brick house dominating their cultivated acres?

Movement opposite draws Rob's attention to Isabella perched on a dining chair crossing and uncrossing her legs. Assuming she's either uncomfortable or bored, he tries to think of something positive to say but Isabella beats him to it, asking Ivy what's on their itinerary after Naples.

'Pompei first. Then we're going to try and organise a boat trip to the Isle of Capri.'

'You will enjoy both,' Isabella assures her.

'The ruins of Pompei are fascinating and Capri is beautiful with its rugged shores and tiny coves. I hope your boat trip takes you to the Blue Grotto, the sea is a magnificent colour there because of sunlight shining into the deep cave.'

'Capri sounds wonderful and I'm sure the grotto would be included. We also have some free time after the boat trip to explore Sorrento.'

'The main square of Sorrento, Piazza Tasso is very interesting,' Isabella remarks. 'It was built over one hundred and fifty years ago and has many sculptures. There are also historic buildings nearby. The church Santa Maria del Carmine is very beautiful.'

'Thanks for the advice, Isabella. I'll make sure we go to the square and the church.'

'Oh, I almost forgot. If you have the time, have a look at the Valley of the Mills, it's only a short walk from Piazza Tasso. It's a deep ravine between two cliffs. You get a good view from the Via Fuorimura.' She pauses, her expression one of embarrassment. 'I am so sorry. I sound like a tour guide.'

Ivy smiles. 'No problem. I think you would make a very good tour guide. From your description of Sorrento, I'm really looking forward to visiting such a beautiful town.'

Place names and street names jog fond memories. Rob raises his head, says distinctly, 'Beautiful place, beautiful girl.' Sixty-year old blue eyes shine with the brilliance of youth.

Embarrassed, Susanna lowers her dark eyes and fiddles with the hem of her dress.

Still immersed in the memory of a delightful day spent in the company of his Italian sweetheart thirty years before, Rob remains unaware that Ivy has noted Susanna's reaction to his rash declaration. Luigi's smile and nod in response to Ivy's questioning look, also pass unnoticed.

'Luigi, you have another sister, I believe?' Ivy says, leaning forward.

'Sì, Maria. She is living end of street.'

'That's nice. Do you live near here too?'

'Sì, I am living...' He hesitates, trying to recall the English words. Shrugging his shoulders, he says instead, 'la prossima strada.'

'The next street,' Isabella translates.

Ivy smiles wistfully. 'How lovely to have all the family so close.'

'Sì, sì. I am having two girls like you.' Luigi beams with pride, then, as if only just realising the implications of Ivy's statement, pokes Mario with his foot, 'Mario, vieni a prendere zia Maria, zia Francesca, Angelica e Bettina.'

'Sì, zio Luigi.' Scrambling to his feet, the boy

races out of the room into the entrance hall. A door slams shut.

Isabella winces at the sound. 'Mio Mario, he makes so much noise.'

'My younger brother was just the same,' Ivy acknowledges. 'In fact, he hasn't changed much. Fifty-one and still playing boyish pranks and laughing loudly at his own jokes.'

'I don't think men ever grow up,' Isabella remarks, gesturing towards her husband and his uncle, sprawled on the sofa, either side of Susanna. Thirty-two-year old Roberto leans against his mother, one hand clinging to her wrist.

The two women exchange knowing smiles.

'Now you must excuse me.' Isabella gets to her feet and after exchanging a few words with her mother-in-law, heads for the kitchen.

'No need to go to any trouble,' Ivy calls after her.

'It's no trouble,' Isabella replies without turning her head.

Susanna rises from the sofa. 'Scusi, I go make a little food for you.' She smooths the creases in her dress before hurrying to join her daughter-in-law.

SEVENTEEN

Food for you. How many times has Rob uttered those words or the Italian equivalent on entering this apartment? Peering towards the open door, he observes his younger self walk into the living room, tins weighing down overcoat pockets, a smile coating his lips. An Allied airman bearing gifts, potent symbols of his nation's new-found status. Victor to vanquished; rations to help preserve life for a few when so many have been slaughtered in the struggle to liberate a city already battered by the retreating army. Saviour a misnomer, he was simply a man overwhelmed by the stench of poverty and the consequences of interminable war, evident with every step he took on the streets of Naples.

He had joined up to help defeat a ruthless enemy, convinced war presented the only possibility of restoring lasting peace to a fractured world. When did he lose faith in this mission, lose faith in his own ability to effect lasting change? Not the afternoon Luciano Zappetti offered his twelve-year-old daughter in exchange for one meal a day, of that he remained certain. Doubts began to surface long before his transfer to Italy or even Tunisia, where for the first time he witnessed extensive bomb damage at close range. Almost all of Tunisia's major towns had been destroyed with extensive loss of civilian life during the six-month air and land campaign against German and Italian forces. No, a young British soldier, blinded during a desert battle, stirred the misgivings that led to an irreversible change of heart. 'They ship the nutters out of here as soon as possible,' the soldier said, referring to the mentally disturbed patients kept separate from those with physical war wounds, at the desert field hospital where Rob was treated for his initial bout of Stomatitis ulcerative. Men who lost their minds somewhere in a god-forsaken desert, the screams and wails heard that morning lodged forever in a corner of Rob's mind, grains of sand irritating sensitive tissue.

The beginning of a second descent into hell,

the sore swelling with every subsequent dogfight, flame and smoke blemishing pellucid desert skies until he could no longer function as a competent rear gunner. His continuing survival no cause for celebration, only a reminder that cheating death did not absolve him from the sin of sending others to a Saharan grave. Not that he expressed such qualms to his superiors when questioned about his diminishing capabilities, preferring instead to focus on physical and mental exhaustion. This they understood, few rear gunners still flying after three years of continuous warfare. Released from his dorsal turret, he prayed that doubts and guilt would fade in the busy atmosphere of a maintenance unit, but they persisted, surfacing whenever there was a quiet moment. The transfer to Italy only compounded the problem, time to ponder past actions and his changing attitude to the validity of war available on a daily basis at a Base Personnel Depot where most were underemployed.

Following his return to England, with the war coming to an end, he experienced periods of relative calm and felt optimistic that mental instability would diminish, if not disappear entirely, when he returned to civilian life. And it did for a while, in the pursuit of seeking employment, learning new tasks, meeting new colleagues, dating new girls. But just when his life should have been balanced – marriage to a loving, caring woman, a permanent job with reasonable prospects – accusing voices began to hound his waking hours and infiltrate his dreams. 'Murderer,' they cried, 'the blood of many is on your hands!' Oblivious to post-war peace, he retreated to an inner world of darkness and despair. Months passed, he went through the motions of work and marriage, lengthy silences convincing his perceptive wife that more than love and care were needed to banish war-borne demons. Persuaded to visit a local doctor, he was admitted to a psychiatric hospital for two weeks, and as a nurse led him down a bland hospital corridor, the hands that had held the Browning machinegun steady for so many ops began to shake violently in a futile attempt to dislodge guilt's gruesome evidence.

Seated opposite a grey-haired, grey-faced psychiatrist, he tried to explain the sense of culpability that engulfed his life, the knowledge that *his* actions had left scores of families grieving for a dead son, brother, father.

'Depressive state,' the doctor declared, 'brought on by insomnia and repeated outbreaks of debilitating ulcers.' He prescribed a course of sleeping tablets and strong anti-biotics plus outpatient visits at the local hospital.

Ulcers healed, chemically-induced sleep ensuring nightmares were held in check, monthly sessions with a younger, more understanding psychiatrist whittling away darkness. Restored, Rob re-engaged with life in all its manifest seasons, helped his wife deal with the trauma of threatened miscarriage and premature birth. The baby delighted, enabling him to focus on the future instead of the past, her future and the part he'd play ensuring her childhood would be the complete opposite of his own.

Three years later, the prospect of a second child held no fears, yet throughout the months of her gestation, Rob was aware of a second post-war unravelling. Sporadic at first, the odd nightmare, a bout of ulcers that took several courses of anti-biotics to heal, a few sleepless nights. Then guilt, the malevolent emotion that had plagued him years earlier, surfaced once again to smother the happiness experienced on seeing his second new-born daughter. Vanquished, he spent sleepless hours ruminating on those denied forever the joy of parenthood by *his* airborne actions. He could hold his baby in his arms, kiss her smooth cheeks, dandle her older sister on his knee, a black and white photograph, taken a few months after a second stint in a psychiatric hospital, proof of his enduring fatherhood.

Laughter filters through fog, warm fingers knock against his bare wrist. Pushing against the weight of past despair, he hears Ivy's cheerful voice, opens his eyes wide to the clear light of reunion. Perched on the edge of her chair, Ivy is explaining to Luigi and Roberto how the shipping line's insolvency resulted in a change of holiday destination, using a series of exaggerated gestures to counter her inability to speak their language. The two Italians laugh and smile, although from their lack of verbal response, Rob doubts they comprehend her lengthy account. Nevertheless, he's proud of Ivy for making a concerted attempt at conversation. He can't imagine Dawn making much of an effort under the same circumstances. For a few moments, he ruminates on Alf lying in bed feigning illness, a convincing performance to gain a few hours' freedom. Why didn't he tell Dawn the truth, clarify his need to visit the war cemetery? Despite his wife's sharp tongue, Rob feels she would understand. A former girlfriend, dead thirty years, poses no threat to a long-standing marriage.

The sound of voices coming from the kitchen, remind him of his own secrets concealed for decades. A painting given as a token of friendship, revealed to Ivy less than forty-eight hours earlier, a former sweetheart preparing food in an adjoining room. Has Ivy guessed the nature of their wartime relationship? Over enthusiastic when greeting Susanna, he had yielded to a sudden longing to hold her close, press his lips to her cheeks. The moment passed soon enough, common sense returning him to his wife's side. Perhaps Ivy interpreted his effusiveness as relief at finding another member of the Zappetti family alive and well; no doubt she's thankful the time-consuming search wasn't in vain. Either way, he vows to tell her the truth when they're back in their hotel bedroom. Tomorrow they will celebrate their twenty-sixth wedding anniversary, a milestone he once thought impossible given the precarious state of his mental health. He remembers their silver wedding anniversary the previous year, Ivy's sister proposing a toast, her brother filling their glasses to the brim, her niece taking photographs of the happy couple. 'I've forgotten the camera,' he says aloud, keen to record the current occasion.

Ivy turns to face him. 'Don't worry, it's in my holiday bag.' She pats the bag at her feet in confirmation.

'I will take la fotografia after we are eating,' Roberto offers. 'I think la strada she good place.'

'Why outside?' Rob queries, wondering what's wrong with a photograph of them all seated at the table.

'The light is better and more spazio.'

'Right. I suppose it will be a bit crowded when Maria and Luigi's families arrive.'

Ivy leans towards him. 'I wish I had something to give the children. Pity we gave away all the sweets.'

'Don't worry about it. I'm sure their grandmother has sweets or chocolate in her pantry.'

Ivy smiles. 'Do you remember that time when I was in hospital?'

'I think so. Why?' Sometimes Rob finds found it difficult to follow Ivy's convoluted train of thought.

'The girls stayed with my parents for a week.'

'And were spoilt with daily sweets,' he says, pleased to have deciphered the issue.

'No, it was the biscuits that impressed. I'll never forget the look of wonder on Frances' face when she told me Gran had six different kinds of biscuits.'

'She's certainly inherited my sweet tooth.' He bends to pat Ivy's hand. 'And your cake-making skills, judging by the delights she served us last year.'

Husband and wife smile at the memory of

afternoon teas in the shade of an upstairs veranda, looking out at tropical plants and a wide expanse of lawn.

'We will eat in a few minutes,' Isabella announces from the kitchen doorway.

'No need to hurry on our account,' Ivy answers politely.

Isabella smiles before turning her attention to her husband. 'Roberto, Luigi, date una mano, per favore.'

The two men rise reluctantly.

———

Soon the living room hums with activity, Luigi and Roberto pulling the heavy dining table away from the wall and arranging three chairs on either side before hurrying into the kitchen to fetch two more. Susanna stands by the dresser surveying the seating, her mouth pursed in concentration. Nearby, daughter-in-law Isabella hovers awaiting instructions, a pile of plates in her hands.

On the periphery, Rob and Ivy sip a second glass of lemonade. 'When Susanna mentioned food,' Ivy says quietly, 'I envisaged slices of cake or a sandwich served with coffee or another cold drink, not a full-scale meal eaten at the dining table.'

'Food is extremely important to the Neapolitans,' Rob informs her, hoping the meal won't be too spicy, anything in that category always results in a spate of mouth ulcers. Stomatitis ulcerative continues to erupt in his mouth, on the top of his ears and on the back of his neck. Nowadays, he can get some pain relief from mouth ulcers by removing his dentures, his remaining upper and lower teeth extracted some years earlier, but he can't sit toothless at a hotel dining table with other tour members. When his mouth is painful, Ivy always cooks soft food: macaroni cheese, poached fish with mashed potato or pureed soup. For dessert, jelly with ice-cream or custard replaces steam puddings and fruit pies, plus she has no objection to him dunking biscuits or even cake in cups of tea.

Loud voices draw his attention to the kitchen doorway where Luigi and Roberto jostle for position, each carrying a wooden chair.

'Basta!' Susanna calls and turning to Isabella, remarks, 'Gli uomini sono sempre bambini.'

Looking sheepish, Roberto approaches the table, waits patiently for mamma's instructions.

'Qui,' she commands, pointing to the head of the table.

Roberto sets down his chair, then twists around to whisper in Luigi's ear.

'Did you hear what he said,' Ivy asks.

'No, but it was probably a warning not to upset the matriarch,' Rob answers in a low voice.

Ivy suppresses a giggle. 'Mamma still rules the roost then.'

'Definitely. It's the same in all Italian families, I believe.'

'Luigi, pronto,' a voice rings out, validating Rob's statement. 'La.' Susanna gestures towards the foot of the table.

Giving his sister a wide berth, Luigi positions the chair and promptly sits down.

'Cheeky,' Ivy murmurs.

'Always was.' Rob recalls an adolescent boy counting gifts, grubby fingers touching each tin in turn.

'Non sederti,' Susanna cries, raising one arm as though about to cuff her middle-aged brother. 'Vieni a prendere due cuscini.'

Without a word, Luigi gets to his feet and hurries to a door on the right of the dresser. But before turning the handle, he looks over at Rob and winks. 'She still molto autoritoria,' he says quietly and opening the door, slips into the dim hallway.

'Very bossy,' Rob translates before covering

his mouth with his hand to prevent laughter escaping.

'Just like our Frances. Sometimes I think James should put his foot down.'

'That's feminism for you,' says Rob, secretly pleased his elder daughter remains self-reliant despite marrying at the early age of nineteen. He leans forward to place his empty glass on the floor.

'Mario no taking long time.' Susanna remarks, bustling towards them. 'Maria a casa soon.'

Rob smiles. 'I'm really looking forward to seeing her. Tell me, does she have a family?'

'Sì, si. Maria, she is marry Vincenzo. They are having quattro bambini. Big boys now.'

Four boys!' Ivy exclaims. 'They must keep her busy!'

Sì, much lavoro.'

'So, what about you, Susanna? Rob asks, looking up at her. 'Did you have any more children?'

Regret shadows her face. 'Scusa uno momento.' She twists around and hurries to the kitchen, closes the door behind her.'

Ivy taps his wrist. 'That was a bit personal, dear. She may not have remarried.'

'I just assumed...' His voice trails off.

Ivy shakes her head, then reaches down to retrieve Rob's glass. 'Why don't you take these into the kitchen?' She hands over both glasses, frowns when he remains seated. 'Go on, I'm sure she won't bite.'

Susanna is bent over the sink when Rob enters the kitchen and quietly shuts the door behind him. 'I'm so sorry, Susanna,' he says, placing the glasses on the draining board. 'I shouldn't have asked such a personal question. I didn't mean to pry.'

She sniffs, then turns to face him. 'I would like many bambini but war...' She shakes her head.

'Damn war wrecked so many lives,' Rob's tone is bitter.

'Sì, but I fortunata.' She gives a small smile. 'I am having much family. Papà, Roberto, Mario, Isabella, Maria, Luigi. Papà e...'

'Luciano was a wonderful man,' Rob interrupts, his declaration bringing a frown to Susanna's forehead.

'Papà he old man but ancora wonderful.'

'He's here? I thought...'

'Naturalmente, this his casa. Papà he in camera. He is having la siesta. I no tell you?'

'No, you didn't.'

'Spiacente!' She throws up her hands. 'I no thinking.'

Moving closer, Rob pats her arm. 'It's ok, Susanna, I understand. It must have been such a,' he hesitates, wanting to use Italian words, 'grosso urto seeing me after thirty years.'

Sì, urto but molto bene.' This day meraviglioso for family Zappetti!'

'Meraviglioso for me too! This is the happiest day I've had in years.'

Once more Susanna frowns. 'Anni? You no happy have vacanza with moglie? You no happy day daughter marry?'

'Yes, of course. It's just that in between there are so many dark days.'

'Buio?' she queries half to herself.

'Don't get me wrong,' Rob continues, so anxious to explain himself he abandons hybrid speech. 'It's nothing to do with my wife or my daughters. In fact, if it wasn't for their love and care I doubt I would be alive today.'

'You are sick?' She reaches out, lays her hand on his bare wrist.

'Yes. I suffer from acute clinical depression.'

'Is very bad?'

FEED THY ENEMY

'Sometimes it gets so bad, I have to go into hospital for weeks.'

'There is medicine for this malattia?'

He nods, conscious now of warm fingers stroking his skin. 'These days the pills help. Dull the pain at least.' He shivers, remembering electroconvulsive therapy treatments administered during the fifties and sixties, sometimes against his will. On the last occasion, he'd plucked up the courage to discharge himself from hospital, fled home by train and bus to Ivy's arms. The hospital, located hundreds of miles away in the north of England, seemed a sensible option at the time, it had an excellent reputation, but Rob couldn't face another bout of ECT.

Susanna touches his cheek with her free hand.

'It was the war,' he explains, staring over her head at a colourful calendar tacked to the kitchen wall. 'Years cramped in the gunner's turret on top of a Baltimore fighter. Years shooting down enemy aircraft. All that carnage and then they expected us to slot back into civilian life and be grateful we were in one piece.'

He sighs loudly, prompting the fingers resting on his cheek to move to his temple where they rub gently to ease the pain. 'They said I was one of the lucky ones. I'd returned intact except for an occasional outbreak of ulcers and these could be treated with the new antibiotics provided at low cost on the new National Health.'

Coated with cynicism, his words fall like hailstones, chilling the warm summer atmosphere, and Susanna shivers, her thin summer dress inadequate protection from the plummeting temperature. Still focused on reminders scrawled in calendar squares, Rob is unaware of the deep concern imprinted on the soft contours of her face, so continues his cruel exposition. 'But I couldn't cope with what I had done, with the brutality I had created, day after day, month after month, year after year.' He hangs his head in shame. 'I wanted peace so much and all I got was my own private hell.' His hands begin to shake, a slight tremor that belies the turmoil within. Then, his head and torso judder as though an electric current has coursed through his body. 'I'm so sorry, Susanna. I didn't mean to go on like this. Not today, not on this special day.'

'Tranquillo, tranquillo, Robbi,' she murmurs, shifting her hands to his shoulders. 'War give many sadness. Mio marito he die, mia madre she die, mio bambino he is having no papà, no nonna. But war many years finish. You have make good life with wife and girls. Oggi is speciale, I am feeling much peace. You no feeling peace?'

Shaking subsides, tentatively he raises his head, risks a glance at a once loved face. Her brown eyes are tinged with sorrow, a sadness he has inflicted with his selfish outburst. 'Sì, Susanna,' he says softly. 'I can feel it, the peace that passes understanding. It's coming from your heart.'

Susanna blushes but doesn't turn away. Instead, she looks directly into Rob's eyes and lifting her chin, presses warm lips to his.

A heavy door slams shut, and footsteps resound through the living room. Startled, Rob and Susanna spring apart, turn glistening eyes to the kitchen door.

'Mamma, zia Maria verra,' they hear Mario exclaim.

Footsteps retreat. Wartime sweethearts exhale and relax.

' Papà, zia Maria ha telefonato a zia Francesca. Lei verrà con Angelica e Bettina.'

'Splendido,' rings Roberto's voice.

'Dove nonna e zio Robbi?' Mario demands.

'Cucina.'

Susanna smooths her dress, then reaches for the door handle. 'We go, Robbi. You ok now?'

'Sì.' Rob follows her into the living room, feels his heart lurch as Mario, beaming from ear to ear, flings himself into Susanna's outstretched arms.

A burble of conversation washes over Rob's head as Ivy and Roberto engage in animated conversation, both parties employing myriad gestures to overcome language difficulties. Although unable to see her face, Rob can tell Ivy is enjoying every moment. Reassured - earlier he was concerned she would consider the hours spent searching for his Italian 'family' a waste of time -- he leans back, one hand on his knee, the other straddling the armrest, the closest he can get to her given the space between their two chairs. Throughout the day, he has experienced this need for physical proximity, bizarre in a man who often prefers solitude. He looks over at Mario, seated at his father's feet, one arm clutching Roberto's leg. Perhaps the Italians' demonstrative nature has somehow filtered through his British reserve? Mario's eyes flick from papà to Ivy, his expression one of intense concentration as he attempts to decipher unfamiliar dialogue.

I suppose half a conversation is better than

none, Rob muses, thinking not of past hybrid dialogue with Susanna, but of a future grandchild's first words. Will he be Grandpa, Pop, Granddad or just an unfamiliar voice at the other end of the telephone on Christmas Day and birthdays? Pushing negative thoughts aside, he forces himself to envisage a summer Christmas, a small boy or girl sitting beside him, chattering about Santa Claus in a broad Australian accent. Little does he know there will be both a two-year-old grandson and a three-month-old granddaughter present at Christmas seventy-six, the baby gurgling in Sally's arms, the boy talking to his 'Poppa' and 'Nana' in a clear southern English accent. Twelve months spent in the company of grandparents while learning to talk, will ensure the child speaks with a distinct English accent until exposure to Australian kindergarten children at age three and a half.

A knock on the front door disrupts both conversation and day-dream. Scrambling to his feet, Mario rushes into the entrance hall to open the front door. 'Zia Maria,' he exclaims, his high-pitched voice perceptible from entrance to kitchen, where his nonna and mamma sit either side of a small table preparing food.

Roberto and Ivy look towards the doorway,

watch a stocky middle-aged woman enter the room, followed by Mario.

Smiling, Rob rises to greet her, feels a moment's concern when she stops in her tracks and stares wide-eyed. 'Buon giorno, Maria,' he ventures.

Sniffing back a tear, she rushes forward, wraps solid arms around his waist, crushing his slight torso against her ample bosom. Seconds later, she releases him, and holding him at arms' length, exclaims, 'Mio zio Robbi!'

'Little sister Maria.' He leans forward, kisses her on both cheeks.

'No little sister now, is trenta anni!' She beams. 'Tua moglie?' she asks, looking over at Ivy.

'Sì.' Rob turns sideways. 'My dear wife Ivy,' he declares, love and delight radiating from clear blue eyes.

Ivy smiles and rises from her chair.

'Che piacere vederti, Ivy,' Maria cries, rushing across the room and almost knocking slim Ivy over with another enthusiastic embrace. 'Sono molto contenta.' Brown eyes glisten. 'Big big celebrazione. I have telephone a mio Vincenzo.' Her expression alters to one of regret. 'Purtroppo, he no come, he is much working. Miei boys also working.'

'Non problema,' Rob assures her. 'Ci sono moltissimi Zappetti a casa.'

'Mettiti a sedere, zia Maria,' Roberto calls, getting to his feet.

Maria glances around the room. 'Dove sono Susanna e Isabella?'

In cucina,' Rob replies.

'Scusi, Robbi, scusi Ivy.' Maria hurries across the room and into the kitchen.

Rob feels rather foolish standing in the middle of the room. 'We'd better sit down again,' he says quietly to Ivy. They head for the chairs.

Settled comfortably but without a glass to occupy his hands, Rob stares into space trying to think of conversation. Tired from emotional reunions and the effort of recalling long-forgotten language, he envies Luciano his lengthy siesta.

Allora, mio amico, all are meet again,' Roberto remarks, getting to his feet. 'Susanna, Maria, Luigi, Roberto e presto Luciano.'

'La famiglia, Rob says softly.'

'È una sorpresa.' Smiling, Roberto walks over to the English visitors. 'La mia bambina Caterina.'

'You have a daughter?'

'Sì, she is having siesta.'

'How old is she?'

'Due anni.'

The same age you were when I met your mother, Rob reflects. 'I look forward to meeting her.'

'Before she wake, we have drink, yes?'

'Thank you, Roberto.'

'And we no drink limonata!' One hand resting on the armrest of Rob's chair, he adds, 'Limonata she is for bambini, sì?'

Rob and Ivy nod in agreement.

Frenzied activity impedes conversation, so the English visitors sit sipping effervescent local wine, bodies turned towards each other to avoid staring at their diligent hosts. Mario, impatient to begin the celebration, has gone down to the street to look for his cousins and aunt. Meanwhile, his parents arrange what seems an inordinate number of glasses and bottles of wine on the table, while his aunt Maria and grandmother march in and out of the kitchen carrying platters of food.

Luigi remains absent, his search for cushions abandoned, Rob presumes, in favour of a snatched siesta. It's either that or a desire to stay out the women's way. *A wise decision,* Rob considers, recalling Christmas mornings when he would retire to the shed while Ivy and the girls bustled around kitchen and dining room. Prior to his father-in-law's death in sixty-three, Christmas Day was always spent a mile up the road in the detached Edwardian house Rob first entered not long after he and Ivy began courting. His mother-in-law, a plump cheerful woman with a broad Derbyshire accent despite fifty years in the south of England, loved to have the whole family around her for Christmas dinner and supper. The 'whole family' comprised three adult children, their spouses and children, plus her son and elder daughter's widowed mothers-in-law. Having never met either of Rob's parents, or any of his siblings, no one ever mentioned *his* lack of relatives.

'I don't know how Luciano can sleep through this noise,' Ivy remarks during a brief lull when all the workers have disappeared into the kitchen.

'He's probably deaf.' Rob leans towards her. 'Not surprising really, he must be eighty-five at least. I do hope Susanna explains how come I'm sitting in his living room. Old people can get agitated when something out of the ordinary transpires.'

'Do you think he'll remember you?'

'Of course. Luigi said he's always talking about the war years.'

Ivy shifts in her seat. 'Living in the past, just like someone else I know,' she says under her breath.

'Sorry, dear, I didn't catch that.'

'I was just wondering how many people are coming to this celebration.' She gestures towards the crowded table.

'Half of Naples I should think judging by the amount of food that's coming out of the kitchen.'

'At least.' She bends to place her empty glass on the floor. 'Any idea where the toilet is?'

Rob points to the nearby door. 'Through there, second on the right.'

'Thanks.' Leaving her holiday bag beside the chair, she hurries to the door.

As Ivy disappears into a dim hallway, Susanna emerges from the kitchen carrying yet another platter. She appears hot and bothered, glances around frantically for a space to put her dish.

'I do hope you're not wearing yourself out on our account,' Rob says, rising from his chair and hurrying towards her. 'We would have been just as happy with a slice of cake and a couple of drinks, you know.'

The platter hits the table with a resounding

thud. 'Why you English no understand?' She turns to face him, eyes flashing, hands on hips. 'Napoletani know food she molto importante. Più importante di amore. We have very old saying, "O Francia o Spagna purché se magna."'

Hands raised in defence, Rob backs away. 'Sorry, sorry, I meant no offence.'

'It means,' she adds in a softer tone, 'it does not matter if we are governed by France or Spain, so long as we eat.'

For the second time that afternoon, Rob hangs his head, prompting a cry of alarm from his volatile host.

'Is ok, Robbi,' she soothes, rushing to his side. 'I am bad woman for the shouting.'

He raises his head. 'Haven't changed, have I? Back in forty-four I was always saying the wrong thing, or you misunderstood, and it wasn't always a question of language.'

Susanna smiles up at him.

'And sometimes I kept silent when I should have spoken. Do you remember the last time I came to this apartment?'

'Sì, you have biscotto for Roberto. Biscotto very hard and he...'

'He spat it out and you were angry.'

'Sì. He very bad boy.'

Rob reaches out to touch her shoulder. 'No, I

don't blame him at all. Those biscuits were horrible. Hard as rocks and if you did manage to chew them up, they tasted like a mouthful of sand.'

'No eat sabbia!'

'And after you had sent Roberto to bed and cleared up the mess, it didn't seem right to say what I'd intended, so I thought I would leave it until our next date.' He hesitates, inhales deeply as though subsequent speech requires extra breath. 'Then I was sent back to Gragnano and I couldn't get away and then I returned to England and I couldn't say what was in my heart, so you never knew that I...'

Susanna sighs, then places a finger on his lips. 'And I no speak same words to you.'

Lifting her finger, Rob kisses it gently.

The sound of voices makes them jump and separate for the second time that afternoon, each looking guilty.

'I have go now,' Susanna murmurs, her lips barely moving. 'I have wake papà.'

Rob leans against the table, his head spinning. Has he consumed ten glasses of wine, rather than one?

'Mettiti a sedere, per favore,' a voice calls from the kitchen and he turns to see Maria standing in the doorway, concern etched on her face. She moves forward to take his arm, leads him over to the chair.

'Grazie, Maria.' He smiles. 'This is the second time you have looked after me.'

She looks puzzled, so he assumes she has forgotten that first meeting, the wine that rendered him unsteady on his feet. Or perhaps she doesn't understand his words. 'Badare,' he says, remembering the verb for 'look after.'

'I am ricordare,' she says softly. 'Papà he contento I cortese.'

'You were always polite, Maria. A beautiful girl.'

She blushes, pats his shoulder before hurrying back to the kitchen.

EIGHTEEN

Immersed in memories of a malnourished twelve-year-old girl, Rob fails to hear the hall door open. Ivy enters the room first, quickly followed by Luigi carrying two cushions, his face crumpled from sleep. Murmuring apologies, he places the cushions on a chair, then moves over to the sofa, sits down heavily.

'I heard him snoring in the room next to the bathroom,' Ivy says, slipping into her seat. 'Hope I didn't wake him when I walked past.'

'If you did, I'm sure he'll be relieved Susanna didn't find him there when she went to wake her father. I wonder what's keeping them?'

'Nothing is keeping me,' a gruff voice says

from the doorway. 'I am pensionato but I move quick for il mio amico.'

Twisting around, Rob watches a frail old man shuffle into the room, Susanna's arm firmly around his waist. Forgetting weary limbs, Rob leaps from the chair, enfolds Luciano in a loving embrace.

'Attenzione, papà,' Susanna warns as the old man sways in Rob's arms.

'Non fare storie,' Luciano mutters, trying to dislodge the hand clutching his stooped shoulders.

'Siediti,' she adds, undeterred by the abrasive tone.

Rob glances at Susanna. 'I'll take his right arm.' Loosening his grip, he turns around, places his left hand on Luciano's right arm to steady him. 'Destra,' he adds needlessly as Susanna reaches for her father's left.

'Andiamo,' Susanna says brightly and together they escort the patriarch across the room, ease him into the chair at the head of the table.

'A tavolo,' Luciano calls, indicating the feast laid out before him.

'Uno momento, papà,' Luigi calls back. 'Aspettiamo Francesca e le nostre figlie.'

The old man nods before helping himself to a slice of cheese.

Still standing behind him, Susanna frowns at this display of bad manners, while Rob takes the opportunity to return to his seat. 'We're waiting for Luigi's wife and daughters,' he informs Ivy.

Minutes pass with excruciating slowness, all present listening for footsteps on the stairs. Maria has already opened the front door and stands in the doorway peering out, shifting her weight from one foot to the other. 'Ecco qua!' she cries suddenly, prompting Luigi to leap up and head for the stairs.

Neapolitan dialect erupts in the stairwell, Luigi's voice predominating; a disagreement between husband and wife audible even in the far corner of the living room. Listening to mounting volume, Rob is reminded of the volatile adolescent who oscillated from offensive outburst to moody silence to friendly dialogue within the same conversation. It seems maturity hasn't subdued Luigi's temper. 'He hasn't changed,' he says aloud, forgetting Susanna standing close by.

'You are thinking right, Rob,' she answers, flinging out her arms in a gesture of exasperation. 'Francesca, she is una santa!'

'Certamente.'

A clatter of footsteps in the hall halt further commentary.

'Papà, mamma,' Mario calls, racing into the

room at full speed. 'Zia Francesca e Angelina e Bettina ecco qua!'

On cue, Luigi ushers his family inside, his face wreathed in smiles. 'Mio famiglia,' he declares proudly.

Rob and Ivy rise in unison and walk forward smiling, their cheeks prepared for a multitude of kisses.

―――

Introductions over, family and friends head for the table, where Susanna stands directing seating arrangements. As honoured guests, Rob and Ivy are placed either side of Luciano, who greets their arrival with a nod, speech or a smile impossible due to the large slice of half-chewed cheese in his mouth. Roberto is next to Ivy, then Isabella, little Caterina perched on her lap. Opposite Luciano sit Luigi and Francesca, while Maria perches on a stool, fetched from a bedroom, and the three older children standing behind their respective papàs. When her family has settled, Susanna slips quietly into the remaining seat beside Rob.

Eight chairs and a stool squashed around a table meant for six, eighteen thighs pressed together, body heat palpable through summer-weight clothing; there's no way Rob can avoid a once yearned for touch. Half of him wants to slip his hand beneath the table, clasp the fingers resting on Susanna's lap, restore long-abandoned intimacy. The other half longs to change places with his Italian namesake, press warm flesh against Ivy's familiar thighs. Then, as though Ivy has read his mind, her sandals touch the tip of his shoes and an electric current of love surges through his body, restoring equilibrium.

Conversation begins to bubble around the table, laughter melding the assortment of Italian, Neapolitan dialect and English. Platters are passed around: crusty bread, a selection of cheeses, tomato salad, olives, gherkins, grapes. Comments are made on the quality of tomatoes, the texture of cheese. Luciano alone refrains from expressing an opinion, preferring instead to concentrate on consumption. Beside him, Rob marvels at his undiminished appetite, unusual in the elderly. Nothing is wasted, the few drops of olive oil remaining on the old man's plate, mopped up with a piece of bread. After completing his meal with a few gulps of wine, Luciano mutters to himself for a few moments, then thumps the table with his fist and slowly gets to his feet.

FEED THY ENEMY

Silence descends like a sudden downpour; family and guests turn to face the patriarch.

Gnarled fingers grip the edge of the table and a creased mouth trembles as tears stain cracked-leather cheeks. 'Grazie a Dio,' the old man cries. 'Grazie a Dio our saviour have return. Molti anni lost but never forgot. Always in our hearts, always in our prayers. Grazie a Dio, our beautiful saviour have return!' Lifting one hand, he bends to pick up his glass, holds it towards Rob.

The rest of the family follows suit.

'Benvenuto, Rob, always you welcome in mia casa. Always you welcome in mia famiglia.'

'Benvenuto, Rob,' the family chorus.

Glasses chink. All except Caterina drink a toast.

Suddenly Luciano sways and drops of wine splash on to the table. Alarmed, Rob and Susanna rise in unison, hurry to the old man's side. Arms encircle his waist, steady him before trying to lower him into the chair. Eighty-five-year old feet stand firm, a hand pushes against Susanna's arm. 'Sederti immediatamente!'

Chastened, Susanna returns to her seat, Rob following close behind. An uncomfortable silence ensues, the family loath to resume conversation in case Luciano wishes to say more, the guests a little cowed by his outburst.

Still standing, one hand gripping the table, Luciano sips his wine, eyes focused on the glass. Lips smack, he looks up, turns to Rob. 'Molti giorni we are sitting this table, mio amico. I no forget. We have talk, we have laugh, we drink the vino.' He chuckles. 'You are wearing the big capotto with the big ... er'

'Pockets, Luciano, pockets crammed with RAF rations.'

'Sì, sì, you are giving molti grossi food. Is call tins, sì?'

'That's right.'

'Is meat tins, is fish tins, is cioccolato, is...'

'Don't forget the puddings, Luciano. You really liked the puddings.'

'Sì, sì, I am loving puddings! Inglese puddings molto bene!'

'The best way to finish off a dinner if you ask me.'

Luciano grins, then a frown creases his forehead. 'Yankee pudding, she no good. Yankee pudding, she senza gusto.'

'Sì,' Luigi chimes in. 'Yankee pudding like eat sponge from bath.'

Throwing up his arms, Luciano roars with laughter.

FEED THY ENEMY

Concerned he'll lose his balance, Rob grabs Luciano's waist.

'Attento, papà,' Susanna calls, but stays seated.

Obedient at last, Luciano clutches the edge of the table as laughter slowly subsides.

'Papà, sedete per favore,' Susanna pleads.

'Fra un momento.'

Susanna sighs, exchanges worried glances with her siblings.

'He'll be ok,' Rob reassures, gently patting her hand.

'Allora,' Luciano continues, 'we have much talk of puddings. We have laughing, we have dancing with sardine. Mia memoria she good, yes?'

'Sì, molto bene,' Rob agrees.

Luciano acknowledges the compliment with a smile, but then his expression alters, dark shadows scudding across his face like thunder clouds before a storm. 'But I have also say, I am remember every tins, ogni food you have bring a mia casa. Food help mia famiglia in very bad giorni when terra she is dying from bomb and burn.' He sniffs back a tear. 'E molto importante, mio amico, I no forget every tin you bringing mia famiglia, she is rischio for you and tuo amico Alfredo. Very big rischio.' Lifting one hand from the table edge, he picks up his glass. 'Now I finish talk and we drink.' Raising his glass, he says in a firm voice, 'Adesso vorrei un brindisi.'

Hands reach for glasses, lift them high. Juice splashes from Caterina's plastic cup as she too follows suit.

'Ai migliori Englishmen del mondo, Roberto e Alfredo!'

Rob blushes scarlet. Incapable of speech, he listens with pounding heart as the family and his own dear wife, echo Luciano's words.

Glasses clink. All, including Rob, drink deeply.

A murmur of conversation begins as Luciano resumes his seat.

Ever the sweet-tooth, Rob eyes the almond-topped torta in the centre of the table, hoping it won't be long before he's enjoying a slice.

He's still savouring the thought when Luciano clears his throat and grasping the edge of the table, pulls himself upright once more. He takes a moment to regain his balance, then reaches for his half-empty glass. 'Alzarsi,' he commands, eyes swivelling around the table.

Cutlery clatters, adults get to their feet and push back chairs, a difficult manoeuvre for those sitting only inches from a wall; older children exchange glances. All turn to Luciano, beloved patriarch and old friend, standing proud as a king overseeing his subjects. Then, to the astonishment of all – they anticipate another toast to Rob or one to Rob and Ivy – a mischievous smile births in the corners of the old man's mouth, grows rapidly until his entire face glows gold.

'Ai migliori Inglese pudding!' he cries, holding his glass high. 'Brindiamo al spotted dick, grazie, grazie!'

'Spotted dick,' comes the obedient response, although children and wives remain perplexed.

Hurried explanations in Italian and English clear confusion and in next to no time, smiles coat every face.

Shared laughter drowns the chink of glasses.

AFTERWORD FROM THE AUTHOR

AN ORDINARY MAN

One of my most poignant childhood memories is of my father sitting in his chair by the dining room fireplace staring into the glowing coals. Minute after minute, hour after hour, barely moving; his eyes riveted to flame and ash.

Sometimes he would be sitting there when my sister and I returned home from school eager to talk about our day. Mum would quickly shepherd us into the kitchen, explaining that Daddy wasn't feeling well, so we mustn't disturb him with noisy play. We couldn't see any signs of illness, but we obeyed anyway, afraid not of our mother's ire but of those shadowed blue eyes filled with pain and sadness.

AFTERWORD FROM THE AUTHOR

After a week or so of eerie quiet and unnatural inactivity, Daddy would disappear from his place by the fire and from our lives. His absences often lasted for months, we were told he was in hospital and would return when he was better. We didn't go to visit him; the hospital was in another town and Mum said it was too far to go on the bus. Occasionally he would come home for the weekend, armed with gifts for his girls: huge lollypops, swirls of coloured sugar that stained our teeth and resulted in numerous fillings; items he'd made in basket weaving or leathercraft classes. I imagined the hospital as a kind of boarding school but failed to understand why my beloved father had to go away to learn arts and crafts. At home, he always mended our broken toys and enjoyed repairing the old radios and clocks he purchased at the local second-hand shop. I was pleased with the little baskets and purses and bracelets but would have preferred my Daddy to remain at home.

When I was twelve, Mum disclosed the nature of our father's illness. She called it depression and explained that sometimes Daddy felt enveloped by dark clouds and couldn't find a way out. Then he had to go into hospital, take tablets and talk to the doctors about how he felt. Depression was a mental illness, she said, which

AFTERWORD FROM THE AUTHOR

meant a sickness of the mind as opposed to a physical illness. She omitted to say what had caused this illness and many years passed before I discovered it had arisen as a direct result of his war service.

My father had been a rear gunner in the RAF during the Second World War, a rank with a very short life expectancy. Somehow, he had survived three years of warfare in the deserts of North Africa. Countless missions against German and Italian troops, firing at a mostly unseen enemy from his cramped position in the dorsal turret of a Martin Baltimore fighter plane.

When he finally returned to England, my father was physically intact but mentally and spiritually shattered. He couldn't cope with the brutality he had experienced and created day after day, month after month, year after year. He had committed violent acts against fellow human beings and to make matters worse, at the time he hadn't thought about what he was doing, neither had he felt remorse.

Today the diagnosis would be Post-Traumatic Stress Disorder. The sufferer would be given counselling, encouraged to talk about his war experiences and given appropriate medication. He would not be ridiculed or told to snap out of it.

AFTERWORD FROM THE AUTHOR

But in nineteen-forty-five servicemen and women were expected to return home from six years of war, slot back into civilian life and be grateful they were in one piece. Those who had lost limbs or suffered long-term physical illness were given pensions and assisted to rebuild their lives. My father was regarded as one of the 'lucky' ones; he had returned with only a slight health problem, the ulcers caught in Egypt that erupted periodically in his mouth and on his lips and the back of his neck. These could be treated with the new antibiotics available to all under Britain's new National Health Scheme. But his mental suffering festered untreated until the very foundations of his psyche were irrevocably damaged.

For the rest of his life, my father was destined to suffer lengthy episodes of mental illness that frequently prevented him leading a normal life and impacted on his marriage and his daughters' childhood.

Although protracted periods of hospitalisation, medication and electric shock treatment failed to completely cure his illness, there were numerous intervals when he functioned normally. Then we went on family holidays, laughed at his jokes and enjoyed lively discussions around the dinner table.

AFTERWORD FROM THE AUTHOR

One such tranquil period lasted for some years. During a hospital stay in the late fifties, my father watched a film about the Religious Society of Friends, commonly known as Quakers. Everything about the Society appealed to him, from the way of worship -- waiting in silence for guidance from God -- to pacifism and dedication to social justice for all. The basic tenet of Quakerism "there is that of God in everyone" also spoke to his condition. Wholeheartedly, he embraced Quakerism and became a loved and respected member of the local Meeting.

At home, he radiated a serene presence at all times, never raising his voice when my sister and I were disobedient or boisterous or interrupted his favourite television programme with our childish quarrelling. He was almost too good to be true.

I have no idea what triggered a return to the dark days when once again he sat in front of the fire staring at the coals. Perhaps he had become spiritually exhausted having given so much of himself during those 'angel' years.

My sister and I grew up, left home for career and marriage; left the England of our childhood to begin new lives on the other side of the world.

Our father visited our homes in Australia twice. During those holidays, he seemed content,

AFTERWORD FROM THE AUTHOR

more at peace with himself. Perhaps this tranquillity was in part the result of no longer having to worry about long periods of unemployment and the effect this would have on his family. After many years lobbying military medical boards to have his mental illness recognised as war related, he had been granted a one hundred per cent disability pension. Or perhaps he had finally come to terms with the role he had played in the carnage of the Second World War.

When heart disease claimed my father's life at the early age of sixty-four, I felt sad and angry he was denied more years of peace. Selfishly perhaps, I also wished there had been more time for me to share my deepest hopes and fears with this sensitive, caring, intelligent, beautiful and troubled person.

Decades after his death, fond memories still nourish me. I remember how he helped me find the faith that sustains me through my own dark days, his acceptance and belief in the life-love I embarked on at eighteen when others, including my mother, could foresee only disaster. When I began mature age university studies at age twenty-seven, he expressed only delight and encouragement. No mention was made of my adolescent refusal to undertake higher education.

And sometimes when I sit in the special si-

AFTERWORD FROM THE AUTHOR

lence of Quaker Meeting for Worship, I recall the sound of his spirit, the words of an ordinary man trying to unload an extraordinary burden.

'An Ordinary Man' first published in The Australian Friend, June 2011

ABOUT THE AUTHOR

Born and brought up in Southern England, Sue worked in clerical positions within the civil service, firstly at an atomic power station and secondly for British Telecom. At nineteen, she married her childhood sweetheart, Mark and seven months later they emigrated to Australia, arriving in Brisbane, August 1970. After three and a half years working as a Library Assistant in a technical library, Sue became a stay-at-home mother to son David, now 44.

In 1978 Sue began a Batchelor of Arts degree at the University of Queensland, graduating in 1982 with majors in English Literature, Drama and French. One week after graduation, Sue secured a graduate position within the University of Queensland Library, where she worked until relocating to Melbourne with her husband in 1999. In Melbourne Sue worked for nine years as Acquisitions Officer at the Victorian College of the Arts Library, now part of Melbourne University, until taking early retirement to pursue her long-held dream of becoming a professional writer.

Since retirement Sue has written six novels: *Sannah and the Pilgrim,* first in a trilogy of a future dystopian Australia focusing on climate change and the harsh treatment of refugees from drowned Pacific islands, Odyssey Books, 2014. Commended in the FAW Christina Stead Award, 2014.

Pia and the Skyman, Odyssey Books, 2016. Commended in the FAW Christina Stead Award, 2016.

The Sky Lines Alliance, Odyssey Books, 2016.

Chrysalis, the story of a perceptive girl growing up in a Quaker family in swinging sixties' Britain was published by Morning Star Press in 2017.

Re-Navigation, recounts a life turned upside down when forty-year-old Julia journeys from the sanctuary of middle-class Australian suburbia to undertake a retreat at a college located on an isolated Welsh island. Published by Creativia, 2019.

Feed Thy Enemy, based on her father's experiences, relates a British airman's courage and compassion in the face of extreme trauma during World War II and his struggle to overcome Post-Traumatic Stress Disorder during his post-war life. Creativia, 2019.

    Sue's current project and seventh novel, *A Question of Country,* explores the female protagonist's lifelong search for meaningful identity through the context of country.

During Sue's employment at the VCA College, a lecturer in Film and Television read some of her prose fiction and suggested she consider scriptwriting as he felt her writing style lent itself to the screen. Using texts from the VCA Library, she studied screenwriting in her spare time, undertook a short scriptwriting course and subsequently, wrote a short drama script *Last Fling* adapted from her short story of the same title, published in 1996. The script won First Prize in the FAW TV Drama Award, 2009.

Since then, Sue has written feature film scripts based on her novels *Feed Thy Enemy* and *Re-Navigation,* plus a pilot episode for a tv series based on *Sannah and the Pilgrim.* So far, she has been unable to find a producer for her work but hopes publication of *Feed Thy Enemy* and *Re-Navigation* may assist in this endeavour.

Creative writing has been a passion since Sue's teenage years when she wrote poetry reflecting her feelings about social issues or newly discovered love. Her poetry has been published in Australian and UK magazines and anthologies. A book, 'New Flowering: selected poems 1986-2001,' was self-published in 2001. She also writes short stories and articles. Short stories have been published in Australian magazines (print and online), anthologies and a US anthology. Articles have been published in Australian and UK journals.

Passionate about peace and social justice issues, Sue's goal as a fiction writer is to continue writing novels that address topics such as climate change, the effects of war, the treatment of refugees, feminist and racism. Sue intends to keep on writing for as long as possible, believing the extensive life experiences of older writers can be employed to engage readers of all ages.